Also by Michael Wescott Loder

Published by Hemlock Lodge Press:
Landscapes & Interiors #1
(personal photography)

Paul Gill & His Long Beach Island Art:
Images from the New Jersey Shore, 1925-1938
(compiler and editor)

The Tenax II: Zeiss Ikon's Precison, Fast-action
Camera

Taken Beyond the Ohio: The Indian Captivity of Marie
LeRoy and Barbara Leininger [historical fiction]

Beetle: The Autobiography of a Virtual Girl

Published by McFarland Press:
The Nikon Camera in America. 1946-1953

Published by Publish America:
The Golden Horn

A strange girl with a strange voice who knows who he is.

I retire to my room, set my books down and stare at them. But I am not seeing them. I am seeing the look on that freshman girl's face when she realized who I was. I feel the darkness, like a storm cloud, moving across my desk. Will any of this ever end? Will any girl ever believe I didn't lie? I take a deep, cleansing breath and open the book Marty gave me. As I turn to page 20, a call slip lifts off and settles back on the page like a suddenly disturbed butterfly. "Huh?" I pick it up, turn it over. The words, 'Hi, Peter' stare back at me

Forbidden Games

Michael Wescott Loder

Hemlock Lodge Press
Kutztown, Pennsylvania
2021

Chapter I   Game Changer

"Aunt Millie just died."

I freeze, ham-and-cheese sandwich halfway to my mouth.

"Who's that?" My fourteen-year-old brother barely looks up from buttering his lunch bagel.

"Your great aunt. You know. You've met her—many times. Remember, three years ago down in Patricks Mills. We all went out to lunch with her." Mom offers the letter she just opened to Arnie. "She was your grandpa Marv's older sister."

"Oh. You expect me to remember someone *that* old?" Arnie refuses to take the letter with a shake of his head. His whole world right now is a knife, cream cheese and one warmed-over pumpernickel bagel.

But I nod. I remember; I remember her well: nice, 'all lady' and always smiling, with white hair like fly-away silk. Doubt she had much to smile about these last couple of years: cooped up in that nursing home that always smelled like pine oil and old diapers… I hide a sigh, but the pain in my chest lingers.

Dad sits up. "Well. It's about time. Who's the letter from?"

Mom checks. "A Mr. R. Jacobs, Esquire, 'Counsel for the Woodbridge Nursing Home.' We're on their 'to-know' list."

"Jacobs? He was supposed to phone right away when this happened!" Then Dad smirks. "I was beginning to think she was never gonna' die." He resumes jamming his toast, his knife scraping across its overdone surface.

Mom holds the letter like a paper airplane ready to launch, thinking. "Woodbridge will take care of the cremation. She already had her plot next to Uncle Walter. Dear, do we have to plan some kind of memorial service?"

Dad barely looks at her. "I don't think so it. Nobody else's left alive who would remember her. Stan was her only child, and he's been dead what … almost three years?"

"Okay." Mom folds up the notification and sets it on the pile of glossy, feel-good pleads for money that are all the mail we usually get.

I reach over and retrieve it, brush off bread crumbs and start to scan it. Mom and Dad may be treating Aunt Millie like a momentary distraction from the work-focus of their lives, but she was always nice to me.

Huh? I wave to Mom, then point to the second paragraph.

She sighs, then takes the letter from me. "What is it, Peter?" She puts her glasses back on and examines the second paragraph. "Dear, Jacobs expects to meet with us. Something about Millie's will? You know anything about this?"

Dad takes the letter and reads. He taps his fingers on the table edge and nods. "Yeah, Tsk. We'd better had. Doubt the place left anything once they got a hold of her money, but who knows?" He takes another bite of toast.

Who does know? Holed up in my room with two summer-reading books yet to finish, I let my thoughts wander to memories of Aunt Millie instead. Cool lady. When she was still in her own place, she always had home-baked goodies ready for us whenever we visited. I can still smell her blueberry muffins and lemon squares fresh from the oven. And, unlike almost every other adult—including *dear* Dad and Mom, she was the one who believed I didn't lie.

I run one of our conversations once more though my mind, her words a balm in the midst of a storm. "You're not a liar, Peter. You haven't been one for a long time. Nor do I think you will ever be one again. I believe you. Keep strong. Someday … someday the truth will come out, and you'll be the one standing tall."

I guess you might say she had more faith in me that day than I did in myself.

She broke her hip. When was it? Three Christmases ago. That was right before Uncle Stan died. I remember Mom moaning about being 'stuck' with Aunt Millie and 'Poor us!'

According to Dad, Woodbridge was the *only* place that had a room that would take her. Dad *had* to sell her condo, had to sell everything. I recall both of them complaining about the hassle and time it took to get everything done. We got a couple of chairs and a desk— nothing else. I still have that desk in my room: slant-front top, all mahogany with brass pulls for the drawers. I got it because she left a note on it saying that it was mine. Thank you, Aunt

Millie.

Later I think about that son of hers. He'd be sorta' my first cousin—although we always called him 'uncle.' The only thing about him I know for sure is that he was in the Air Force and flew bombing missions out of Thailand during the Vietnam War. The guy must have been a fool for glory since he stayed for 200 missions—twice what he had to. Maybe that's how he got sick and why he didn't have any children. If he had, they'd be getting whatever is left of Aunt Millie's estate—not us, as if that matters.

There was a girl too: little Mary. Mary? Where'd she fit in? She had to be living with Aunt Millie back then—at least she seemed to be. She was always hanging around the condo whenever we came to visit. We would play together. I recall a Star Wars LEGO set: brand new with all its little pieces still sealed in their bags and Mary offering to share. "Yeah …" I nod as I remember Arnie and I sorting pieces, Mary reading the instructions and snapping bricks together. I wonder what happened to her. No one has mentioned her since forever …

Dad reaches the attorney for Woodbridge the next day. They agree on an appointment for the following Saturday at 10AM. Surprise: all of us are expected to be there—if possible. Well, I'll miss one pre-fall cross-country run, but, so what? So Saturday dawn I dig out a clean shirt, my best black jeans and a purple-and-green tie and make myself presentable. Even comb my hair. Arnie puts on a clean polo shirt.

Walking out to our garage, I turn my face toward the

morning light. "Mmm …" Sunshine feels so good today. It would be nice if … if this was a new, new-morning, the first day of the 'rest of my life.' But it isn't. It's same-old, same-old, and I've lost the last relative who believed me—other than my brother. I sniff and rub my chest before getting in the car.

Of course when we get to the home, Attorney Jacobs isn't there yet. So we stew around in this lobby straight out of a thirty-dollar motel—with ugly chairs, six-month-old *Reader's Digests* and a television on the wall running talk shows nonstop. I finally walk out and hang by the outer door until I spot this fat, bald dude in a grey suit come waltzing in. In one hand he's carrying a briefcase. The other is flashing his out-stretched palm, reaching for Dad's attention. I rejoin the others, but ignore the asshole when he starts making friendly toward me. I can spot hypocrites from half-a-mile, and this guy has to be right out in the open, ready for the grand prize.

Some lady in charge opens her outer office for us. She adds two uncomfortable stacking chairs to the three already there, sets a shoe box on the table and leaves with a firm click of her inner office door. We gather around the table and the process begins. Actually, it's over almost before I can get my butt into the least uncomfortable position. To summarize: this is Millicent's most recent will. She signed it in April. Each of the four of us will receive a thousand dollars. The balance of the remaining funds that had been set aside to cover Mrs. McClure's expenses at Woodbridge will go to the Arts-and-Recreation fund of the Woodbridge Nursing Home—to further their activities helping seniors.

What a crock! All other parts of her estate, known and unknown, are to go to David Bain. *Dear old Dad ...* "Tsk-tsk."

Attorney Jacobs then turns to the box. "These are the personal items that Mrs. McClure still had in her possession. You are welcome to any of these items, if you want them. Otherwise, Woodbridge will dispose of them. Go ahead, take a look and take your pick. There were a few clothes, but I doubt you'll be interested in any of them." He sighs, gives Dad a glance that includes a smile and sits back, hands knitted together over his fat stomach.

Mom lifts the lid and all four of us peek in the box. All I see are a couple of small leather boxes, a bundle of what might be letters tied together with a pink-and-blue ribbon and a pile of photographs. Mom lifts out the photographs and begins to leaf through them. Underneath where they had laid, I spot a sprig of dried flowers, then a tiny brown, snap-closed packet. *That's it!* I edge closer, then wait until Mom and Dad start to ooh-and-ah over some ancient photo. Lawyer is staring out a window, his brain in some cloud. Fingers in the box and a quick palming and I have the packet. *Got it!* It goes in my right front jeans pocket, and I'm back with the crowd. Only Arnie notices my move. When he raises an eyebrow, I shake my head and put a finger to my lips. He nods and says nothing.

That's pretty much all of it. Dad agrees to take the whole box and signs a receipt for the contents. Jacobs is all serious now, commiserating over our loss, saying Millicent is no longer suffering and in a better place. We'll receive our

checks when the will clears probate, etc., etc. *All bullcrap*.
Then he shakes hands all around. Tells Arnie how much he is
growing into a handsome young man. When he shakes mine,
he gives me a close look. "Peter, sorry to hear you still don't
talk."

Not to you, asshole. I give him a weak smile and turn
away, letting my hand go limp.

"Well, enjoy the memories," Jacobs manages before
bending down to retrieve his case and waving us out the door.

I'm almost back to the car before I realize that Dad
isn't with us. *Huh?* He and the lawyer are still talking by the
home's door. Mom, Arnie and I wait until these two are
finally done. Dad rejoins us, whistling under his breath before
catching our looks and shutting up.

We take a different route home. Without even a word,
Dad turns on Saks Boulevard and we head up into the hills
north of our neighborhood. He takes a right into a new court
—its asphalt still black and uncracked—and drives to the
turn-around before parking. *Hmm.* Not much here other than a
few new evergreens. "We'll be only a minute," Dad says
before he and Mom get out. They come together and, holding
hands, walk out to one of the house sites. A moment later,
Dad's got his left thumb extended high overhead. *What'd you
just win, Dad?*

"What's this got to do with Aunt Millie? Why'd Dad
stop here?" Arnie whispers.

I stare at my parents' backs and shrug. "I don't
know." Maybe this has something to do with Aunt Millie, but

I doubt that part. This is Dad's dream world: Hanscomb Heights: new homes for the one percenters. He's wanted to live up here ever since I can remember any conversation about where one should live. If we could afford to live here, we sure wouldn't need to be splitting wood to feed our wood stove.

Dad and Mom turn around, still squeezing hands, and return to the car. As they get in, I note a smile on Dad's face like he'd just eaten a loaded scoop of double-fudge ice cream. Mom's eyes are trying to smile, but she's not pulling it off.

Back home, we all fall into easy chairs and veg-out. Maybe Mom and Dad are thinking about the few times they've bothered to see Aunt Millie these last three years. How they talked about going to see her only a week ago, and how "We all wait too long." Then Arnie starts talking up lunch and that finally moves us back toward a normal Saturday schedule. Of course that packet is burning a hole in my pocket the whole time, but it's my secret. I will share it with Arnie, but not yet. Not until I'm sure that what I snatched is what I think it is. If it is, maybe this will be a better morning after all.

After lunch, Mom takes out the pictures and fans them out on the dinner table. Some are black-and-white and look old. I recognize a snapshot of Dad when he was my age, all big grin and flat stomach. There's a shot of Mom and Dad together, both still young, holding a baby between them. It takes me a moment before I figure out that the smiling baby with bright blue eyes is probably me. The next picture of me shows a brown-once-blonde-haired, skinny kid with a big grin, standing on a back deck next to Aunt Millie. "You were so happy then Peter, I wish you would smile that way now."

Don't bet on it, Mom. I don't smile for people who believe I'm a liar. ... But I sure have gotten a lot taller.

The little leather boxes turn out to hold jewelry, but nothing worth more than sentimental value: Aunt Millie's high school ring and her late husband, Uncle Walter's, college ring. A well-worn simple band is probably Aunt Millie's wedding ring. A strange pin ornamented with tiny pearls that set off a monogram of three Greek letters turns out to be Uncle Walter's fraternity pin. Mom decides that a Russian cross belonged to Millie's grandmother. I manage to snag the dried flowers from the trash can after Mom throws them away.

I head to my job at the local farmer's market, so Arnie can't talk to me alone for most of the afternoon. Walking through the garage, I look up at the taut wire that crosses overhead—regulation volleyball height. For five years I've worked to make sure I never touch that wire with ball or hand. Good enough? Am I good enough? I sigh and head out.

By 5:30PM I'm back, and Arnie's through waiting. Manners and patience go only so far with that kid. Still, he knocks first before invading my room within minutes of my return. He knows that my room is my fortress and cave. No one, not even Mom or Dad, dares enter without a knock or permission. The padlock on the outside that I use whenever I leave is not just for show. It goes on the inside when I'm in my room.

Into a chair and "Okay, Bro, what'd you snatch?"

"This," I answer. I set the little brown envelope with its snap flap on my desk.

"What is it?" Arnie peers at the miniature packet, then, when I nod, picks it up.

"It's an envelope for a key to a safe deposit box. You get it from a bank."

"Ooh … Does that mean that Aunt Millie had some kind of box at a bank Woodbridge or Dad don't know about?"

"Maybe. But the name of the bank, and the number of the box are right there, and now I have it."

"Is the key inside?"

"No. That's why I think Woodbridge let it get away."

"So what good is it? Can you get in without a key?"

"You can't get in without the key. I have the key. And, my name and your name are on the authorized list for the box. Aunt Millie told me all about it when Mom and I visited her last November right before Thanksgiving. She slipped me the key and told me it was yours and mine. I think she was gonna' give me the envelope too, but then she couldn't find it."

"Wow! How come I didn't know about this?" Arnie still has the packet in his hand. He opens the flap and looks in, then sets it back on my desk.

How can I word this? "Ah … Aunt Millie gave me the key because she said she knew I would never tell anyone."

"… Because you almost never talk to anyone—except me. Not since you were eleven, anyway."

I nod.

"So what do you think's in the box? When can we check it out?"

"Banks are open late on Thursdays," I answer.

"I can't wait that long! What if it's full of gold, or old baseball cards or stock certificates—who knows what?"

"I doubt it. Suck it up 'cause we aren't going sooner."

I put the packet in my left-hand desk drawer. After Arnie leaves, still moaning with curiosity, I move it to the hidden compartment behind the desk's central drawer panel. The key is already there: a long, flat type with many teeth. *No, Arnie, there won't be gold or certificates or anything valuable like that. But maybe it will have answers: answers for me, answers to questions that have haunted me for the last three years.*

I pick up the dried flowers, tied together with the same colored ribbon used to hold the shoe box's letters together. A slip of paper hangs from the ribbon. I puzzle over the tiny, faded letters, written in a child's hand. "For Great-Grandma, love Mary."

Chapter II   The Bank Box

Sunday, Dad and I split a cord of wood. The usual routine: Dad runs the splitter while I do the grunt work— picking up logs, setting them on the fulcrum, then dumping the split firewood in our wheelbarrow. It is hard work, and requires attention. Otherwise, a half-split log can pinch a finger or a two-pound piece can fall on a foot. Today I can't concentrate and drop two pieces on Dad's foot and mine. "Ouch!"

"Hey, Peter. What's the problem? Pay attention!" Dad demands, yelling to be heard over the rumble of the splitter's engine. Dad's good at yelling.

I shake my foot, willing the pain to go away. Ugh!

Dad sighs and closes the blade on the next log. When it snaps open, I fish out the smallest piece and wait for Dad to reposition the remaining log for the next cut. I guess I'm more curious and nervous about going to this bank than I thought. And today, as every day, I still wonder how it is I can work with Dad at all.

Somehow Arnie survives until Thursday, as I knew he would. But by then I'm antsy myself, so I get Arnie to tell Mom we're headed down to the Freeze after dinner.

"Be back before dark," is all she says.

I give her a quick, silent smile, and Arnie and I are out the door, one of our cloth grocery bags in hand. Bank is open until eight. We get there at 6:30. I slip over to a side office. When the bored-looking young man in dress suit and tie looks up, I wave. "Excuse me. We need to get into a security box."

"Ah. Okay. I guess I can help you. Do you have your key?"

"Yes."

"You're talking to someone other than me," Arnie whispers as we follow the attendant through a gate and over to a tiny desk. I shrug. When I have to, I can talk, but not to Mom or Dad, or anyone else who still thinks and says I'm a liar.

Guy sits down at a computer, types in a password and mouses through several screens. "Number?"

"Twelve-five-two-four." I open the packet and pull out the key I had put in there.

"Name? Photo ID?"

"Peter Bain." I show him my new driver's license.

"Bain? Aren't you the kid who accused …?"

I give the guy a 'die-right-now look.'

"Okay." He let's it go and opens another screen, hands me a corded marker and points to a sensor pad. "Sign here." I do.

"This way." He leads the way through this huge circular doorway and into a long room lined with tiny metal doors. He counts off doors with a finger, then stops at one three feet off the floor. "Your key?"

I hand it to him. He inserts it into one of two slots, then inserts a second key on a ring he had taken out of the drawer by the computer. He turns each one, opens the door, and pulls a metal drawer part way out. He takes out his key. "There you go. There's a table just outside the vault in that alcove. When you're done, put the drawer back, close the door and take out your key. Let me know, so I can sign you out. We close in an hour."

"Thanks." Arnie and I wait until the guy is gone, then I grasp the handle and pull the drawer out. "Oh, my god!" *This thing must weigh a ton!*

"This is so cool," Arnie whispers.

"At least the asshole had enough courtesy to shut up."
I lug the drawer into the cubbyhole the banker had pointed to
and set it down on the table with a "thunk" then look around.
No cameras pointing here. Good. I hinge back the lid.
"Hmm." Another packet of letters lies to the front, secured
with the same pink and blue ribbon the photos in the shoe box
had been tied with. Farther back, a small canvas sack fills
most of the remaining space. I lift it out and almost drop it.
This is where the weight is. Underneath are several paper
documents. *Okay. Time to dig in.* "Open the sack, Arnie."
Arnie does, and dozens and dozens of gold coins, each one in
its own plastic snapcase, spill out on the table. "Huh!" I takes
me half-a-minute to get my stupid mouth shut.

"Wow!" Arnie picks up one. "This one has a leaf on
it." Another. "This one has a deer, or is it a gazelle? on it.
Hey, this one has a woman's profile. It's a U.S. coin."

I do a quick count. There must be at least fifty coins
here. I will my hands to stop shaking. "Okay. Put them back
in the sack."

"What?"

"We're not taking them with us."

"Not even one?"

"Arnie, if you take one, what are you going to do with
it? Buy ice cream at the Freeze?"

"How much are all these worth? Thousands?"

I do some fast and rough arithmetic, nod, then add,
"Yeah, but if Woodbridge finds out, that sleazy lawyer of
theirs will claim every bit for that place. Something like

'unclosed' expenses. Or Dad will make it disappear. That place and Dad already took everything else she owned with that bullshit will."

Arnie stares at me. "Bullshit?"

"Yeah. 'Arts support fund.' Give me a break."

I begin to unfold the documents. Two are bundles of stock certificates. One holds shares in Apple Corporation! I flip through the bundle, doing a quick count. 3200 shares total! "Wow." My mind is spinning now. *Aunt Millie, you sure were no fool. These have to be worth a fortune.* The other bundle has certificates for two hundred shares of General Motors. *If these are old shares, they're worth nothing. Well, win some, lose some.* I take a deep breath. Here are some answers to my question as to where all of Aunt Millie's money went. I refold both bundles and place them back in the box. Two other documents look like municipal bonds. Later. I want Woodbridge to be cold and old before taking these somewhere. "Woo-who. There's our college educations, Arnie."

"All right! What's that?" He points to the next paper.

I unfold it and trace the words "It's ... a birth certificate? 'Mary Beng Soo, San Francisco General Hospital, December 3, 2.... Mother: Lie Beng Soo. Father: Unknown. Informant: Stanley McClure, Grandfather.' Huh? This is a birth certificate for a granddaughter of Uncle Stan's. Why'd Dad say there were no other relatives left? Why didn't the will mention her? And what happened to the mother? Who was the father?" Now I've got even more questions, but the name on the dried flowers begins to make sense. This is the

Mary I remember. This is *her* certificate, and she is or was Uncle Stan's granddaughter. Did she die or move far away?

"That birth date: she's less than a year younger than you, Peter."

I nod, then try to figure out the relationship. Uncle Stan was Aunt Millie's son, my dad's first cousin—although a lot older. So this unknown mother, Stan's daughter, would be my second cousin. So little Mary has to be like a third cousin, or something like that.

I turn to the letters, aware that we have to be out of this place soon, plus still have to get the ice cream cones to keep ourselves clean with Mom. I untie the ribbon. The first envelope contains five color photographs. All show a little girl with straight, dark brown hair and light brown skin, smiling, waving to the camera or about to throw a ball to someone. In the last picture she rests in Aunt Millie's arms, tired but smiling. "Wow." That's the Mary I remember.

Well, I have some answers: I know who this Mary was and I know where some of the money went, but I still don't know quite why Dad is so determined to erase this part of the family.

I retie the ribbon and put the letters into the grocery bag. Whoa. The back envelope feels heavier and has my name on it. I rip open its flap, and a large key with a number stamped on it drops out. Inside is a sheet of folded note paper with writing and a receipt of some kind.

Okay. Enough for now. I put that into the bag as well and close the box back up. I carry it back to its hole in the vault, shove it in, close the door and remove my key.

"All done?" the attendant asks as we leave the vault.

"For now. Thanks."

"Sign out. Thank you."

"No problem. Have a good one." Arnie and I head for the Freeze.

One more week until school starts. My summer weekday job picking peaches is over, so Arnie and I have five days to kill this mystery. When Arnie isn't in my room, I return the bank key and add the birth certificate to the secret compartment then go to bed.

Next morning, 9 AM, Monday: Mom and Dad are long gone to work, Arnie and I have made quick work of breakfast. I clean up and bring out the envelopes from the bank and set them in a pile on the dining room table. Arnie pulls up a chair and watches. I start with the letters from the shoe box. As I figured, they are useless : Christmas letters from Mom and Dad to Aunt Mille, Older letters from Stan. "Hmm."

Dear Mom,

I have a lead on what happened to Mila Soo. I intend to fly to Bangkok on Tuesday to follow it up. I will not give up until I know what happened to Mila and can verify this girl who might be my child. I know 25 years is a long time, but I cannot give up now when I feel I am so close to answers.

I try to make sense of what I am reading. Uncle Stan was in Thailand. He flew two hundred missions, so he had to have been there close to a year or even more. So was this Mila Soo someone he met over there? Did he have an affair with her? Did she have a daughter, this Lie Beng Soo who gave birth in a San Francisco hospital 15 years ago?

The other letters don't add anything. I put all of them back into the shoe box except the letter from Uncle Stan, then turn to the letters from the bank vault. Many are from Stan and all seem to relate somehow to this vanished cousin of ours.

"I am so glad you have time to see Mary. She is so looking forward to staying with you next week …"

"She misses her mother so much …"

"I only wish my health was better. Doctor I just met with thinks that the prostate cancer may be related to Agent Orange exposure, but, of course, the VA is in total denial. I just hope I can keep working.

"Please take care of my *hlan saw*. She is all I have. I only wish I could have been a better grandfather for her.

"She is so independent—far too grownup for someone only twelve. Every time I come home, she already has a supper ready AND has started on her homework. I am so glad you are going to be able to spend time with her again. What a kid!

"Will see you this Christmas …"

"Whoa …"

"What is it, Pete? Oh. That's the Christmas …"

"Yup. That's the Christmas Aunt Millie broke her hip

—the month before Stan died."

"So ... what happened to Mary? It sounds like she was living with Stan. What happened to her?"

I shrug. I remember Mary, but Mom and Dad have not spoken her name, nor have I seen even a trace of her since Aunt Millie's fall. But if she's still alive, all that gold and Apple stock belongs to her, not us, not Dad or that nursing home.

The last envelope is the one with the key and a letter. It has only my name on it: no address, no postage. What is it?

I take out the piece of note paper and catch a whiff of lavender. It is the smell of Aunt Millie. I open the sheet and begin to read.

```
Dear Peter,
      If you are reading this letter, it is
because I am dead and you have the bank
number. Good work. I know how much you have
suffered these last few years. The world can
be cruel and unfair in many ways,
particularly to children. I am sorry you
ended up a victim.
      But now I must ask for your help in
finding someone who has also become a victim,
my great-granddaughter, Mary Beng Soo. I know
you have met her several times. When Stanley
died, I was so weak and ill from breaking my
hip, I could do nothing for her. Now I am
told I cannot recover enough to return to my
home. Stanley is dead, and I do not know what
has happened to Mary. She may be in foster
care. I spoke with your mother and father
concerning her, but, just as they have denied
```

you and your own problem, so they have
denied that Mary could even be a relative.
They say she has been taken care of—whatever
that means. I am sorry. They are lovely
people in many ways, and I do love them, but
they fail the imagination test almost every
day.
     Two days before I fell, I rented a
locker and parking space behind the North
Shore Mall. The rent is paid for ten years—
same as the bank security box. The key should
be in the security box with this letter. I
put several boxes of records in the locker. I
told Stan to fill it up once I knew I was
never going home again. I do not know if he
did, but there may be something in there that
might tell you where Mary has gone to. This
is your task now, Peter. I will get this into
the security box somehow. Maybe my friend Tom
can manage it. Please be willing to undertake
this mission and task. I think it will help
you. She was all I had in the end—besides you
and Arnold—and it breaks my heart to think
that they took her away from me. Love and
courage and thank you, *Aunt Millie*

Millicent Bain McClure, January 31, 20----.
Storage unit gate digits: **4133**

    I tent my fingers, trying to think—although my
struggling lungs are getting in the away. It's over two and a
half years since Aunt Millie fell, two years since Mom
suddenly bought a new Mini and Dad a new set of golf clubs
and his first Audi ... one trip to Vegas, one to Mexico since
then. Yeah, things sure got better for Mom and Dad after

Aunt Millie fell, but not for Mary. I know something came to my parents after Stan died, but supposedly not much. So what happened?

Chapter III   the Locker

My eyes meet Arnie's. "I guess the locker is the next place to check. I don't see any other clues here—not yet anyway."

"Road trip?"

"Yeah. Sort of. About ten miles."

I am under strict orders never to drive anywhere as just Arnie and I are about to do. Something about putting all the eggs in one basket, but neither Mom nor Dad will be home before four. We have some time. I don't plan to take the main roads anyway.

The old Volvo sweet and caring Daddy has gifted me for getting to my job is definitely not a babe-magnet, but it gets us there. I circle around the mall, spot the sign for the storage units and drive down an alley to the entrance. I key in the four digits from Aunt Millie's letter, and when the gate rolls back, I drive through and turn into an alleyway between lines of garage doors. No attendants, but maybe that's why people like these places. Lots of privacy.

"There's the number," Arnie points out. I stop and we get out. The lock on the side of the door will respond to some kind of card, but I don't have that. Instead I insert the key from the envelope and, as I turn it, the locker door rolls upward. Half-way up and a light turns on inside. Arnie and I walk in a room the size of a small bedroom, both of us ducking a little and tapping the overhead door as we do so.

Place is pretty packed. A row of six stacked cardboard boxes line up against the right wall. Several tables and chairs I vaguely remember from Aunt Millie's apartment and a dresser topped by two old, non-rolling suitcases take up the back wall. Sort of what I expect. What I do not expect is the sofa set against the left wall with its neat set of sheets, pillows and blankets on the cushion. "Huh?" It's actually a futon, and the bedding looks like it goes with it. A small table with a desk lamp and an office chair on rollers sits in the middle of the concrete floor.

"Looks like someone's made themselves comfortable here," Arnie whispers.

"It does," I whisper back.

Several books lie in stacks on the nearer boxes. I pick one up. Ninth grade algebra. The next one down is *History: Ancient Times to the Modern Era*.

"More like living here. But why, and how do they get in here?"

"Don't know, Bro." Arnie sits down on the futon, then stretches out. "Not bad if you open it up."

Something else is bothering me. I trace a finger across the edge of the table, and I know: no dust. If someone has been living here, it has to be recently. How can they stand this heat? I'm sweating so badly the moisture is starting to drip inside my shirt. Even with the garage door open, it must be close to a hundred degrees in here.

I start opening boxes but know I won't last long. First box contains sewing materials: printed cottons and velvets, and in the middle, a sewing machine. I remember Aunt Millie making me coveralls for playing in a sandbox. I wonder if she used this machine.

I try another box. Lots of file folders filled with paperwork. Might be worthwhile, until I realize that all the files cover tax records from the 1990s. *Crap.* "Check the drawers, Arnie."

"Got it."

Next box is full of old kitchen utensils. *Double crap.*

"Just underwear in this one." With a grin, Arnie holds up a pink bra for my inspection.

"Put it back." I sigh.

"Old jeans and sweatshirts in this one."

"Okay. I think we're done for the day." We have to be back home and settled before the dear Dad and Mom get off work, and this heat is the pits. "Let's go." I carefully put back everything as close to original as possible. We both exit, pull down the door and set the lock.

"What a zero place! Man, I thought this place would be full of antiques or paintings or something cool."

I nod and feel a silent mode coming on, even from my brother. I get in the car, wait for Arnie to belt-in, back out of the driveway, turn and head out of the gate, pausing to make sure it closes behind us. We're on our way.

"How big was Aunt Millie? I mean, around here?" Arnie motions to his chest.

"As I remember, she wasn't small … Wait a minute! That couldn't have been her bra, could it! Or those jeans or those sweatshirts. That's stuff girls wear. That bra looked like it would fit a twelve-year-old."

"So whose is it? This Mary girl's?"

I nod, but do not pretend to understand. Not until I am turning into our driveway do I remember that we never checked the suitcases on top of the dresser, or the boxes underneath the top ones.

Okay. That takes care of Monday. Parents do not have a clue, so on to step two—whatever that is. That night I lie awake, staring first at my window, then the ceiling. I now have access to a locker full of stuff, almost none of any interest to me and with no obvious value, and still have the cousin question. What are we going to do about it? I suppose I can tell Dad or Mom, let them deal with it. They'll probably just throw everything out. Dad and Mom hate keeping old records and worn-out clothes. But, no. I never share anything else, and I'm not about to now. Not yet, anyway. Aunt Millie asked me to do this search, not my parents.

We could wait for cooler weather, go back and go through those boxes I missed, and the suitcases, one by one. I could check the internet, county records. I know Mary exists. I used to play with her—build LEGO, play video games, watch movies—but I have no idea where she is now, or even if she's alive. So who was, or is using that locker? Mary—a kid younger than I am? No, no, no … Not possible. Well, not yet, anyway. There was no food, no toilet, no heat, or cooling.

Only thing it would be good for is staying out of the rain. I guess I'll start with the internet … tomorrow.

An internet search Tuesday morning reveals no records of a Mary Beng Soo. Stanley McClure does show up with records from the war. I learn he was awarded the Distinguished Flying Cross plus a bunch of air medals, commendations, etc. I suspect that cross was one medal that didn't get handed out in the chow line. Millie does not show up except for a short obit the local paper published two weeks ago. "Millicent nee Bain McClure, widow of Walter McClure, successful local industrialist, etc." So far, pretty much a bust. I try county records, but cannot find any recent stuff on line. I'll have to go to the courthouse. If she went into foster care, where would records of that be? Not online, apparently. For two seconds I wonder if there is anything new on Dennis Tiltman, 'beloved coach and teacher.' Then I shake my head. I know that going there will only renew the pain.

After lunch, Arnie and I go through the safety deposit box records once more. We find more pictures of Mary, only older. She no longer looks as happy as she did when she was a kid. "What do you think, Arnie?"

"She looks suspicious, maybe shy, cautious," is Arnie's take. I see pain too. I know what that is, and feel a kinship. *Poor kid—you've gotten screwed too.*

Tucked in another envelope, I find a copy of Lie Beng Soo's death certificate. I calculate and realize that Mary's mom died when she was four. Cause of death: asphyxiation due to drowning. That sounds weird, but the paperwork gives no other information.

First day of school. "So, you going out for cross-country again this year?" Good old, concerned Dad. He is sure that if I play *his* sports and make the right moves, somehow everything will get better.

I nod. Volleyball is what I really want to play, but cross-country is what it'll be. I've already started running every evening. Usually Arnie goes with me, although he's going out for volleyball now that he's old enough. I set a pace so he can keep up, which is not as fast as I want to go, but I get the workout I need.

"I hope you're not thinking of volleyball."

I wouldn't tell you if I was, but I am. Why do I feel bolder, freer this fall? Maybe several tens of thousand dollars' worth of gold and stock certificates in a bank do that. Maybe plans to make this my last year in high school.

"Well, give our regards to Mrs. Shipton. She's always been a good friend."

Mrs. Shipton was my English teacher in tenth grade. First teacher since sixth grade who treated me like I was normal. *Yeah, I'll say 'hi' to her.*

I let Mom kiss me on a cheek and let Dad rub a shoulder. Arnie and I are out the door and headed for the Volvo. Belted in and ready, I back toward the street and almost run into Denver Jack. "Hi, Jack." I call out after blowing out a sigh of relief at my close call.

"Hi, Peter; Hi, Arnold," Jack replies with a stiff, cautious wave. He waits while I finish getting the car out onto the street, then waves again as we drive off. I guess Jack's as low on the mental functioning scale as one can get and still live at home and take care of himself. I think he's eighteen, but it's hard to tell. Nice guy and friendly—as long as you never call him 'Denver Jack' to his face. Not sure why, but it usually sets him off into screaming and sobbing. Of course the local bullies call him 'Denver Jack,' anytime they get a chance. I have my problem, but not one like Jack's. "There, but for the grace of that which animates all of us …" I whisper.

"Amen," Arnie responds.

The first day each fall is always the worst, but now that Arnie's in ninth grade and we're in high school together, maybe we can protect each other —to a limited extent. I once thought that as the years went by, some people would forget. Maybe the younger kids would never have heard about my supposed lies or Mr. Tiltman's suicide and leave me alone. If you figure three hours of hell each day last year instead of eight the way it started then, yes, maybe things have gotten better, but, no, the whispers, confrontations and harassments have never gone away completely.

No sooner do Arnie and I make it through Truman High School's front door but the first call goes out. "Hey, look who's back. Pete with the lying peter. What a dick!"

Pretty lame stuff. I ignore the laughs and keep moving. "Who was it?" I whisper to Arnie once we turn a corner.

"Jason Small, same punk as last year, right?" Arnie

answers.

     I nod. *One of them. Some things never change.* I give my locker a once-over before spinning the lock dial and lifting the handle. I never used to know from day-to-day if it will be booby-trapped or the handle covered with grease. That's the main reason the principal lets me have a lock. Once I opened it and got a flour bath in the face. Once it was a whole stack of porno mags aimed at gay men. Today, it proves to be innocent, and I put my hat and lunch inside and head for homeroom, weaving my way around the clang of other lockers being opened and sneakers squeaking on the newly-polished floor. Maybe this will be a better year.

     Classes are still the same: teachers direct me to seats either in the back or to one side. That's fine. I don't have to worry about watching my back that way. As my classmates shuffle in, most turn their heads away, noses lifting or wrinkling like I've just farted. The whispers pass around me, like I don't exist. I raise my hand for first class roll call but otherwise keep my silence. As the classes proceed, I take careful notes in longhand, moving through several sheets in every class.

     All my classes are honors or advanced placement—senior level stuff. I know a lot of other students resent that too, but studying hard is one thing no one can take away from me. I earn my grades, even with the silence. Back in middle school, several teachers were sure I was cheating. My social studies teacher tried to set up traps. He failed.

     I still get a lot of sighs, but I am still here. I will make it through this year, lies or no lies.

After school, I'm down by the track, changed into sweats and ready to roll. "Hey-day, Pete," Ryan Demsworth greets me. He's one of two guys in my grade who are openly gay. Nothing that could have ever happened to me can faze him.

No one hassles him either—not at six-foot-two and maybe close to two hundred-thirty pounds. He probably would have been an outstanding halfback but for his orientation. He knows that football is out of the question—not unless he wants to get killed every game. Cross-country is pretty loose. Guys and gals, we just go out and run and have fun. First day back, so coach takes us around the track, then sends us off on a path that will eventually bring us into the downtown, then back along the river. It will get harder, faster and longer later.

I notice several new faces. Must be freshmen. By the time we turn onto the river trail, one of the girls, a little, freckle-cheeked blonde in red sweats, is having a hard time keeping up. I fall back and give her a smile.

"How do you guys do it?" She pants. "I've been running a mile every day for a month, and I'm beat already."

"Hey," a junior calls out. "No talking to the coach-killer."

Blondie makes a face like 'What's he talking about?' then it dawns. "Oh. Sorry." She leans-in, pushes and passes me.

So much for meeting a girl. Sigh. But that is what my life is. I ease into a ground-eating pace, pass my teammates one-by-one and cross the line in the stadium three car lengths ahead of the former leader. That's why I'll never be cut from the team—much as certain individuals, including the team captain and the coach, would love to do it.

I walk it off, then ease over to open doors that lead into the main gym. Men's and women's volleyball teams are hard at it. Arnie is out there, moving the ball. I wish ... I so wish that could be me in there. *Do I dare? What will it take?*

Chapter IV   The Northside Library

For reasons I cannot understand, "Modern" European history begins in 1789 with the French Revolution. Since I am officially mute, I get research and written assignments—lots of them. Fine with me. Books don't accuse me of causing a hero coach to kill himself. For my first assignment, I recall a library book on the Reign of Terror that might be perfect for supplementing whatever *wikipedia* might start me with. On the way home, I stop off at Cross Creek, our local branch of the public library, but discover that the book is no longer in the library. 'Weeded' it seems to make room for new novels... I search the library's catalog and luck out: the missing book is available at the Northside branch.

I wave to Nancy Upton, my favorite library worker. "You can order it, Peter, and we'll have it here for you by Thursday," she tells me when I point to the entry on the computer screen. Unlike most people, Ms. Upton is nice to me. Sometimes I wonder why. The rest of the staff here, like everyone at school, try their best to ignore me.

"What if I drove over there? Could I just pick it up?"

Only a raised eyebrow reacts to my speaking. "You could. Put a hold on it, and check the box that says you'll pick it up at Northside. You could get it tonight. They're open until nine."

I hesitate. Mom and Dad will be okay. Maybe no one will know me there. Would be nice to walk into a place and not have someone start whispering 'There goes the coach killer. there goes the liar.' "Okay. Sure, I'll do it."

By supper I have Arnie primed so he can go with me. He tells Mom that he needs to go over to Northside to pick up a book he needs. Would it be okay if Peter drove him?

No sense in drawing attention to what I might want or need.

Mom looks at Dad. I pretend to concentrate on my broccoli. "I guess. You both will be home by nine?"

"Scout's honor," Arnie tells them.

We head for the door.

The ride is uneventful. Driving is getting easier for me. That's got to be a plus toward my independence if I bail out next year—like I plan.

Unlike Cross Creek, Northside has its own parking lot. The place is busy inside, but I wait my turn at the circulation desk.

A middle-aged lady dressed in a polo shirt logoed with a dragon deep in a book is standing there. The words 'Fantastic Summer Reading' are the shirt's message. "May I help you?" she asks.

"Picking up a book titled *Reign of Terror*. By Livingston. Supposed to be on reserve for Bain for pick-up this evening."

Lady eyes the circ terminal. "You're fast. It must still be on the shelves. Marty, could you go get this book for this gentleman? Here's the call number."

Hmm. Marty-girl must be some kind of student assistant or page. I take in the view: young, cute, nice figure covered with a similar library-logoed polo plus jeans. She sweeps back her long, dark, mahogany-streaked hair from her smooth-skinned face as she takes the slip from the lady. "I can get it," she whispers in a soft, husky voice that surprises me, and heads for the non-fiction. Arnie and I tag along behind, Arnie grinning, staring at her butt and rolling his eyes at me. This kid would never give even a first glance at any girl his age or older at school, but one minute 'off the rez' and he's eyeing every potential beauty. I just shake my head. For me, they are probably all off-limits, no matter where they live.

The girl runs a finger along a low shelf, checking off numbers. "Here you go." She lifts off a thick tome, stands up and hands it to me. "Thanks, Marty," I tell her.

"You're welcome. No problem." For half a second, our eyes meet—her hazel set in lids that hint of East Asia searching my blue. Suddenly she grins, lifts her right hand as if to wave but then turns away. I catch a whisper "night … shining," as I open the book. Yup. This is the one I remember.

I take it to a table and begin to leaf through it, already mentally taking notes. I grab a couple of slips of paper, flip to the bibliography and start scanning citations. That one, maybe that one. I start writing.

Arnie has wandered over to the YA section. He rejoins me, several novels in hand, sits and begins reading the blurbs inside the dust covers. He clears his throat, once, twice and points with his lips behind me.

"What? Oh."

Marty is standing there beside me. "If you're interested in the French Revolution, this title might interest you. We just got it in last month. Ah … I read it and learned a lot." She offers me a book. *Glory, Equality and Fraternity: A European Bloodbath, Parallels to our Modern Revolutions* reads the title. Sounds deep, but different. But is there a parallel to the madness of 1789 and the conflicts going on now in the Middle East and elsewhere?

"Thank you. That does look useful. Thank you." I accept the book and set it down on the table. Now I do give Marty-girl more than just a glance as she heads for a book truck near the fiction section. She gives me a nod and another smile and I feel my heart beating in my chest, so strong that I place my hand there.

Arnie and I are home by 8:30PM. "How'd it go?" Mom calls from the living room as we walk in. Arnie leans into the room far enough to wave a fistful of books at her. I retire to my room, set my books down and stare at them. But I am not seeing them. I am seeing the look on that freshman girl's face when she realized who I was. I feel the darkness, like a storm cloud, moving across my desk. Will any of this ever end? Will any girl ever believe I didn't lie? I take a deep, cleansing breath and open the book Marty gave me. As I turn to page 20, a call slip lifts off and settles back on the page like a suddenly disturbed butterfly. "Huh?" I pick it up, turn it over. The words, 'Hi, Peter' stare back at me.

Chapter V   The Tryout

I do not know what to do. It is as if I have walked into an overhead beam. 'What …?" is all I can manage. No one knew me at that library—nobody. *This is a new book*. Marty told me that. Would she? Did *she* …? "No." I let out a deep breath. *This is totally crazy*. For five years not a single girl, or guy (besides Ryan and Arnie) has spoken to me, except by accident or out of ignorance. For five years, I have spoken to no one unless I can trust them, or I know they do not know me. I have never been in the Northside branch before.

I pick up the slip of paper, check both sides and shake my head, then drop it into the center drawer of my desk. I put the library books aside and turn to other homework. Pre-calc, stats, English, physics, German all take time. By ten, I'm wiped. I print out some of my writings and calculations, shut down my old laptop and get ready for bed. M*arty, whoever you are, did you slip that greeting in the book?* Why? I see that smile and beauty as I brush my teeth, I see the motion of her hips and body as she walked back to her cart. I see that flick of her hair. As I head back to my room, I realize that the soft whistling I am hearing is coming from my own mouth. And as I slip into bed, a revelation comes to me: *a beautiful* *girl was nice to me today.*

You would think in a high school as big as ours, I'd be able to disappear, but this has never happened. We are so big that the academics has two different schools. If you are in School A, you take all your classes there. You never see anyone from School B, except for sports and other extra curricular activities. Take this Marty girl for example. If she is in my own high school, but in School B, unless I like the same activities she does, I'll never meet her. and once you are in A or B, that's where you stay all the way for four years. Maybe I can get ahold of class lists. But who in the administration is going to help the 'lying kid who never talks?'

I could return both those books to my local library, but I'm won't do that. Not if returning them directly to Northside will allow me to see friendly Marty again. Of course, there is no way I can know if she will even be there. Maybe with school, she's stopped working there. Well, I guess I have to take a chance.

I make it back to Northside the following Thursday, but do not see Marty. Still, I do my best. "Please tell Marty that the book she recommended was a real help. I did use it for my paper."

The librarian looks at the discharge line on the computer. "I'll tell her when I see her."

"Thanks. She's still working here?"

The woman nods. "Marty almost never leaves here. Sometimes I think she believes this is her home."

"Hmm ..." I smile before leaving.

Volleyball ... Volleyball? I do not think of myself as a jock. I just like to run and play volleyball. Running I may do, but volleyball? Coach Tiltman is what got me in trouble in the first place. Do I dare? I cannot ask anyone, because they will all say no. Mom and Dad will say no—not just no, but hell no. Coach Allison will say no. The rest of the team will probably hate me. But maybe this year will be different.

First fall week after Tiltman killed himself, I got slapped and shoved around so many times I lost count. Second day of classes, half the volleyball team grabbed me, pulled me into a corner and spent half-an-hour poking and pounding on me. By the time they finished, I couldn't even walk straight—but I never said a word, just stumbled away and went to class. "Liar, liar, coach-killer," their whispered shouts still echo. All those guys are gone now. The last member of the team who played under Tiltman graduated over a year ago. Maybe ...

I have six years of practicing behind me: hitting that ball over that taut line stretched across the garage again, and again. This is Arnie's and my private world. Dad thinks we are practicing basketball. Arnie is good too. He has to be: he's the one who has been setting me for the last three years. And this year, he's gonna' make the team. But, oh-no, Dad won't hear of *my* playing.

Under the "great" Coach Tiltman, the men's team made States twice. Coach Allison has not been so fortunate, and, checking the tryouts, it does not look like it's going to get better. Well, no guts—no glory. On Wednesday, instead of running, I find myself rapping on the Coach Allison's office door.

"Come in," the thin voice rasps. Coach Allison always sounds like he's smoking two packs a day. Not sure why, since I know he doesn't smoke.

"Bain? Why aren't you out there running?"

I take a deep breath. I know this will be hard, but it is what I want, what I feel has to carry me now. "Coach, I want to play varsity volleyball?"

Mr. Allison, chokes and gags. It takes him half-a-minute of sputtering before he can manage the expected "No. No way. You're too late anyway." His lips are quivering now and he starts running his fingers through papers on his desk.

"Team rosters aren't due until tomorrow. First game is next week," I point out. *Is it so hard to speak now because I have been silent so long?*

"Bain, we started practice two weeks ago. If you wanted on team, you had to be there then. Where's your physical?"

"Already turned in for cross-country. Try me."

Mr. Allison slams his hand down on the desk top. "Bain, I will not have some lying … guy on my team unwilling to 'fess up to a false story that killed my friend. And who won't talk in class."

"You want to beat Freeland this year? Try me." That one hits home. Freeland High is *the* traditional enemy. We haven't beaten their varsity in six years."

"No!"

"Let him try, Coach. Give him a chance," comes a girl's voice from behind me—that same husky soft voice I just heard last week. I turn, mouth gaping, and there stands Marty girl, dressed now in sweats and a tee-shirt, ready for some activity.

"You think I should?" Surprise and confusion are rippling across Mr. Allison's face.

"Yes, I do," she answers firmly.

Coach takes a deep breath. "Okay. One shot. No, two shots, then you're out of here." He heaves himself to his feet, grabs a ball and heads out to the court where several members of the men's team are already warming up.

"I'll spot the net for you," Marty tells Coach.

"Thanks, Marty." He pitches the ball to me. "Serve me one from that side. Everyone, I'm giving a late-comer two serves."

"Bain? What's he doin' here?" Bernie, the team captain, asks, but he walks off the court with the rest.

I take a position behind the line and pop the ball. It's not my favorite, but I know it will work. It floats up high and deep—looking like it'll sail out for sure. When it lands, it's six inches in bounds, deep right corner. Coach, who was going to let it go, just stares. "Shit," I hear him whisper. Someone rolls the ball back to him and he returns it to me.

Now he's ready. He shifts back, alert for wherever that ball might go. Several team members take up positions on the court in back and in front of him.

I leap and overhand the next shot straight down the middle, clear the net by an inch and plant it straight on the floor two inches from Coach's left foot. No one can return a volleyball coming at them at thirty-miles-per-hour. Coach jumps aside.

"Wow," I hear several schoolmates whistle.

"Coach, are you all right?" I ask.

"Yes, dammit. I'm fine. You did ..." He pushes away the other players. I just gave him two serves that every opponent hates or fears. "Okay, everyone, let's get practicing. Bain, I want you at the net. Let's see if your ball handling is as good as your serves.

"Coach," Bernie cries. "Do we have to?"

"Just play. I make the decision here, and I haven't made it yet," he growls.

The game starts. The ball soon comes my way. I set it for the middle hitter, again and again. Seems like the ball is headed my way a lot. Well, maybe it's time. This time I take a set and pound it down Bernie's throat.

Volleyball is not a contact sport, or isn't supposed to be, but intimidation is the name of the game. If your opponent fears you, you're half way to winning. Bernie just got something no volleyball player wants: a ball in his face so hard it knocks his glasses off. "Holy shit, man! What are ya doin'?"

I hear Arnie cheer from somewhere behind me.

"He touched the net" someone from that side calls out.

"It was a clean kill," Marty yells back. I forgot my lady supporter is still watching the net.

I don't answer, but pass the ball back to the next

server on our side. We play until our side hits 25 points. The other side has managed five.

We go into drills, including me. I play nice, moving the ball, setting it up, then killing it on the return. By the closing time I have the feel for the other players—who's good, who's not, who will work with me, who wishes I was dead. As the players, guys—and the gals from the other court —roll balls back into the net bags, I turn and walk over to stand in front of Mr. Allison.

He stares at me a long time. "I can't do it."

"Can't or won't?" I stare back at him until he looks away.

"Half the teachers, the other coaches, the parents of the older kids, they'd have my scalp on a pole."

"Coach, I never lied. I do not lie. I haven't told a lie since I was ten years old. This is what I want to do, have ever since I remember. Thank you for letting me try out today. Maybe we'll beat Freeland with the team you have, maybe the team might even make districts this year, but ..." I don't say anything more. I figure I don't have to. The board has promised any coach a bonus if his or her team makes the playoffs. A fair deal, since playoffs mean extra work for everyone. Second tier social studies teachers don't get overtime, and he has two kids in college, and another a senior in high school. That bonus will mean a lot.

"Coach?" It's Jason Patrick, one of Arnie's classmates. "Let him on. We need him, please. I know we do." Several other team members are gathering. When Coach looks around, the other younger players nod agreement. Only the seniors and juniors are holding back.

Coach wets his lips. "Okay. Come back tomorrow. I'll let you know then."

"Thank you," I nod and smile.

I'm heading for the showers. Tomorrow's okay. I figure by stalling, Coach has a chance to save face. I'll have to let the cross-country folks know, but that will keep. I look around, hoping to spot Marty girl, but I don't see her anywhere. *Marty, whoever you are, I owe you one—big time.*

Chapter VI Martina Sofia

I'm heading for my car, Arnie beside me, when standing by the exit is Bernie and several of the other seniors. He moves in front of me. "Hey, asshole. Who do you think you are? You made me; you made the *whole team* look like shit today."

I knew that doing this might not be popular. "Sorry. I just want to play."

Knuckles press against my chin. "Okay. You can serve; you can spike, you can set. What else can you do?"

"I can give the team everything I have."

Bernie steps back "He's gonna' 'give the team 'everything he has.' Did you hear that? This another lie of yours, Bain?"

I shake my head, once more wrapped in my silence.

"If you want him to speak to you, you've got to be

nice and not accuse him of something he never did," Armie butts in.

"Oh. So little brother knows all the answers." Bernie pauses. "You were smiling out there. Did you like hitting me?" I shake my head. "Okay. Get the fuck out of here." He stands aside and Arnie and I leave.

"Bro, you were awesome out there."

I nod. *It was worth it, even if I don't make the team.*

"All those nights bouncing that ball back-and-forth … but I didn't think you were *that* good."

I shrug. "You worked with me. You were a great help."

"Think Coach will let you on?"

I shrug again. "Maybe. He sure doesn't want to end up in Freeland's swimming pool again." This is a long-time tradition. Losing coach gets tossed in the host team's pool. Mr. Allison gets wet every year.

"Hey, wait up." I stop. Marty girl comes trotting out after us.

"Thanks for your help," I tell her.

She blushes. "Everyone should have a chance."

Arnie gives her a smile. "So, you out for volleyball too?"

"Ah-huh. Thought I'd try it again this year. Not sure I'm gonna' make it. Played last year, but Mrs. Hertz makes the cuts tomorrow before the rosters are due."

"Maybe Peter here can give you some pointers." *Thanks, Brother.*

Marty laughs, a deep chuckle. "Maybe."

I need to keep this conversation going. She is so beautiful and so nice, and she's a girl actually talking to me. "You a student here, but in B School, right?"

"You guessed it. Tenth grade."

"I wondered why I'd never seen you before."

She puts a finger to her lips, as if lost in thought. "Oh, I think you have, maybe you just don't remember." She smiles, then shakes her head, as if that sentence was no more important than a wisp of smoke.

"How long have you been a page at Northside?" We have reached the Volvo now, but I'm suddenly in no hurry to get on home.

"Two months...? Two-and-half October first. I like working there. It's fun."

"Maybe Peter will want to do all his library research there," Arnie puts in.

Ouch. Thanks, Brother. Cool it, would ya.

Marty gives me a serious look. "Maybe it would work. The staff talks to you there. Yeah, I know. I've heard all the stories."

"But you are talking to me anyway ..."

"I make up my own mind; I live my own life. No problem. If you say that you told the truth, that's the end of the story."

"Do you think I should remain silent?"

"I don't know ... Silence can be a lie. You believe in truth, I take it. I lie all the time." She looks away, face suddenly grim. "We all do what we have to do."

"Even right now?"

"*Touché*! Maybe."

"So what's your full name, where do you live? Can I …"

"Ah … Martina Sofia. I live over in Taneytown. I don't have a phone, if that's what you were digging for. Although you can reach me at the Northside most non-school hours when the library's open. My email address is MarSo4133@Allmail.com. I check my mail there when I work."

"I don't have anything to write on," I stammer.

"If you don't remember, I'll give it to you next time you stop by Northside. Just remember, I am a liar. Nothing I just told you might be true."

"Can I give you my number?"

"Not now. I've got to go."

"Were you the one who left me the note in the book?"

"What note?"

"The one that said 'Hi, Peter.'"

"Maybe …"

"How'd you know my name?"

"See if you can figure that one out yourself? Have a good one." She waves and sprints across the parking lot to where a dark grey Mercedes is waiting.

See if you can figure it out. How am I supposed to do that? "Let's go home."

"That has to be the longest conversation you have ever held with anyone in this entire planet outside of yours truly. You could've just put her information in your phone."

"Thanks. Not a word of this to anyone."

"My lips are sealed."

"Word gets out that Marty Sofia is making eyes at Peter Bain, and she'll lose every friend she has, plus get the attitude check from her teachers."

"Why's she doing it?"

That's the million-dollar question, and one I have no answer to. *And why did she put herself on the line for me— literally?* I merge into traffic and head for home, or, as it really is: the *domicile*, the house where I sleep and study.

What a screwed-up mess! My mind is like swamp city as I get ready for bed.

After five years I dare to take on part of this *stupid* world where I live, and blam, a cool chick walks into my life at the same time. I so did not plan on that. What does she see in me? Someone to feel sorry for? She said she's a liar. Maybe she thinks I'm a liar like everyone else does, so misery goes for company. I don't know. I only wish I can forget about her long enough to get to sleep. I roll over to try my left side, but it's no more comfortable than my right was. I roll back the covers, wait until I feel the chill, then roll them back up again. It's gonna' to be a long night.

I know that it's pointless to look for Marty in the school halls, in the cafeteria or in our school library. If she's in School B, she's in an entirely separate set of buildings, the other side of an access road and two lines of trees. Still, I find my eyes drifting, taking note of girls in a way I have never bothered to do before. I spot the freshman blonde from cross-country who made the error of talking to me. I give her a smile anyway. She cringes and faces away. I almost laugh. I think about laughing a lot. Sometimes it's the only thing that keeps me from banging my head against the hallway walls.

At the end of the school day, I'm standing outside Coach Allison's office. I've got my cross-country sweats with me in my gym bag. No sense in getting high hopes, but I'm ready either way.

When I knock, Coach waves me in. "You want to know what I decided?"

I nod.

"I talked with the principal this morning, and the superintendent. They are not happy about this. I'm not happy about this. But legally I can't keep you off the team. Oh, I could. I could tell you the same things I told you yesterday, but you're sharp. If the others are willing to play with you, I think this team can do great things this year. So ... yes, go practice with the team. I'll make a final decision before our first game. I could say yes now, and your name is on the roster, but if the rest of the guys won't work with you, it *won't* happen. Understand? Oh, and I already let Mr. Gross know you're dropping cross-country for volleyball this fall." He pauses and runs a hand across the top of his head where there used to be hair. "I was surprised that Mr. Gross didn't seem surprised at all."

I nod, but cannot keep from grinning.

After a couple of laps around the gym, practice is

drills and games. Every five minutes or so, Coach stops us
and subs someone in or someone out. Then he switches
positions. I'm on the same side of the net as Bernie and the
other seniors. I lay up for them and play nice. I also show
them that I can return the ball so it will drop right next to the
net anywhere I want it to. No one returns those shots,
although the other front line makes valiant attempts, some of
which go flying off in wild directions. I use my roundhouse
serve—an arcing shot that starts toward one corner on the
other side but always ends up somewhere else. Only two of
those get returned. When we break, no one wants to block
opposite me. Coach fixes that. "If you guys want to win every
game, you got to be able to face every opponent, even the
toughest." Soon everyone on the other side was trying in any
way he can to block and return my shots. I keep making it
harder and harder. By the time Coach called quits, the whole
team is down to just tees and shorts but still covered with
sweat, the opposing guy playing *libero* most of all.

As I'm heading for the showers, Coach stops me.
"They needed that."

I nod and smile. *We all need that.*

The buzz in the locker room snaps off the moment I
enter. I know twelve other guys are watching me the whole
time I undress and head into the showers. I hurry up and get
in and out and re-dress. As I grab my gym bag and backpack,
Bernie steps over to block me. I face him and wait as he
studies my face. Finally he shrugs and punches me on the arm
so hard I tremble. Then he nods and walks off.

"What was that for?" Arnie asks as we head for the

hall.

"The Alpha Male reasserting his dominance" I answer.

"I have no idea what you are talking about."

"Look it up. Part of social dynamics."

She's waiting outside the gym door when Arnie and I come out. "Hi, guys."

"Hi, yourself," Arnie answers as he waves to Marty.

"Hey, can I get a ride from you guys. My ride didn't show."

Whoa, this is going fast. "Sure. I think we have time. Where to?"

"The 'Y'."

"You doing volleyball there too?"

Marty laughs. "No, meeting someone else." Gallant Arnie opens the front passenger side for her and she hops in. Arnie gets in back, and we're on our way.

All the noise in the world is outside. Inside the Volvo we move in a glass-and-metal cage of silence. I keep glancing at her. Twice I find her staring back, but she says nothing, although once she sighs. Is this a good silence? Each traffic light I feel the thread of silence stretch tighter and tighter, my own throat caught between a desire to hear her strange voice, and this world so like the way I always live in now myself. "You can just drop me off in front." Her voice snaps the tensioned thread."

"Okie-dokie." I signal and pull into the sidewalk next to the handicapped ramp.

"Thanks, guys. See you whenever." She pats my arm then is out in a dash and running up the steps, her backpack and gym bag in her hands. I follow her butt, trace her slender legs, taking in the curves, then spot the lone guy waiting at the top of the steps. He leans in to give her a quick kiss on her cheek, then takes her backpack, holds the door open for her and they disappear inside.

Arnie gets out and moves to the front before we drive off. "Well, that was sweet while it lasted."

"Thanks, Arnie." That touch to my arm had felt so warm, so personal. Now it is just numbness, four icicles raking my skin instead of four magic fingers.

"Hey, Bro, I was rooting for you."

"I know. Thanks." I head to the domicile, my throat so tight that I know I can't say a word, even if I wanted to.

The rest of the week moves along. Another pickup load of firewood has arrived, so Arnie and I both help with the splitting two evenings. The wood shed already has close to three cords—more than enough for this year, but Dad hates to see a half-empty bin, so we keep at it.

I continue to note Marty at practice. She's always the first one there, checking the nets, getting out the balls. She's a hustler on the court, going for every ball in her zone, no matter how unreachable. No wonder Mr. Allison has a soft spot for her. Other than one quick wave, she has no time for me. Volleyball is keeping me busy—far busier than cross-country ever did.

Wednesday, I'm heading for the showers after

practice when Ryan joins me outside the locker room. "Missed you on the runs. Say, you are out for volleyball? Heard Joey Hernandez say he saw you out on the courts."

"Yeah. I'm giving it a try."

"Good luck. You're gonna' make it."

"What do you mean?"

"If you're half as good at volleyball as you are at running … That's what I mean. But I also know you're finally scouting the girls. You're gonna' make that happen too."

"What are you talkin' about?"

"Pete, don't act like a dumb shit. Half—maybe more than half this place—thinks you're gay. They think that you accused Coach Tiltman of trying to rape you 'cause you went for him and he turned you down. But I see you. Every time I'm coming in from my run, and volleyball's finishing up, you're staring at the girls team. I know hunger when I see it."

Oh my god! I stifle a snort. *Am I blushing? Gad. Marty must think me some kind of stalker-dork.* "Thanks for the heads-up."

"No problem. They don't do anything for me."

"I guess not." I shake my head and head in for a shower.

On Thursday, I note Mr. Smelz, our principal, sitting up in the bleachers watching. Does this mean trouble? Or maybe nothing at all.

Saturday morning, Arnie and I wash all the family cars. Then I crawl under the Volvo and check for rust and spray-paint the obvious spots with black Rustoleum. After lunch, I head to the farmer's market where I work half of every Saturday at the indoor veggie stand, plus—now that the fall veggie season is in full gear— all day Sundays. I unpack melons, tomatoes, oranges, peaches and early apples, open boxes of mushrooms and mist-spray the lettuce to make it look fresh. The rush is always in the mornings, so Saturday afternoons I get a chance to organize things and take inventory. Sunday mornings are so busy, particularly after eleven, that I spend all my time making change, unpacking and bagging. By four, as I am every Sunday, I'm whipped and ready to go home. One last cabbage head to bag for some lady so fat she has to turn sideways to get down the side aisle when I hear the voice. "Got any rutabagas?"

"Middle of the third aisle," I tell her without daring to look her way. I smile at the cabbage lady and count out the dollars and change. "Thank you." I head over to the third aisle.

"Do you really think I might want to eat rutabagas?" Marty tells me with a wink as I grab a bag and approach her. "But I will take these carrots and those cucumbers."

"This many?" I take the carrots and bag them, then walk over to the baskets of cucumbers. "Big or pickle size?"

"Those." She points at a pint of medium-sized. I turn the basket upside down into another plastic bag and wait. Marty pulls a wallet out of a back pocket and counts out three crumbled and dirty bills.

"Need fifty cents more."

"Oh." She fishes out a Sackie and hands it to me. I don't see the dollar coins too often, so I hesitate until I realize what it is. I hand her change from my apron. "Everything going okay?"

"No. I'll catch you later, Peter," and she walks off without even a wave.

I so wish I knew what's going on.

Chapter VII   First Game

First game is Wednesday night against Port Lenape, an opponent of mixed reputation—same as us. Tuesday practice I spot Ed Clancy, ace junior reporter for the on-line and paper rag that pretends to be our high school newspaper. I keep working on my sets—still my weakest area, when I hear Ed's high-pitched voice calling to Coach. "That's Bain, isn't it? What's he doing out there?"

I don't hear the rest of the conversation, but catch Coach walking him back behind the bleachers. *Well, that should put the shit into the fan.*

Before we head for the showers, Mr. Allison pulls us over for one more pep talk. It's too late for improvements before the game, but he works hard to sooth the nerves and build the confidence. "Okay. Showers, men, but be ready for the bus at 6:30PM—here. Oh, one more thing: Bain. What do you think?"

For a second I'm not sure if he talking to me or the team. I hold my breath.

"He's good—real good," Clarence, one of the seniors admits. No one else seems to have words, but several nod.

"Okay, Bain, let's get you a uniform. We'll see what happens tomorrow."

Arnie tells the folks that I'm going to watch the game. Dad makes noises about going too, but after Arnie begs him not to come to the first game, he lets just the two of us go. At quarter-to-seven both the women's and men's varsity teams are on their way to Port Lenape. I spot Marty in the back where she chats with her team mates. The long ride to Port Lenape takes us over a ridge and along a deep valley before we reach the river and the school. I spend the whole ride silent, ignored even by Arnie as my hands slowly twist and turn, wrapping and unwrapping each other in a slow dance, like ten boas trying to squeeze each other to death. Why am I so nervous when all I want to feel is joy?

Nice gym with new LED overhead lights. Ceiling is lower than ours, but still legal height. Something to keep in mind. I suit up, but after we volley awhile, Coach points to the bench which I will warm along with the freshmen, and the three sophomores. Clarence puts on a red polo, so he's going to be *libero*. Good choice.

I'm here. Is this what being part of a team feels like? Am I really part of *this* team?

Tonight, it's best out of four. Women play their first game while we watch and cheer. Marty starts at right front. She knows the game, although I cannot say she's anything special, but she sure hustles. They win, 25 to 18. Now it's our turn.

Port Lenape's men's team is a lot better than their

women's team. It's a squeaker, 25 to 22, and I thought they were supposed to be an easy opponent. Their *libero* is really good, passing our shots again and again and feeding them to the front line.

The women head back onto the court, and again we win, 25 to 16 this time.

The men's second game is also a back-and-forth squeaker, but this time, we lose, 21 to 25. They must have our plays down and score six points in quick succession. "Oh, God," Arnie whispers to me. "We are so dead. Those guys haven't even broken into a sweat this time. Look at our guys, even Clarence looks like he's ready to collapse." I cannot disagree. I want to play; I want to be out there so badly, but can only sigh and wait. Will it happen? Please, I want to be out there so much. *Please, let me play.*

The women play, and ours win again, so they are done for the night. Out the men go again. Again we lose 25 to 17.

A fifteen minute break follows, then our six are back on the court again. Port Lenape takes control and has nine points on the board before we get one point. But then we seem to rally and get up to seven before they take off again. By now, the bleachers are full of screaming Porties yelling and cheering. Their score mounts. It is now 22 to 15. three more and we're history.

Allison signals for substitution. "Bain, I want you in for Jervis." I ditch my sweatshirt and head for opposite side of the court and in front row, rubbing my numb thighs as I go in. "Go for it, Bain," I hear Arnie call after me.

"Thank you," I whisper. "Ready, Bain?" I nod. *I am so ready!*

I stretch and wait for their serve and lay up for center, who dumps it left and short. Our serve and our point. The serve is now mine—which I'm sure is what Coach intended.

I toss up the ball and jump serve it straight at their *libero*, who bangs his knee as he dives for it. He lands on his right hand. When he gets up, he's still shaking his right hand. Score is now 22-17. They never score again, never even return one serve. I float the ball, spin it low, spin it high, drop it on the line. I make sure every serve is different, each one tailored to the players I've been watching the whole evening.

Our few supporters, the women's team and a few parents, are going wild, the rest of the gym silent. I play the entire fifth game. Final score: 15-3. When the last point goes up on the board, our team is silent. Even our cheer for the losers sounds anemic. Back in the locker room, I feel the eyes studying me. Finally, Bernie comes over. "Bain, you saved our sorry, weary asses out there. That make you feel good?"

I sigh, smile and nod, "Yeah, it felt real good—not for saving ... for winning."

Then one of the freshmen starts to clap, then another, then another until the whole team is applauding, quietly, gently. I stand, and when I do, Bernie puts a hand on my shoulder "To State!" he yells. Then everyone does cheer with a roar.

On the ride back to school, I can feel so many eyes watching me. I lock eyes with Mr. Allison. He looks like he wants to break into loud laughter. I turn around and look back. Marty meets my gaze, eyes peering over her cheap-looking glasses and the textbook she is holding. She gives me a smile and a thumbs up. All is right in this world for the moment.

"You did it! You really did it!" Arnie chortles as I unlock my car doors.

"Let's get home," I respond. "Still got social studies and English homework to do."

As we're getting out of the Volvo at the domicile, Arnie whispers. "Better get rid of that silly-ass grin you've been wearing all the way home before Dad or Mom see it. How am I to explain it if you aren't part of the team."

I chuckle, trying not to crack up. Then I zip my mouth in a firm, sour line and head inside.

I have to get back to that locker and do more searching; I have to find out where Mary Soo ended up, and right now that seems like the only place that will give me a clue. When will I have time? No time, it would appear when the shit hits the fan at breakfast. Newspaper over breakfast is Dad's sacred morning pleasure. Normally he pays almost no attention to the sports section, but just reads the news and editorials. Mom heads right for the crossword puzzles. But Dad wants to read about the game Arnie was in, even if he only warmed a bench. "Arnold, I thought you said you didn't get to play last night. Sounds like you made the fourth and fifth game happen. Listen to this, Helen: Bain, a junior, served an unreturnable ending to the fourth game, blanking

Port Lenape for the final eight points.' That's real good. But how'd they think you're a junior?"

Silence.

Dad's head slowly rotates so he is looking at me. I continue to eat my greek yogurt. "Peter, that wasn't you, was it?"

Silence.

"Peter. Would you cut this silence crap out and answer me! Was that you or Arnold?"

Arnie butts in. "Dad, it was Peter. He's on the team. He's the best player we've got."

"I wasn't talking to you. Peter, answer me. Did you, have you, gone out for volleyball when I specially ordered you *never* to do that?"

I nod and keep eating, stripping the inside of the cup with a finger so as to get the last remnants out.

"Well. This is a fine how-to-do! My own son won't talk to me and disobeys me. I bet you talk on the court! I bet you talk to your coach and teammates. I know you talk to one-or-two of your teachers. But, no. You will not talk to your own father or mother." Dad stands up suddenly enough to drop his chair on its back. His coffee spills and spreads over the open paper. "Damn!"

"Dear, please." Mom gets up and runs for paper towels. Dad stares at the browned newsprint, then grabs and folds the sports section into a ball and drops it into the waste can. "You will tell Mister Ellison, Allison, whatever the hell his name is, that you can't play. You will tell him this afternoon. And if you won't, I will. Understand?" He pauses then resumes yelling. "What were you doing these last few years out in the garage? I thought you were playing basketball. God, you lied, you're still lying."

I get up and walk back upstairs to brush my teeth and get my books.

"Do I have to take that car of yours away? Do I have to enforce a curfew? What will it take, Peter?"

Arnie's waiting at the bottom of the stairs. Together the two of us head for the driveway. Neither of us look back.

"You never told him you were practicing basketball, how can he accuse you of lying?"

"I know, Arnie. Doesn't matter, does it?"

"Coach will shit a brick now when he finds out you can't play. Particularly after the way you played last night."

I sigh and shake my head in sorrow. "I had to try; I had to know if I really was any good. Maybe I can get back on cross-country." *No use getting angry. No use at all.*

When I hit the gym, Mr. Allison is waiting for me. "Peter, come into the office." I follow him inside and sit down in the chair he points to. "Your dad called me, then stopped by to talk just half-an-hour ago—after he went and met with the principal." He sighs, then hits the desk with his fist. "I'm sorry. I can't let you play." He's shaking and slowly waving his hands around, as if not sure where to put them or what to do with them. "I took a risk. And I will admit it, I did it against my own instincts. But you *can* play volleyball. And I think the team, even the older players, are accepting you. I could have been … Well, I talked to Coach Gross. He said he'd be happy to take you back. And … I'm keeping you on the team roster—just in case things change in the next two weeks. As long as you're actually playing before the end of the season, if we make districts, you'll be good to go for that as well."

"Mr. Allison, you are being more than fair. Thank you."

"Thank you for giving us what you have."

I give him a salute and head out the door.

Bernie's waiting by the court. "What happened, man? I hear your dad won't let you play."

"That's the truth," I answer.

"Man, we need you. Shit. This isn't fair! What's with your dad? He some kind of dickhead?"

I shrug. "He has issues. Thanks for your vote of confidence. I like playing with you guys." I nod and head for the exit. Maybe I'll get back to running tomorrow. "Arnie, I'll stop back and pick you up after practice. Give me a call when you're done."

Arnie gives me a wave. "Okay …"

"Wait!" It's Marty, sprinting over from the women's court. "What happened?"

"My dad called the school and told them not to let me play."

"He can't do that!"

"He can and did. He spoke with the principal, and now I can't play."

Marty looks around, her face a map of confusion— like some cuddly little kitten just bit her. "Well, that's shit.

I'm sorry. Hey, I gotta' go, but, that is really chicken shit. I know I shouldn't say that about your own old man, but that's what it is."

"Thanks." I shrug, add a weak smile and leave.

I don't talk to my parents. I will not say anything to them. There's no point in doing that. Dad claims I lie all the time. I long ago figured that silence is better than being accused of saying something he thinks is a lie. And no, I never lie—ever—not any more, not since I was ten years old.

Chapter VIII   Two steps to the right, two to the left

I figure the other shoe will drop the next morning. To my surprise, Dad says nothing: nothing about my driving to school, nothing about being grounded. I sense him watching me, his eyes peering over his glasses and the top of the paper —like a floating frog watching for a fly. He waits in vain, for I keep my silence and proceed with my own breakfast routine.

"You'll be home after cross-country?" he finally asks.

I nod and keep eating.

"I think we'll both be going over to the Northside library again tonight," Arnie puts in. "I want to return the books I took out there and pick up some new ones."

"Doesn't Cross Creek have what you need?" Mom asks.

"They have some, but Northside has a lot more."

All true. Northside is twice as big a library as our

local. *Thanks, Bro. I owe you one.*

    I'm eating my lunch, my 'frugal repass' as I call it—alone, as usual. I'm half way through the mystery pudding when Ed Clancy, star cub reporter of the high school rag, pulls up a chair and sits down next to me. Lunch is not his goal. He has no food or tray with him, but he's obviously smelling raw meat and hungry. "I heard you went out for volleyball this year. Coach even put you on the team. I asked him about it, but he wants no publicity. Give me a break—please, pretty please. I heard about Lenape. What's going on? Give it to me straight from the horse's mouth."

    I give him a laser stare that should melt even his pea brain.

    "Look, Pete. (Is it okay I call you Pete?) I need a story. Someone's holding out. I know you never talk to anyone, but I also know you can, 'cause you talk with your teammates and brother."

    I continue to study his flushed face. Guy is so skinny, I suspect that he runs everywhere and can never sit still for even five seconds.

    "Look. *The Mariner* used to be an award-winning student paper. Now we can't even get twenty kids to pick up the free copies when we put them out."

    "You publish online," I give him that much.

    "Huh? You can talk! Yeah. We do. Leslie and Jaxon have been working hard to get the on-line copy out. I know no one reads print anymore. This whole school walks around with their iphones or ipads glued to their fingers. But they aren't reading the online version either. Anyway, back to this story. I thought you were permanently banned from ever playing volleyball. What changed?"

Kid does not know I'm off the team. "Listen, I don't want to talk about it, and I was never banned. If we get through the season, maybe I'll talk then, but not now."

"Will you give me an exclusive?"

I sigh, and nod, then shovel another bite of grey pudding into my mouth.

Ed pauses, his notepad and pencil poised above the table. "Ah … okay. I guess I'll see you around." He gets up. "Why did you make up that story about Coach Tiltman molesting you?"

I look at him again and shrug. Does it matter what I say? "I did not make up a story. It happened."

"So why did Tiltman write that letter?"

"I do not know. I do not pretend to know what went through his mind. And if you do not believe me, don't expect me to talk to you."

"Ah … ah … Okay. Ah … have a good one." Ed folds his arms around his steno pad, lips hanging out like his next word just got stuck in his teeth. Then he shuts his trap and walks away.

I 'm not sure why I spoke to Ed at all. I'm not sure why I want to go back to Northside either. It certainly looks like Marty has a boyfriend, and a pretty serious one judging by the easy way he kissed her at the 'Y'. If he's the same guy who was picking her up in the Mercedes that first night after practice, I've got no better chance with her then winning the Lotto. I guess I still want to know how she knew who I was that first night I met her. "Hi, Peter" still burns through my mind. And why is she so nice to me? No other girl has ever been.

Arnie elbows me as we enter the library. "Hey, Bro. She's here."

"I can see that. Thanks." I head for the adult non-fiction and begin checking history titles.

I'm tilting out French history titles to check the covers when I sense someone beside me. "Hi, Peter."

I straighten up. "Hi, Marty."

"Found another title for you." She offers me a newish book, its dustcover a splash of photographs and prints.

Wow. "Ah … Thanks." I take the book from Marty and give her a smile. "You're sure taking care of me." I don't dare tell her that the French revolution report went in on Friday.

Fingers to her lips, she looks away, but then her eyes meet mine. "That's what library workers do," she whispers, then gives my closer shoulder a quick rub and leaves.

What is this all about? "Marty, I …" But she's gone. I walk to the end of the shelves and look around. Marty's already standing by the circulation desk, talking to one of the adults. Arnie is picking through the YA fiction titles. *If he would read his texts as often as he reads fiction, he'd have straight-As. What am I supposed to do? Climb back in my hole? She's a friend. Take it.*

"Excuse me. Marty?"

She turns away from the other library worker she was listening to and gives me her attention. "Yes?"

"I have something here that I promised you." I hand her a folded piece of paper on which I have written my phone number, domicile address and e-mail address.

"Oh?" But she takes the slip, unfolds it and nods. "Okay. Great. Thanks." A brief smile and she turns her attention back to where it was, the slip of paper disappearing into her right jeans pocket.

I stare at her back, then shrug. "See you around," I manage and return to my own table.

Next day, I'm heading for the gym to change for running when Josh, one of the sophomores on the volleyball team, waves. *Now what?*

"Hey, Peter." *He sounds friendly anyway.* "Listen. I know you're off the volleyball team. Not sure what happened, but, you know, you really know your stuff. I want to be a first stringer so bad, and all Coach does is bench me. Could you, you know, would you, be willing to give me some pointers?"

I freeze, memories, *bad* memories in full flood. This was me five years ago. This was me pleading with Coach Tiltman for some extra instruction. I breath in slowly, pulling it all in, like the doctor always is telling me do when he's giving a physical. Finally I manage. "Sure, Josh. After I do my run, I should have a few minutes. I'll stop by the court." Dad won't let me play, but I have heard nothing about coaching. I give Josh a wave and he hi-fives me. *That* surprises me, but whatever.

I run hard and make it back to school in near record time. Coach signs me off and I change and head for the volleyball courts.

"Hey, it's Big Bain." someone calls out. "You coming back on?"

"Can't," I answer and look for Josh who's trying to hit line drives. The trouble is that half are hitting the net and not going over. I watch, taking in his serve, the way he positions his arm and where he hits the ball. He's contacting too high on the ball, which drives it down instead of over. After five serves, I'm ready. "Josh?"

"Yeah. I stink. I know."

"You have power and you know where you want to put that ball, but it won't go over the net, right?"

"Yeah." He punches the ball and it almost hits him as it bounces back from the net.

I pick up a ball. "Match my posture. Good. Watch the ball and contact it at the height of the toss."

Josh does. The ball clears the net, but it's a floater. Anyone can return those. "Try again, but snap through."

Several other players are starting to gather around to watch. I can almost feel Coach Allison standing behind us. I take Josh's serving arm and move his elbow where I want it. "That's better. Try again." This time the ball has a bit of power behind it. "Work on it that way," I suggest. "See if that helps." I back up to the bleachers and sit down to watch. Coach is working with four servers now, including Josh, telling them all the same thing I just told them. Once he glances my way and gives me a nod that I take to be a thank you. Bernie walks by, his body covered in sweat. He pauses, frowns, then gives me a wave. "Wish you were out there," he mumbles and moves on.

I can't stay long, not with concerned Dad always wanting to know why I'm late or early or whatever. So when Arnie is done and ready, we head out together.

"Josh is the worst server on the whole team," Arnie moans as we get in the Volvo.

"You're probably right, but he'll get there if he works at it."

"Yeah, but in the mean time, he gets to play at least some of the time 'cause he can dunk, and I bench warm 'cause I'm a freshman."

"I'll do what I can," I promise.

Sometimes I think my life is becoming a ball bouncing back-and-forth between the gym and Northside library. I still do most of my studying in my room, but find the back tables and computers of Northside productive in their own way. Tonight I'm there alone, Arnie declining to go with me this time. It is nice to be able to know that I'm in a room with someone who is friendly, even if she's busy shelving books or helping patrons. I spend an hour there, using some library books and reference volumes, but I will admit I cannot concentrate the way I can in my own room. Marty gives me no attention except for a smile and a wave when I arrive, but I find myself watching her instead of doing the work I've come here to do. Finally I admit defeat, pack up my duffle and head for the door. "See you," Marty calls to me as I open the outside door. "You too," I answer.

As I head for the Volvo, I check out the vehicles in staff parking, wondering momentarily how Marty gets here. A sprig of flowers catches my eye. I stare at the bunch of white plastic blossoms taped to the antenna of an ancient, blue-green Volkswagen bug. *Cute! I wonder who that belongs to?* Marty must get a ride here somehow. I know she has no wheels, or else why would she have asked me for a ride to the Y. Maybe she rides in that old bug.

I've e-mailed Marty, thanking her for her help in the library and for getting on the team, even if that was a bust. Tonight I have a reply. Ah! Great … maybe.

Dear Peter,

U R 1 fantastic VB player!! I M so glad you did try out this year. I know thats something Uve wanted for a LONG time. Keep UR fingers X, the seasons still new. Maybe U will get to play yet. Sorry I had to ask U for a ride. I hope those rides will end soon. ITMT, I'm rooting for U. See you again soon, LUV,   MARTY

Short, sweet. What does she mean that she 'hopes those rides will end soon?' Does that mean she will have a different ride? Does she plan to break up with that guy we saw? How does she know I've wanted to play volleyball for a long time? Well, she does know who I am. I guess everyone who's ever heard of Tiltman knows.

I guess doing a little coaching on the side was not

enough. The men's volleyball team barely win their next match, then lose the one that follows. Arnie gets to play during the second match after it is clear that there is no hope of a win. He scores three points, so I suspect his days as a bench-warmer are numbered. Dad goes to that match and actually watches the whole thing. Arnie thinks he was afraid I would be there and try to play despite the ban. If true, he is disappointed. I'm ten miles away in the storage locker going through the file boxes. The two suitcases are both locked. I hesitate to break into them so concentrate on the files stuffed in the lidded boxes. In the third box I discover correspondence that leads me to decide that Great Aunt Millie was an extremely astute business lady. Most are letters between some guy who must have been her broker and herself, ordering him to buy or sell certain stocks when they reached certain levels. She bought those Apple shares when they were less than ten dollars a share—against the wishes of the broker who stated firmly that he was sure the company would soon go bankrupt! There were other shares mentioned, but I can find no traces of them. Maybe they got sold to pay for the nursing home. I do find a bundle of what appear to be United States savings bonds—at least twenty or more, none cashed in. Again, the same pink and blue ribbon used before secures them together along with a stickie on which Millie had written: "For Mary."

I take a deep breath. "Mary, dear Mom and Dad really screwed you over by refusing to help Millie and Stan, didn't they?"

I finally hit paydirt—sort-of—in the fifth box. Letters

between the county orphans court and Millie and Stan, first relating to Mary's mother, then to Mary.

'DNA evidence presented here confirms the relationship of the dependent child Mary Soo to the plaintive, Stanley McClure. However, the court must consider the physical and mental health of McClure in this matter. He has a well documented history of mental and physical disability including a discharge from the armed services due to on-going medical problems. The petition of the county youth and childrens' services is thereby accepted, confirming the assignment of Mary Soo to the care and custody of this court.'

The letters go back and forth, with Aunt Millie providing testimony. Then I find what may be the final letter: 'Since Daniel and Helen Bain have declined the guardianship of Mary Soo requested in the will of Stanley McLure, the court directs that Mary Soo be placed in foster care until she reaches the age of majority at 18, or is adopted.'

Millie and Stan asked my parents to take care of Mary. Which makes sense: we're the only other relatives— but they declined! *Why?*

I carefully return that last letter to its envelope and sit back on the futon. *What was, is, wrong with people? You don't just throw away flesh-and-blood, even if they aren't that close a relation. What were they thinking?* And it seems that Millie and Stan both pleaded to Mom and Dad to take her.

I don't know what to think. Here's another dead end. It's getting late. Time to go. I carefully return the boxes to their former places, matching up the dents the higher boxes have made in the lower boxes. *Well, some answers here.*

Where next? Homework. I got to keep up the 'A's if I want to do what I plan to do. I'm about to leave when my eyes settle on the neatly-folded pile of sheets and blankets on one end of the futon. "Mmm …" I open up the pad I brought with me and beginning writing, then rip out the sheet and carefully fold it and lay it inside the stacked sheets.

I lock up the storage unit and head home, thinking about Mary the whole time. The courthouse should be able to tell me what foster home she went to, and if she was adopted or not. I guess that's the next place to go and check.

I'm up in my room slaving away at Senior-level statistics when Arnie, just back from the last game, knocks. I let him in and he fills me in on the loss. Done, he sighs; I sigh and shake my head. This fall was my only chance, or would be if I follow my plan to get out of here.

"Oh, and I saw Coach Allison and Bernie talking to Dad after the game. I couldn't hear what they were saying, but Bernie was getting pretty worked up."

We stare at each other. Maybe …?

Chapter IX   My Back Story

I run, then play volleyball. Everyone knows I can't go out in uniform for a game, but no one has said I can't practice with the team. I call sets to Clarence, trying to help his part of *libero*. I work on serves. Josh is better. All of his serves clear

the net, but he still needs more power. Next game is on
Wednesday. Maybe they'll be ready.

"Peter." I turn to look at Coach as Arnie and I are
about to leave. "Your dad and I talked after last match. He
didn't say, but ... but maybe if you talked to him, he might let
you play."

I don't know what to say. ... Or do, for that matter. *If
I kiss up to Dad, give him what he wants, then I get to do
what I want? But will that mean that he gets to continue to
believe whatever he wants to about Tiltman? Does that mean
he can still believe I'm a liar?*

"Thanks, Coach. I do want to play; I do want us to
win, but I think the ball is in my Dad's court. He has to
apologize for refusing to believe me. If he does, I will happily
speak to him."

"It's that important?"

I nod. "You know the hell I've lived with. I never
lied, yet almost everyone in this school, this whole freakin'
community, still believes what I said happened, didn't—
including my own father and mother! How am I to deal with
this?"

"Come into my office. Let's talk about this." Coach
leads the way and I follow. Arnie tags along, then stops and
takes a bench outside.

Mr. Allison points to a seat, and I sit. What now?

He takes a seat behind his grey, steel desk and, hands
clasped together, stares at me over the top of his glasses.
"Would you be willing to tell me what happened with Dennis
five years ago? Tell me in your own words. I will listen."

I find that, even though I want the words to come out, that my throat is tight and dry. It takes several deep breaths before I can sniff and speak. "Do you really want to hear this?"

Coach nods. "He said in his letter that you were the worst volleyball player he had ever tried to coach, and that you wouldn't listen to anything he told you. I don't think that's true now. You can't be as good as you are now if you were *that* bad five years ago. You know, you're a natural athlete. That doesn't just suddenly pop out of a locker."

"When I was ten years old …"

"Was this before you went to Dennis?"

Please, throat, open up. Let me speak. "Yes, it was two years before I went to Mr. Tiltman. Anyway, I did something at home, something I shouldn't have done. Dad caught me. I lied about it, tried to get out of it. He believed me at first, then found out the truth. He told me that he would never trust me—ever—again. I guess, kinda' like the boy who cried wolf." I shrug. "That's where it started. I wanted Dad's respect; I wanted him to be proud of me. I swore I would never, ever lie again, but he refused to believe me. Told me 'Once a liar, always a liar.' It was so unfair.

"I've always loved volleyball. I can't explain why. I just always have. Spring of seventh grade I heard a rumor that Mr. Tiltman was planning to retire at the end of the school year. He was the best. You know that. All those trophies out in the hall case are the proof. I told Dad and Mom I wanted to see if I could get some private coaching. They said okay. So I approached Mr. Tiltman. I asked him if he would give me some private lessons, offered to pay for them out of my allowance. He acted real cool. 'Not a problem, come down to the gym after school.' Said he'd be happy to work with me. So I stayed after school and went down to the high school gym where he and I met. I practiced serves for over an hour while he stood on the other side of the net, catching or returning the shots. When we were done, he told me to go ahead and take a shower and head home. Then he did this strange thing. He gave me a hug. You know, kind of a sideways hug, pulling my shoulder against his chest.

"And I didn't think anything about it. I mean, it was weird, but I thought maybe he was just trying to be nice or encourage me, or something. But when I came out of the showers—dressed, ready to go home, he was standing by the entrance to shower room. Just standing there. So I said 'Good night, see you tomorrow,' or something like that. He looked kind of distracted, like I wasn't even there, but then he said, 'Great. We can go at it tomorrow.'

"This went on for, I don't remember, maybe two weeks. I got those hugs after almost every practice. Only later did I realize that I got them only if no one else was around. And each time he would pat me on the chest or thigh."

Mr. Allison nodded. "There are rules about touching we all have to follow. Why wasn't anyone else there?"

"I don't know. But one Thursday. I remember it was a Thursday. We had both been working hard. I'm heading for the showers 'cause he always insisted I do that before I headed home. And he said 'I'm sweaty too. I'll take one too before I head out.' I didn't think anything about it. I showered, then, as I turned the water off, realized that he was standing right there wearing only a towel. 'Hi,' he whispered in this strange voice. 'Come here.' I didn't know what to do. So I walked over to him. 'Let me give you a rub-down,' he said. And he started rubbing me, only he wasn't rubbing my shoulders." *Why do I always start crying when I get to this part?*

"Finally I couldn't stand it anymore. 'Please,' I yelled. 'Please, I need to go home.'"

There's a knock on the office door. I jump. Arnie and Marty are standing outside, pale faces staring in through the large glass window that looks out onto the suite of coaches' offices. "Are you okay?" I hear Arnie ask. I can barely hear his voice through the glass.

I give them the okay sign and a wave.

"This happened just that once?" Coach asks when he has my attention once more.

I nod and blink, trying to clear out the tears.

"And he touched your privates?"

"Tried to. I kept squirming and giggling every time he reached for me. Finally he let me go. Kinda' apologized, then."

"That was it?"

"That was it? Well, sort-of. Next day I told my dad I didn't want to go for lessons any more. Dad got angry. Wanted to know why, since he'd had to pick me up late each day, and hadn't wanted to take the time. I couldn't say. So I went back, only Mr. Tiltman didn't seen interested in my volleyball any more. I didn't hit the showers afterward either.

As I was leaving, he came over and told me I should forget what happened. He warned me that I should never-ever, tell anyone. And that if I did, I would be in deep trouble. He was right, 'cause when I told Dad what happened and why I didn't want lessons anymore, he wouldn't believe me. But then he finally did go in and spoke with Mr. Smelz. A day later Mr. Tiltman ran a hose from his exhaust into his car and killed himself, and everyone was blaming me, including my own parents."

"You know what Dennis wrote in that suicide note he left?"

"Ah-huh. He wrote that I was the worst volleyball player he had ever tried to tutor. He wrote that he told me that, and when he did, I threatened to accuse him of making sexual advances at me unless he kept teaching me. Then he wrote that by carrying out that threat and lying about what happened, I had ruined his reputation and life … He sure ruined mine."

"So you stopped talking to anyone who did not believe you?"

"Yeah. I guess that's it in a box. You know, I figured that if I never said anything, no one could accuse me of lying." I'm trying to breathe slow and natural, but it's hard, like pulling fog in my lungs, instead of just air. I sniff, wipe my nose. *This is why I hate to tell this story*.

Coach is sitting back, staring off at a calendar. "Violet—his wife—had died that December. We—my wife and I—used to go out to dinner with them. They seemed such a happy couple. Never had any children, though. I always had thought they couldn't for some reason." He takes a deep breath. "We think we know people, but sometimes there are secret parts that we never see. I wonder if this was the first or only time ..." Coach sighs. "Okay. I do believe you. Which, from what I hear, is more than the school counselor or the principal, your teachers or your parents ever did—or do. I do not see how that gets you to play the sport you love, or gets your dad to believe you, but ... I will talk to him again. See if I can work something out. Okay?"

"You've been honest with me all along, sir. Thank you." I stand up.

Coach stands as well. For one moment his hand comes up, as if it intends to pat me on that back. Then it drops. He chuckles. "The language of body communication is not what it used to be. See you tomorrow."

I nod and head out the door.

"What was that about," Arnie challenges as I leave and we all head for the exit. "Marty's hoping for another ride to the 'Y' and you're inside yapping with Coach."

"Sorry, Marty; sorry, Arnie. Coach wanted to know my side of the story concerning Mr. Tiltman, and I told him."

Arnie slams to a halt so hard that Marty almost runs into him. "And you told him? Did he believe you?"

"He acted like he did," I answer. "Let's get going. I can explain all this to you sometime later, Marty, if you want to know."

Marty grabs the outside door and holds it for the two of us. "I think I already know the story, but sometime later."

Driving to the 'Y,' I ponder my own thoughts. I feel

freer, yet sadder too, as I think about what I just told Mr.
Allison. That moment when I realized that Mr. Tiltman was
reaching for my penis, is still so *real* and fresh in my mind
that I feel the sickness inside growing again. For years I beat
myself around, wondering *if* I had just refused to shower after
those lessons, maybe nothing would have happened. *If* I had
pulled away from his hugs, maybe nothing would have
happened. How could anyone *not* believe what I know
happened? The self-blame is long gone now. The silence has
helped in that way. No locker tricks yet this year either. Is the
school finally forgetting? Dad hasn't.

"You okay, Peter?"

"I'm okay. As good as it gets, Marty."

"Hmm." Front of the 'Y' is in sight. She picks up her
backpack and cradles it in her arms as I slip into the 'no-
parking-zone' in front. Dude is standing waiting.

Marty gives me another arm rub like she did last time
we took her to the 'Y.' "See you around." She unfastens her
belt and jumps out, then opens the backdoor to retrieve her
gym duffle bag.

""Hey, Martina. Where the hell you been?" The dude
who's been standing there yells. I miss what happens next,
but suddenly I realize that he's grabbed her by the neck and is
almost lifting her off the ground. "Don't you dare talk to me
that way. Ouch!" Marty must have just stepped on him in
some way, 'cause he lets go and starts bouncing around on his
left foot. "You're a bitch, you know that."

Both Arnie and I are out of the Volvo now and
closing in. Marty waves her free hand. "Don't. Leave him

alone. It's okay. I was late. Ricky's just a little upset, right?"

Ricky's taking in both of us. "Who are these guys?" he snarls.

"Cousins. Cousins nice enough to give me a ride over here when you didn't. Okay? Everything is okay now, right? All right?"

"Yeah," Ricky answers, one hand still rubbing his right foot. "Sorry I was such an ass."

"See you guys at practice tomorrow?"

"We'll be there," we both say before getting back in the car, Arnie joining me up front. I put my seat belt back on and wait until Marty and Ricky are part of a crowd, Ricky carrying the duffle bag. After they disappear inside, I start up the car and we head home.

"What was that all about?" Arnie yells before I'm even merged into traffic. "Cousins? We aren't her cousins. Was that bullshit, or what? And who is that jerk? And why is she even puttin' up with him?"

"I don't know," is all I can answer. Cousins? Another one of her lies? Or is that the truth in this case. "I don't know," I repeat. "Let's get to the domicile and find out what the home front is like."

Martina equal Mary? Is that even possible? It's starting to rain, the evening streets turning to shiny blacks and street lights glare. Got to concentrate on the driving. That note in the French Revolution book? She left that for me. I know that. But did she know who I was the moment I entered my name on the library book request form? I try to remember what Mary looked like the last time I saw her. She was just a kid. There might be a resemblance, but Marty's voice is definitely not anything like the voice Mary had.

The supper table is a sea of silence. Even Arnie and Dad are reticent tonight. But their eyes keeping moving to rest on me. Arnie wants me to play. Dad is waiting for me to show my hand.

Okay. Let's try this. I get up from the table and grab the memo pad that lives by the phone. I write. 'If I speak to you, will you let me play volleyball with the school team.' I tear off the sheet and lift it up, studying it, wondering. Then I lay it down beside my father's plate, facing him. I resume my seat and wait. I sense that Arnie and Mom are both staring at the sheet as if it will explode at any moment.

"What's this?" Dad asks, his mouth already forming an angry line. But he picks up the paper and reads. "This more of your nonsense, Peter?" he demands, holding it out like it might bite him and eying me over the tops of his glasses.

My lips move, but the sounds won't come. I try taking several deep breaths, my head and body nodding back and forth. Finally ... "No, sir."

Dad continues to stare, his eyes getting bigger and bigger. I stare back until his gaze drops back to the words on that paper. "Did you just say something to me?"

"Yes, Dad. I did."

"Tired of your own lies?"

"No, sir."

"So, now, you want me to believe you?"

"It would be good if you would believe me. But if you do not want to, that is your decision. I just want to play the sport I love."

"Dan, please," Mom interrupts. "It's what he wants to do. There is no harm in it, is there? The team wants him; Coach wants him."

"Helen!" But Dad continues to hold that paper, his other hand's fingers drumming on the table. "Okay. I'll call a truce. I'll call Mr. Smelz and Coach Allison and tell them that you have my permission to play." He lays the paper down. "I still do not trust you. But Mr. Tiltman's blood is on your hands, not mine. Is that what you wanted to hear tonight?"

"Thank you, Dad." I pick up my fork and resume eating, but Arnie lets out a cheer and grabs Mom and gives her a hug.

Dessert is usually ice cream and tonight is no different, but somehow with Mom serving, the dishes get cashew bits, cherry sauce and whipped cream. "Thank you, Mom," I tell her, and the smile she gives me is almost worth the sad knowledge that neither one of them believes I told the truth.

Bedtime: I lie in my bed, staring at my wall and the poster of a cloudburst over the Grand Canyon. My stomach hurts; I want to cry but the tears won't come. Five years! Over five years *I* held out, waiting—waiting for Dad to back down and back me up. Now I'm talking anyway. I'm the one who gives in. For what? In order to play a few games? Is it really worth it? I don't know. I wonder what it will feel like being back on the court. I wonder if I can be strong about anything.

Will I do what I plan to do when I turn eighteen? "Peter,
you're a whimp, after all," I whisper and let the tears come.

Chapter X   A First Date?

I'd missed that third match—which we lost—all three
games. Girls won again. I guess everyone must know I'm
back because when I walk in the gym, instead of
discouragement I see smiles and waved hi-fives. Okay,
everyone sees me as the magic wand, but can I make it
happen? I pitch in, doing whatever Coach tells me to do.
Seems like he sees me as more of an assistant coach than a
player because I spend half the practice helping with serves.
But I do get into two games and get a chance to work on my
spikes. As before, no one wants to be on the other side, but
Arnie and Clarence are game and by shower time, they can
dig and return half of what I throw at them. Next game's on
Monday, three days away.

Arnie and I, our faces filled with smiles, are headed
for the parking lot when I hear Marty calling. "Hey, guys,
wait up."

"What's up, 'Cousin' Marty," I answer.

Marty actually blushes. "Had to get him off me
somehow. Say, you back on team? For good?"

"Yup. I guess so."

"So, you caved to your Dad?"

"Yeah." All the good feelings I had just felt being out

there on the court pour out through my feet.

But then Marty grabs my right hand in both of hers. "It's hard, I know." I turn to stare into her soft eyes. "You *did* what you had to do. I guess we all have to do that sometimes." She nods, suddenly grim, then gives me a sad smile before letting go of my hand.

"Thanks, Marty," I manage. "You need a ride?"

"Nope. Not tonight. Got to go to the library anyway. And hey, It's really great you're playing. See ya." She hustles off through the lot, leaving me with a bunch more questions, none of them asked or answered.

As I'm unlocking the Volvo, I hear the distinct sound of a Volkswagen bug heading out and spot a flower-sprouting antenna. That's got to be the same one I saw at Northside. Maybe one of the other students here works there and is giving her a ride. Or … is that Marty driving? *Naa. No way.* She's too young. How old is she? Am I actually thinking she might be Mary—who has to be only fifteen. She said she was in tenth. *E-mail her. Ask her. She may even give you a truthful answer.* Gad, I hope she really isn't my cousin, 'cause I do have hots for her, despite Ricky.

"Feeling good, Bro?"

I nod as I wait for the traffic light to go green. "Yeah. The playing feels good, real good. I never thought I'd crawl to Dad to beg to play. But being in the game … I never thought it would mean so much, but it does. *Better than I felt last night.* So I crawled. I guess I'll feel really good on the day Dad apologizes to me for not believing me."

"He will, … or I hope so." Arnie slumps back in his seat. "You figure out why Marty called us cousins last night?"

"I don't know. Maybe she was just trying to get Ricky-dicky to back off."

"She slammed his foot with her heel. I saw it. I think she can take care of herself."

"Then why does she put up with a bully-jerk like that?" *There, I've asked the next million-dollar question.* "I'd never grab any girl like that."

"Yeah, me neither. Speaking of girls … You know that freshman blond you were trying to be nice to the first day of track?"

"Yeah. What about her?"

"Her name is Vicky Sutherland, and I asked her to join me for Sundaes at the Freeze around eight."

"Ooh. She is cute. How'd you wing that?"

"We're in English together. She asked me about you. And I, not to let a chance go by, took it from there. Do I get transportation tonight?"

"If you have your homework done."

"Geez, man! It' s Friday, for cryin' out loud! You aren't gonna' act like you're our dad and mom, are you?"

"Nope. Just covering my own ass."

"So, bring your own date."

"Like who?"

"Marty."

My hands tighten on the steering wheel. "She's got her own boyfriend, as if you didn't notice."

"So? That doesn't mean you can't poach. She's at the

library tonight. Give her a try. Library closes at eight, be there before it does."

It feels strange to have my own kid brother giving me the dating advice. I guess it figures. He's had several dates and one brief 'steady' in eighth grade. I think the steady part lasted one week, but it's all more than I've ever known—which is zero. "I'll think about it."

"Do more than think. We can both swing by the library around seven, You make the move, then the three of us can pick up Vicky and all go to the Freeze together. Afterward, you can drop Vicky and me off at her house to say hi to her parents and make sweet talk, you take Marty home, come back and get me and we go home together. Sound like a plan?"

"I have to work tomorrow, remember?"

"Come-on. It's only an ice cream date. We'll all be home and in bed by ten."

It feels like my heart and hands are dipping in ice water. "Okay," I finally manage.

"Okay? Thanks, Bro."

"You're welcome."

So, at just past seven, Arnie and I are easing into a drive-through space at Northside. I scan the lot and note the VW with the plastic flowers at the far end where the staff park. If *that's how Marty gets around, then she's still here.* Inside, I don't see her at first, then spot her back in the librarian's office. She and the woman who I think is the head honcho are talking. It looks lively. So lively that no sooner do

I spot Marty, but the librarian closes the blind that shields the office from the circ desk and public view. Well, I guess we wait and see if she comes out. I take a seat in the periodicals section, next door to circulation, and begin browsing an *Atlantic Monthly*. Arnie goes over to the movie section and looks for new DVDs.

"I'm sorry, Marty. I can't let you do this anymore. Tonight's the *last* night. And that's the way it's going to have to be," I hear head honcho say as Marty steps out of the office and closes the door.

"Hi, Marty."

She gasps. "Oh, hi, Peter." I'm not sure if she looks ready to cry or explode.

"Sit a moment, please."

Marty freezes, confusion now the obvious emotion. "Okay ..." She takes the nearest seat. "What gives?"

Now my tongue has peanut butter-itis. "Ah ... I ... Listen, when you get off work tonight, how'd you like to join Arnie and me for a sundae at the Freeze? Arnie's bringing a girl. I thought maybe ... maybe you'd like to come too. I don't want to be the parlor lamp for those two. We ... we could just talk, or enjoy the sundae." *Is my face hot or what?* "What do you think?"

Marty's lips quiver. "I ... I can't. If I leave at eight ... Damn. This is complicated. Look, Peter, I'd like to. I ... I *want* to—you're my shining knight—but right now ... tonight is not the time. You saw me in with Mrs. Sawyer? If I leave here at eight ... This is so messed-up."

Is a ride to the Freeze complicated? I wait, silent. I do

not know what else to do. Marty too is silent, lips now pressed together as she stares at her hands.

"We can get you home. It can't be that far to your place in Taneytown. I don't plan to be at the Freeze past nine." Marty shakes her head and waves her hand for me to shut up. I close the magazine and put it back on the rack. "Arnie and I will be here until closing. It's up to you. Please?" I give her a long, still-hopeful look then walk away to join Arnie who is picking out R-rated movies, checking titles and putting them back.

"No go?" Arnie asks without looking my way. "*Clockwork Orange*? I thought it was X-rated."

"It was. The rating changed. I guess it's no go." *But what does she mean by 'shining knight? She said that before. I thought she meant night—like opposite of day.*

"Marty doesn't want to come, or she's got a date with Ricky-dicky?"

"I don't know. Something about she can't leave here at eight."

"So, is she leaving earlier. We can leave here earlier. I'll call Vicky and tell her we can come earlier."

'If I leave at eight.' 'Tonight's the last night.' Last night for what? I don't know, so I find a computer, log-on and start on my stats homework.

Ten minutes until eight and I'm logging off and collecting my notes on a flashdrive and there's Marty at my elbow, her dark blue windbreaker already on. "Can we leave right now?"

"Ah, yeah, sure." I stumble to my feet and grab the

X-country jacket I earned last year. "Arnie, let's go."

"Coming." He grabs his book bag and heads for the door, passing a dozen other patrons making last-minute checkouts.

Marty and I fall in behind him. "Oh. This is great. Thanks for joining us." I can feel I'm glowing.

"Problems solved, I hope." Marty still sounds worried and grim.

"See you later," the clerk at the desk calls to Marty as I open the exit door.

"Thanks, Wanda," Marty answers. "I owe you one."

I think half this town is at the football game, so the Freeze has only two other customers when we get there at 8:15. "What do you want? I'm treating," Arnie tells Vicky as the four of us approach the counter.

Vicky shakes her head and pulls this huge red wallet out of her beltpack. "Mom says I should never let the guy pay on the first date."

"Marty, what about you? May I buy, or you want to go dutch?"

"Peter, I'll let you buy, but I will be modest. No banana splits or triple dips."

I chuckle. "Thanks. I will be modest myself."

Marty orders a chocolate sundae but does allow the cashews when I insist that's okay. I order my usual dusty road: powdered malt, whipped cream and cherry over vanilla. We take a table away from Arnie and Vicky, who seem to be more interested in talking than eating.

For several minutes silence surrounds our table, broken only by the sounds of plastic spoons tapping the edges of the glass sundae cups. I want to talk, but have no idea how to start a conversation: I'm Peter Bain, the guy no girl will ever even look at. *Talk to her! I don't know what to say!* I'm Peter … and I'm eating ice cream with a beautiful girl who seems to like me. *Oh, God, I'm on a date and my mouth won't work!* I pinch my thigh under the table, but it still doesn't feel real.

Marty crunches nuts, licks her spoon and pauses. "Peter, I have to be back at the library by 8:45. I hope that is not a problem. Sorry."

I nod. "No problem. If that's what you need, I can make it happen. But why? It's closed now, isn't it?"

"Wanda is staying for me. She promised to let me in."

"In?"

"Yes. In the library."

"Don't you need to get home?"

"Please don't ask me so many questions. I live by lies, but I don't want to lie to you."

"Ah?" I stare at her and catch a brightness in her eyes. "Ah … Okay." *And I was just about to ask her about her family and what she likes or does besides volleyball. So much for small talk.*

"Peter, I know you're in advanced placement courses across the board. What are you going to do next year? You won't have any classes left to take, will you?."

Where's this come from? "How do you know what courses I take?"

"I got nosy."

"Who says I'll still be around next year?"

"What do you mean?"

"If a college has the courses I want, and the high school doesn't offer them, I can head out a year early—which is what I plan to do. I'll be eighteen November fifth next year. Why wait around?" *There, now you know something that no one else in the world other than Arnie knows.*

"I wish I could do that."

"Are you in the gifted program? Are you taking any advanced placement?"

"I'm a sophomore. I wish."

"Why do you hang out with that Ricky guy?"

"I said, 'no questions.'" Marty takes a deep breath. "He has access to things I need. He knows things that could get me into even deeper trouble than I already am."

"You're in trouble? I'm sorry. I shouldn't ask."

"What will you do for college?"

"Use the money I've saved from working at the market."

"That can't be that much. Who's paying for that old Volvo of yours? Who's paying the insurance, the gas, the upkeep?"

"You're right. It won't be easy."

Then she covers my right hand with her left. "You think *we* could do this? Do this together. I mean, light out early?" Her hand moves to rub my forearm, then settles back on the table. She scoops up the last melted remains of her sundae.

"Marty. I hardly know you. How do you know me?"

"Peter, you've known me all of my life. Think about it. And it's time to go."

I get up, brain spinning, and arm-wave to Arnie and Vicky. No response. Finally I walk over to their table and clear my throat several times.

"Oh! It's time?" Arnie gets up, picking up his empty ice cream tray in the process. He grabs Vicky's and leads the way to the counter where we all leave our dishes. At my car, Arnie and Vicky climb in back and Marty takes the front. "Seat belts."

"Must we?" Vicky asks.

"Use the one in the middle if you want to," I answer. Marty giggles.

On our way. Marty leans closer, her elbow on the center consol, then lets her head touch my shoulder. "Thanks. It was good to get out. And thanks for the sundae. So many people are kind and watch out for me, but you just like me—I think."

"Yes, I do," is all I can think to answer, then, "Hey, what about pizza sometime?"

"I would love to go out for pizza with you."

"What kind?"

"Hawaiian."

"Not sausage and mushrooms? That's my favorite."

"That's okay too." It sounds like Marty is actually smiling as she rubs my arm.

All but one back room light are off at the library when we turn into the lot—empty except for the flowered

VW and a white Corolla. "Back door," Marty whispers and eases back upright.

"Okay." I stop and wait as Marty lets go of me, unbuckles, gets out and walks quickly up the steps to the back door and knocks. A woman I recognize as circ desk Wanda steps out, holding the door for Marty. They exchange greetings then Marty waves in my direction and disappears inside. Wanda also gives us a wave, then heads for the Corolla. A minute later, she is gone. I hear Arnie and Vicky sitting up and looking around. "Man. All of a sudden, this place is like dead," Arnie whispers.

I nod. The library lights are off. Except for the VW, the parking lot is empty. Where did Marty go? It feels like the library swallowed her.

Chapter XI   Victory & Death

Sometimes I wish I didn't have to work every Saturday and now, every Sunday. How nice would it be to kick back with someone like Marty and go for a ride in the mountains, or down along the coast. As I bag cucumbers and weigh grapes, the dream that first floated last night grows and moves out of the market. All the pleasures of a guy dream fill my inner mind: on a beach, babe beside me, all oiled skin and wet bottom. What does Marty look like in a swim suit? I spot a dressed-up guy headed my way and Bam!, my dreamworld implodes. *So Ricky-Dicky, what can I do for you*?

Up close, the guy looks to be at least in his mid-thirties wearing this grey, pin-striped suit with a red power tie. Hair has just the right air-blown and brushed look, his facial stubble making him a Brad-Pitt-want-ta-be. To me, he reads fake-fake-FAKE. I smile.

"What do you have in vine-rippened tomatoes?" Ricky asks.

"All but the plum-shaped are vine-ripened," I reply with a smile. *That is true, whether you believe me or not.* "The larger ones over here are the heirloom variety we carry."

Ricky eyes me then studies the tomatoes. "Okay, I'll take a dozen of these red ones, and two of the heirlooms. How much?"

I tell him, and start bagging. As I'm lifting the tomatoes off the scale, I suddenly feel a hand on my arm, pushing upward. "Lift it higher, liar. No cheating on the scale."

I pause, then return the tomatoes to the scale and move my hand away. The needle does not move. "Three fifty," I tell him.

He hands me a twenty. I make change, making sure that I give him the dirtiest and crummiest bills. "Yuck. Listen, kid, I don't know what you're trying to pull with Sophia, but stay away from her. If you know what's good for yourself, stay away. You understand?"

I turn away and head down the aisle behind the produce to help the next customer. "Hey, asshole, I'm talking to you. I saw you hanging out with her. Stay away or a lot of people will get hurt, Sofia most of all." Customers are staring at the guy. Bill, my boss, is already moving to place himself between Ricky and myself. This is not good karma.

"I'll take that basket of the red potatoes," a white-haired woman in a teal jacket points.

"Certainly. Anything else?" I empty the basket's contents into a plastic bag and hand it to her. As I'm making her change, I note that Ricky is gone.

Monday: game night. It's at home, so no bus ride. Arnie and I eat a quick supper in the domicile before heading back to school in the family car with Mom and Dad. By 7PM, we are both out on the court warming up. Girls are warming up in the second court. I see Marty among them, first time I've seen her since Friday night. I try twice to catch her eye, then give up and concentrate on moving the ball where I want it to go. *You have to understand, it is just a ball, a sphere, governed by the same laws of physics as any other sphere. Make it do what you want it to do.*

I play the second half of the first game. Jefferson is supposed to be the second best team in the league, but we're up, and I don't give them much of a chance. We win 25-15. Girls win their first as well. I play the entire second game. Arnie gets to play as well, and I am happy to watch his confidence began to match his skills. We win our second, 25-12.

Then it's bleacher time to cheer on the girls' second. Marty starts, but I know she is struggling. She looks tired and has no concentration. Coach takes her out after five minutes. The girls gain the lead, but then drop behind to lose, 19-25.

Third game for men's goes super well. We pound Jefferson and walk away, 25-8. But women's fourth is a disaster for our side: 12-25. That's the first match they've lost all season and it takes the topping off our own killing. What went wrong with Marty? I don't see her on the bench. Did she hit the showers already?

"Freeland's this Wednesday. You ready?" Bernie gives me one of his punches on my arm—lighter this time.

"Yeah. I'm ready." I present my knuckles and he taps them with his own.

"We are *so* going to win this one."

Dad and Mom come off the bleachers to join us. "You play well, Peter," Dad admits. "Great games," Mom adds. "Arnold, you're good too."

"Thanks, Mom; thanks, Dad," we both reply. "Bernie, catch you later," I add.

"Later," he agrees.

The four of us are out in the lot, heading for the car when I spot Marty standing by the Mercedes talking to Ricky. I stop and stare. Arnie joins me. "What is it?" Dad asks. I hold a finger to my lips for silence.

"In. In now!" I hear Ricky order.

"No!"

I can't follow the next couple of sentences, then "That's it. I'm reporting you tomorrow." With that, Ricky gets in his car, slams the door, revs the engine and races out of the lot and onto the street without even pausing to check for traffic.

Marty, alone, watches until the last screech of tires

reaches our ears, then she turns and walks away, toward where I can see the blue-green Volkswagen with its plastic flowers on the antenna. *Oh, Marty, Marty ...*

"What was that about?" Mom wonders. "I hope that poor girl isn't in trouble. Tsk. Seems like girls are getting into mischief so much these days. Used to be only boys made trouble."

I just shake my head. The Volkswagen leaves the lot, stopping before turning out on the street to take the opposite direction Ricky had.

Tuesday is one big team push. What will it be this time? Who will end up in our pool? By six, we're all soaked with sweat and exhausted. Heading home, Arnie is a bundle of nerves and anticipation. "Three wins, one loss! Wilbur Memorial and Kennedy will be pushovers. We beat Freeland tomorrow and it's playoffs for sure. Pete, I think we're gonna' make it. Man, I am so up for this."

"Don't count chickens ..."

"Pete, don't be the wet mop now. We are gonna' win tomorrow. You *know* that."

I say nothing. Instead I try to think about the exam in stats I will have on Friday.

Maybe I am a little nervous; maybe I do want to win this one more than any of the others. Maybe I should not have promised to keep Mr. Allison out of the swimming pool. But if I hadn't baited him, would he have let me try out?

Arnie and I return to the gym early in my car. As we

cross the student lot, I feel a new chill in the air. *It's fall, stupid. Volleyball season is half-over. What do you expect?* Soon it will be dark when we cross these painted lines and I'll be glad for the buzzing overheads lighting our way.

Out on the court and warming up, I feel, can even smell, a different atmosphere tonight. But it's not that raw outside air snaking in. The opposing bleachers are actually filling up. Many of the Freeland students are carrying what look like posters. I step off the court and watch the opposing players, sorting and checking their moves. What is it I should know?

"Hey, coach-killer, you playing tonight? Why aren't you in jail?"

I continue to watch the opposition, not even sure who called out, or from where in the stands, but now I can peg the emotion. These guys are not just another team. They know that this year—for once—they could lose, and so they are not just an opponent. They're an enemy. Out of the corner of my eye, I note the refs standing around, talking. But when I turn their way, one of them, a stranger, tall and overweight gives me a hostile look. *Keep cool. Play the game. Do not listen or watch the other side. Concentrate.*

Girls play first. They struggle but finally pull off a 25-22 win before the lively, but mostly quiet crowd. Marty is out there, but I can tell her heart isn't in it. Why? She's always put everything into the game before.

Now it is the men's turn. I start tonight. From the first serve, the crowd goes wild. But every time the ball comes my way, new posters emerge in the Freeland side bleachers: "Kill

the liar. Take out the liar. Coach killer!" I play, but it is
harder, and they are a good team—the best we've played yet.
Twice a Freeland player rams the ball at me. I block both, but
the boos and liar chants get louder. It is like every Freelander
is determined to wrap me in a shroud of sound and bury me.
Final score is 25 to 18, our win, but the final minutes are a
chorus of boos that neither the Freeland adults, nor the refs
make any attempt to stop.

We're toweling down, sipping gaterade and breathing
real quiet as the girls get ready to go out again. "What is
wrong with this place," Clarence calls out. "They're a bunch
of animals tonight."

They are. What am I to do about it?

The girls win their second game. Not by much—I can
tell that Freeland has their second wind. The next game will
be a killer.

We head into our second. Again, I experience this
perfect storm of boos, shouts and shaking signs. Still, we win:
25-20.

Now it's the girls turn again. Marty does not play.
Halfway through that game, I see her get up and head for the
locker room. As she disappears, I catch a movement in the
bleachers. Was that Ricky moving out? I barely notice that the
girls take the third and the match.

Now it's our turn again. Two minutes in and I drop a
curve onto the opposite side six inches in from the right edge.
"Out," the fat ref calls, pointing for the serve to change.
"What!," screams Bernie. "Whoa," cries Mr. Allison. Even
half of Freeland can't believe the call. I say nothing. I just

stare at the ref—the same hostile one from before the game—who returns my gaze with one so evil, so full of hate and glee, that I know. *Peter, there is no way, not tonight.*

Three plays later, when the same ref calls me for touching the net on a return even though my hand was easily three inches above, I know this has to end. I signal to Coach to take me out.

"Put Arnie in for me," I whisper when he calls for a sub and approaches.

"Arnie?"

"Yes. Arnie for me. Just do it. It's the only way we'll win tonight."

"I'm going to take that ref and see to it he never covers any of our games again."

"Coach, please. Just do what I ask. You won't regret it."

"Oo … kay." Mr. Allison turns and signals Arnie to go in.

"Here's your chance, Arnie. Don't hold back." I hi-five him and head for the bench, the air filled with the cheers and jeers of the Freeland crowd.

I wait three minutes, long enough for our team to recover and Arnie to start doing his thing. When he pounds the ball into their captain's chest so hard that the guy falls to the floor, I know it will be good. I walk out, followed by a chorus of boos.

I don't wait around. Mom and Dad are here. They'll get Arnie home. I also know that neither will understand what was going on, or why I'm leaving. In the locker room I change slowly, cooling down, letting the hurt settle. Am I happy or am I sad? Is this what I wanted, or expected? I don't know.

I take a deep breath, put on my coat and head out the door. And run right into two sheriff's department deputies, male and female, a guy in a suit, and a gal in a windbreaker and slacks with an iron grip on Marty's arm, trying to haul her out the back door. Ricky is standing by that door, holding it open. The moment the woman has a free hand on the door, he ducks outside.

"What's going on?" I ask, trying to sound as neutral as I can.

"Just stay back," The male deputy cop orders. He moves to place himself between the struggle and myself.

I do not move and repeat, "What is going on?"

"Just go back inside," The cop, all red face and broad shoulders, pushes into my personal space.

"Pete, help me," Marty screams. "Get the fuck off me," she then yells at her griper.

"Why don't you let go of her and leave her alone?" I ask, thinking I'm sounding reasonable.

The male cop grabs my wrist and tries to shove my arm behind my back. He may be big, but there is no way I'm going to let him move my arm unless I let it move. He pushes, his face getting redder and redder. "Get back in there!" he screams. "I know you, you lying son-of-bitch. You're going down, right now." I back toward the wall, hands out where anyone can see them, arm not moving. The cop brings back his right fist, I duck and his fist hits the wall so hard I can hear the tile crack "Aaah!"

The woman pulling at Marty screams and goes down, and Marty is gone—the outside door snapping shut. The male cop is spinning in circles, waving his limp hand. Female cop is trying to grab him, calm him down. "Stop it. Jesus Christ, Pat!" she tries. "You, (that's me) stay right there."

"Yes, ma'am," I answer. The crowd in the gym, our crowd, is roaring, The woman who had hold of Marty is groaning and trying to get back on her feet with the help of the suit-guy.

Pat manages a deep breath. "You're under arrest," he groans."

"Charges?"

"Interfering with an arrest, assault. Ruth, cuff him, God-dammit, and get him the hell out of here."

"I'm calling an ambulance," she answers. "That hand looks like it is broken."

"Help, get help, right now," The guy in the suit is back inside. "Mr. Ogden is down."

"What?"

"He's laying at the bottom of the steps. He's bleeding and breathing funny."

Oh, Marty. What did you do? I get out my cell phone and punch 911.

Ruth, the female cop, turns around and stares at me as I get through to the operator, request an ambulance and give directions. When I hang up, she produces cuffs. "Your hands, please."

"Yes, ma'am." I hold out my hands and let her cuff

me. She gently takes my arm and together we head out the door as I make out the sound of an old Volkswagen bug heading out of the lot at high speed.

Chapter XII   On Bail

We move outside, down the handicapped ramp, away from the bedlam going on in the gym, away from the crumbled body at the bottom of the steps (tended by the other couple I suspect are from county foster care, or some such agency) and away from Pat the Bad Cop who is seated on the steps, nursing his hand and crying. "I'll get you, you liar, coach-killer," he yells.

"Shut up, Pat," Ruth calls back to him, then to me. "I'm taking you to that patrol car. I want you to get in back and not to make any fuss. You understand?"

"Yes, Ma'am." An ambulance turns into the lot.

"I know you did not lose your temper, nor did you touch him, so be cool. I'll call your parents as soon as we get to the station and have them pick you up." She sighs. "This is just one god-damn mess!"

I get into the patrol car. Ruth gets in front and starts radioing, first a dispatcher, then someone, then another someone. Except for codes and occasional profanities, I can follow little of the conversations. A city cop car pulls in, then another. Sounds like a riot is starting up in the school. "Okay. We're out of here," Ruth puts the car in gear and we leave.

So I'm getting to spent my first night in a jail—actually the local lockup at police headquarters. When we get there, Ruth relays the charges that Pat is insisting on, adds that she thinks it's a pile of shit and recommends that I be released on my own recognition. Sergeant gets on the horn with Pat and talks. Result? Sergeant declines Ruth's suggestion and tells me to make myself comfortable in the second right-hand cage. Sounds like the best option. Left-hand cage already has two drunks inside. They both stink. I try to phone home before I turn my phone and wallet in. No answer. I leave a message. Of course Dad doesn't show up to get me out. Why am I not surprised? I find a bunk with clean sheets and one blanket but just curl up on it to wait and see. It is going to be a long night.

Sigh. Regrets? Why did I stand up to that cop? Why? *Because he was a jerk?* He called me the liar. *Was that it?* Was I doing it for Marty? What was happening there? Why were they picking her up? Ricky? He's the rat, obviously, but why? I'm the problem? Marty's leaving him for me? Is that it? What a world!

An hour later the first casualties from the post-game riot start to show up with bruised faces, fingers in splints, bent glasses. My cage gets crowded to the point I'm sittin' on one end of the bed next to four schoolmates. They nod and give me embarrassed glances, talking in whispers to each other. The two standing smell like they were drinking. I watch and wonder at the power of imagined injuries to egos gone ape-shit. For as long as I can remember, we've always lost to Freeland, and our coach has taken a bath. Tonight we won, and I'm hearing that their players and their coach refused to get wet. I gather our whole team—and half the audience—insisted. A fight started. Their coach and their entire team ended up in the water, along with half our team and a bunch of others. Fists were flying and guys were getting dunked and held under. I guess no one drown, but someone is dead. The county sheriff's office and the state and city police are still there. All over one volleyball game—not even a football game! I shake my head. No game is worth a life. Wait! I bet the dead person is Ricky. Nothing to do with the game. Freeland can all go soak their heads, along with the referee who was out to get me. What? A ref did end up in the water? 'Tripped,' everyone was claiming. What a night, and we still have Wilbur Memorial and Kennedy to play in the regular season. I close my eyes, trying to block out this … this screwed-up world. An hour in a cell and I already feel so dark and deep that I wonder what ever happened to love, smiles and freedom. I can't even phone anyone! Hard times and this cold, hard-surfaced space is making it worse. Six other guys in this cell, yet I have never felt this lonely before.

No word from family all night. *Can't expect Dad or Mom to worry, can we?* Parents drift in, claiming their sons, whispering, then smacking their sons on the backs of their heads as they leave. Sleep is impossible, but by dawn I once more have the cell to myself.

It isn't Dad who bails me out at eight in the morning, but Mr. Allison. "Okay, Peter, You're free to go home. Get a lawyer. I don't know what happened to you after you left. I just found out you were here an hour ago, but I gather Pat Monihan's after your blood."

"Thanks, coach. What's the bail?"

"A thousand, but I only had to post a 'C' note. Don't worry about it. Get on home. I figure you're good for it later. Just be glad you aren't some poor black kid. You'd probably be in the county jail right now and the bail would be ten times higher." He pauses. "I probably shouldn't be saying something like that."

I give him what I hope is a reassuring smile. "It's okay. You're black. You're entitled. Ah ... thanks for bailing. Can I get a ride back to school to get my car?"

"Sure. I have to get to work myself."

I ride up front, my empty stomach talking to me, my brain foggy as a creek bottom. Zombie-itis.

Coach keeps looking my way. "You aren't planning to go to classes, are you? You don't look well." *You mean I look like shit.* "What'd you do?"

"Some governmental agency, maybe Family Services, was trying to haul Marty Sofia off. I happened to blow their secret snatch by showing up. Guy cop was not amused, decided to bust me. Took a swing at me and rammed his fist into the wall instead. Broke the wall tile and his hand. Then Marty got away."

"Whoa! A cop took a swing at you? Why would Family Services, or the cops be after Marty? She's a good kid, pretty straight arrow as much as I've ever seen."

"I don't know, sir." *But I intend to find out.* Maybe she's supposed to be with Foster care, but isn't.

Coach drops me by my car. I thank him and head home. I'm pulling into the domicile driveway when I see Jack out taking his morning walk. "Good morning," I call out as I get out of the Volvo.

"Hi, Peter."

"Lovely day." *I will not let what happened last night put me in a foul mood.*

"Yes. Thank you, Peter." He stops and walks up the driveway half way to where I'm standing, his face all smiles.

"Question for you, Jack. And please don't be offended. Why do you hate Denver?"

Jack's face does a blank, then he looks up and stares into my eyes. "It hurt me; he hurt me."

"What? Who hurt you?"

"Denver." Jack is blushing now, struggling with some memory that he does not want. "I … I hurt. He made me hurt him. I did not like it. Denver hurt me." He's almost crying now.

"I'm sorry, Jack. I shouldn't have asked. Please, I won't mention it again."

"He hurt you too?"

"Yes. It's okay. Please. It's a nice day. Cold, but nice. Enjoy your walk."

"Thank you, Peter. I will. He hurt me."

I stare at Jack's back as he walks on, arms swinging a little too high, his steps careful and deliberate. Who would hurt you, Jack? Who's Denver? Is that why you don't want anyone to call you 'Denver Jack?' I shake my head and go inside.

Of course the house is empty. I presume Arnie is in school and my dear parents have gone to work. I eat a breakfast, shower, open my books and, as I stare at the pages, know that it is of no use. I lie down on my bed and don't wake up until the rest of the family gets home

Supper is like strange. Arnie is full of noise, filling me in on the rest of the game and the riot afterward. Dad and Mom are the silent ones, their faces blank, whether from shock or anger, I cannot tell. "Man, you should have seen the look on that crooked ref's face when I returned the first ball that came my way. We got this volley going, back-and-forth, five times, never getting close to me, then bam! I had it, killed it straight in their libero's face. And after that, rest of our guys are setting me up, every chance they had. Every time I'm getting the ball, it's like their cagers were cringing! I was pounding them, and they never returned a single shot."

"How'd you do it?" Dad finally manages—ignoring me.

"Who do you think was returning my balls and shots for five years, Dad? Arnie's as good as I am. Volleyball is not a one-person-only game."

Dad's eyes wander over the table and settle on me as if seeing me for the first time at the table. "Oh."

As I'm loading dishes in the washer, Mom joins me at the counter. "Your father and I have discussed this whole situation. We're sorry, but in regard to what you did last night, you're on your own. You are going to have to learn what getting into trouble can result in. Your father did contact the lawyer who dealt with Aunt Millie's estate. You remember Mr. Jacobs? If you feel a lawyer will help, you may contact him. Other than that, that's all. We do love you, but fighting cops is not acceptable."

I would rather die than deal with that slimy Jacobs, but a lawyer might be a good idea. "Thank you, Mom, for the suggestion. I'll consider it. I know how bad this whole thing looks right now."

Mom lays her hand on my shoulder, squeezes, then walks away. *My dear loving mother*.

I am still so tired, but sleep will not come. So much to think about. Marty, where are you? Who are you really? Where are you living? In the 'Y?' In the library? Do you even have a home, anywhere? What was Jack talking about? Who was Denver? Only Denver I can think of is John Denver, the singer. But he's been dead for years, long before I was born and probably before Jack was born as well. Why can't the world let the liar label go? What do I have to do to make the world understand that what Tiltman did to me was real, did happen? Oh. Marty, I miss you. You've believed in me. You always have. Why?

I get up at five and send Marty an e-mail. Then I work on the homework I didn't get done due to the night in the local lockup. Maybe I can use the experience for a human society paper? I'll think about it. Now I have to be ready for that stats exam.

A glance at the paper headlines causes me to pause and read an entire article. "Charges being weighed against

Truman HS student" the headline reads. "A 15 year old, 10th grader at Truman High, is being sought in connection with the death of the assistant director of the City's YMCA. Richard Ogden was fatally injured in a fall down the high school's steps on Thursday while assisting in the arrest and detention of a girl going by the name Martina Sofia. According to Sharon Huff, agent with County Children and Youth Services who was in the school directing the detention, Sofia is really Mary Soo, an escapee from the County's youth detention home close to two years ago. It is not clear if Ogden fell or was pushed by the student. Charles Booth, Valley's District Attorney, stated on Friday that if Sofia did push Ogden, he will definitely bring adult charges of either voluntary manslaughter or homicide against her. As of now, Sofia remains at large"

"Shit. Tsk." *Well, some of this is not a surprise. Sometimes two plus two add up to make four. Sometimes when you add, you get more.*

On to school. Every class is different now. I can feel the change when I enter a classroom. The voices drop or fall silent, then everyone takes his or her seat. None look my way. Walking the halls, I note my classmates standing aside, giving me room. I haven't noticed many taunts this year, but now they are conspicuous by their absence.

Except for newspaper Eddy's visit, I cannot remember when I haven't spent lunch break at a table alone, unless Arnie joins me. Today is no different, except that guys keep coming by my table to give me smiles and nods. Girls are giving me smiles too. Whoa. What a strange world!

I walk onto the volleyball court. "Oh m' God! Oh my God!" one of the girls scream, and as one, the boys' and girls' teams turn to face me and begin to clap. The applause turns to hoots and yells. Then Bernie and the other seniors and juniors are standing around me, thunking me on the back. "We won! We did it."

"How? I left?" I ask.

Bernie raises a hand and the crowd goes silent. "Pete, for six weeks you've been showing us what we can do. But no one thought we could do it without you being there. We needed you to win. But last night, Arnie here, and all of us knew we had to do this on our own. *You* gave us the right stuff. We just didn't know we had it. Thank you, guy. We're going to States. I know it. This is the greatest moment in Truman volleyball history. What do you say? We get practicing and really make this happen?"

More cheers and yells, and the ball starts moving.

I need to concentrate on school work and the next few games. Marty, the storage locker and its unfinished business must wait. But a lawyer? On Friday I get a notice of a hearing set for November 15th, a Thursday afternoon. That's just over two weeks from now. I run down the attorney listings in the yellow pages without seeing any name I feel like contacting. Then I remember one letter in among the letters that Aunt Millie and her broker were exchanging. Something and something ... I reopen the phonebook and look again. Ah ... Hess, Hess and Hidderschmidt. That letter was 20 years old. Is this the same guys? The same firm? If so, this is going to take money. I retire to my room and sit at the desk, fingers tapping its leather-covered surface. I have the thousand promised from Aunt Millie's estate. Got the check a week ago. Now it's in a new account in the same bank where that safety deposit box is. I already had an account at Mom and Dad's bank, a joint one with Mom, but I am past trusting either one. I hate to break that thousand so soon. What about …?

Chapter XIII   Dealing in Gold

I go downstairs and dig up last Sunday's paper. Yup. There they are—week after week, the same full-color ads: "highest prices for gold and silver." I take down two addresses and hours. Saturday morning I go to the bank and the safety deposit box and remove two gold Maple Leaf coins. Gold content is right on them. No dealer is going to argue over that, and each is one ounce, so no argument on weight either. I have until 12:30 to get to work, so I head to the first gold shop, checking the current price of gold on-line before I leave.

Werley's is not what I would call the best looking establishment, but the heavy-duty bars on every window are certainly all business. I also note that the street-side windows have view-blocking blinds in place. One other car is in its little lot, but a young man gets in it and pulls out as I park.

The inside is bright and clean with showcases

sporting various silver plates, cups and urns. Behind the main counter are two serious doors that look like they were once part of a bank. Fit-looking guy with thinning hair and white goatee is sitting behind the counter reading the *Wall Street Journal*. He looks up and gives me a suspicious smile when I come in. Is it because I look so young? Come to think of it, how many teenagers have honest access to gold coins? "Good morning?" he ventures.

"Mister Werley? Would you be able to give me cash for two gold coins?"

"Maybe … Do you have them with you?" The guy sits up, pushes the newspaper aside then takes a velvet cloth from under the counter and lays it on the glass.

I produce one of the coins, still in its plastic case, show it to the guy, then set it on the velvet. The guy studies my face, his eyes searching for something, then he picks up the case and drops the coin out onto the velvet, his eyes dilating despite the frown he is trying to show me. "What do we have here?" He produces a loupe and, using the lens, goes over the coin. "You have the other?"

"It's the same," I answer. I get it out and set it beside the first. The dealer pops open the case, but does not give the coin as close examination as he did the first. "Hmm. Where did you get these?"

"My great aunt died. I inherited them."

"Do you have any proof of this?"

"Look up the obit. Millicent McClure. She died in August. The twentieth, I think it was."

The dealer, Mr. Werley it seems, rubs his little beard

and taps the counter top twice with his free hand. Then he reaches back under the counter and pulls out a well-thumbed, dark-blue booklet. He pretends to consult it, flipping through several pages before pausing and looking up. "I can give you six hundred."

"Is that each?"

"No. Six hundred for both."

"Well, I guess I'd better being heading over to Ralph's. Perhaps he'll give me something closer to their current value."

"That's what these coins are worth currently. Ralph will tell you the same thing, or less."

I pick up the coins and recase them, pause, then return them to the counter top, all the while staring into the dealer's eyes. "Your ad in the paper says 'highest prices paid.' Now I'm not sure what that means here, but the current price for gold as of an hour ago—according to the *Wall Street Journal* online—is twelve hundred an ounce. Since each of these is an ounce, I would expect their current market value to be something closer to twenty-four hundred dollars. No, wait." I hold up my hand to his shaking head. "I know that you're in a business and need to make a little money on every transaction. If you gave me twenty-four hundred, you might not make a cent. But I also know that these are not just little disks of lump gold, but minted coins which sold forty years ago for more than their weight value at that time. So ... I think you can make me a lot better offer than the low-ball price you just quoted." I fold my hands together and wait.

The guy sighs, picks up one of the cases, takes out the

coin and examines it again. "How about seven hundred each. That make you feel better?"

"Maybe, but I would feel a lot better, enough to part with these, if you offered me nine hundred each."

"Ouch! No way!"

"You're still making at least three hundred each at that price, more if you are selling them as maple leaf coins. That's more than six hundred dollars."

"Eight hundred—each."

"Eight seventy-five."

"Eight fifty."

I ponder that offer. Not as much as I would like, but I suspect I'm pushing my luck as it is. 1700 dollars will be enough to do what I need to do right now. I might get more if I get a broker to sell these, but he or she will want their cut, so I might not be ahead.

"Eight sixty," the guy offers.

My eyebrows go up. "Okay. Eight hundred and sixty dollars for each of these coins. In cash." I offer the guy my right hand, palm up.

Mr. Werley shakes. "You have a photo ID?" I shrug, get out my wallet and hand him my driver's license. He studies the picture. "Peter Bain? You're not even seventeen! Are you sure you're the one who inherited these?"

I nod.

"Wait. You're the kid everyone accused of lying that made that coach kill himself. Huh. I personally think that coach was probably lying himself. Where do pedophiles go? Where the kids are: coaches, teachers, Scout leaders."

Well, what do you know. Someone believes me for once.

"Okay. Leave the license on the counter. I will need a copy to go with the receipt. Be back in a minute." He turns to one of the doors behind him, spins a dial, sets numbers, opens its latch and goes inside. I wait, slowly rotating my license card in my hand and counting the minute and a half that passes before he returns with a heavy-looking, thickly padded envelope. He sets this on the counter, then waits while I open the end and look in. "Go ahead. No one else here right now to peek over your shoulder while you count." He's smiling now.

I pull out four larger packs of twenties, each banded together. I count. Each one holds 20 bills or 400 dollars. A fifth packet holds six twenties. I nod and shove the packets back in the bag.

"I like to deal in twenties. Big bills make customers nervous and they're harder to cash. You want your own copy of the receipt?"

"Please." He rings one out, then takes the two coins, the receipt and my license and lays them on the bed of a copy machine. He makes two copies and hands one copy and my license to me. "Thank you." I watch as the two coins disappear into the slot of a steel box bolted to the wall next to the armored doors, we shake hands again and we're done for today.

As I leave, a couple comes in carrying a cardboard box. I glance inside as they pass by: silverware. Well, it looks like he gets enough business.

I put the package in the trunk, out-of-sight, pause and

look around. A hint of chrome and grey almost out-of-sight at the turn of an alley and I am on high alert. I would know that Audi anywhere. "Damn." Well, if Dad's in the car, he can't see the Volvo from there. I get in, back the car up just enough to get around the couple's Plymouth and ease out of the back exit of the lot and into a narrow alley. I keep the speed slow and quiet until I hit a through street, turn and head for my new bank with my security box and second checking account.

All but 40 dollars of the cash goes in the account, then I'm on my way to work, but checking the rearview mirror more than I usually do.

Chapter XIV   Lawyers

We have our last two games this Tuesday and Thursday. The first of November, volleyball will be over—unless we make the district playoffs. That is looking almost certain at this point, so we—guys' and girls'—are good to go at least until mid-November, past the hearing date. I am moving in a world that is changing so quickly that I can't keep track of what's next when I wake up in the morning. I'm willing to talk to Dad, but now he's avoiding me. I have to play my heart out, get perfect grades, get through a trial, find the one girl I think I care for. And I have to keep working at Bill's in order to afford the wheels and the freedom they are giving me.

Monday, first class break and I'm on the phone to

Hess, Hess and Hidderschmidt. Older woman's voice answers
with the three guys' names and "How may we help you?"

"Good morning, ma'am. I would like to make an
appointment with either one of the Hesses."

"Well, that may be difficult. The elder Mister Hess
passed away three years ago. His son is still here, but he's
semi-retired and not accepting new clients. Would you like an
appointment with Sylvia Hidderschmidt?"

I do a quick shift. "Well, I was really hoping to speak
with Mr. Hess. You see, my great aunt was a client of his—
one of them, anyway—for many years, and this matter
involves her."

"Who was your great aunt?"

"Millicent McClure."

"Just one moment." She puts me on hold, but is back
with me in less than a minute. "What is your name?"

I tell her.

"Tom comes in on Tuesday and Wednesday
mornings, from nine until 11:30. Could you be here this
Wednesday at ten?"

That will most likely wipe out a whole morning, but
Dad and Mom don't have to know. "Okay. I will have to miss
half-a-day of school, but I will be there."

"You're a student?"

"Yes, ma'am, a junior at Truman High."

"Just a moment," and she has me on hold again. I
really need to get to my next class. I start walking down the
hall, almost running. "Bain? Can you make it Wednesday at
noon? Would that be better?"

"Yes—definitely. Thank you. I will be there then. Yes. A-huh. Good-bye." Phone in my pocket and I'm in the classroom as the second bell rings.

We, both guys and girls, demolish Wilbur Memorial the next night. I play in the three men's games, but only for a few minutes. Arnie gets in the whole third game and scores seven points and assists in three more. He's on a roll.

Wednesday I let the office know I have an appointment with a lawyer over lunch break. The office assistant calls the law office to confirm and I'm good to go. I leave at 11:30 and I'm walking in the law offices at quarter to.

"Good morning. I'm Peter Bain. I have an appointment with Tom Hess for noon. Am I too early?"

"No. Please have a seat." The gal behind the window picks up a clipboard, adds forms and hands it to me. "If you would fill these out, we can get started." I take the clipboard and get busy.

Mr. Thomas Hess, Esquire, turns out to be a blunt and buff looking guy in a well-worn charcoal-grey suit, his white hair Marine Corps short and his face weathered and lined. "Bain? Please come in."

I follow him into a long room dominated by a walnut-finished conference table. He points to a chair then takes a seat himself across from me. The assistant brings in a set of file folders and my paperwork and sets them in front of him. He starts reading. As he reads, he talks. "My father worked with Millie McClure for many years. She and her husband were close friends. I did not know her nearly as well as he did, but quite a lady. Smart as a whip. She knew what she wanted. Dad was in line to handle her estate some day. Haven't heard from her since my father died, but that's why I agreed to meet with you. So, where do you come in?"

"Okay. Sir, I have several problems. One does have something to do with Aunt Millie's estate. She died in August." Hess nods. "Yet a lawyer for her nursing home named Jacobs claimed that the costs of her care in the nursing home had eaten up most her estate, and what they still had access to was going to the home to support their arts program or some such thing. According to a will that this Jacobs guy produced, each of the members of my family was to get a thousand dollars, and that was basically it. But then my dad is supposed to get all of whatever Woodbridge didn't have use of—whatever that amounts to. I smell a rat here, but I don't know how to approach an investigation. For one thing, Aunt Millie had a DNA-proven great-granddaughter who was shuffled off to foster care after Millie broke her hip and her son, Uncle Stan, died at about the same time. No provision was made for her. I want to know what happened to her and why she was suddenly out of the estate. And finally, I have been accused of resisting arrest and assaulting a police officer —both false, but I need a lawyer to help me defend myself.

"Whoa. When did this happen?" Tom Hess is now taking notes on a long, yellow pad.

I tell him, pointing out the date of the hearing.

"Okay. I remember reading about this in the paper. It

got coupled to a possible homicide. Bain, you have a long
history of getting into trouble without trying to, don't you?
And this happened because of this Marty Sofia girl—whom
you believe was getting hauled off to God knows where.
Correct? All right. Let me fill you in more on what I know.
As I said, my father was the McClures' attorney for many
years. Walter and Millie were good friends of the family.
Walter and Dad used to golf together. Stan and I went to
school together and were friends—not close, but friends.

      "One of the reasons I agreed to meet with you is that
we had heard that Millie had died, but then no one contacted
us. We were her lawyers, had been for years. It seemed
strange.

      "Walter developed, grew and ran his own business.
Did quite well. After he died, Millie kept her share in the
business but also made a number of astute investments. She
was not a poor woman. There is no way that she should have
been forced to give all her money to a nursing home to cover
their expenses. She could have bought the place. She should
have been able to receive the very best care anywhere for as
long as she lived. So something is not right here. And this is
something I think—from a personal point-of-view, is worth a
look into.

      "The whole situation with her great-grand daughter
also sounds suspicious. You're telling me that they did a
DNA study and that it proved that she was definitely a
relative of Stan's? Yet the moment Stan was dead, she was
shuffled off to foster care?" Mr. Hess pauses. "I wonder. We
should have a copy in the files of either Millie or Stan's will

from before Millie's accident. Hmm. Okay, back to that in a minute. Now, tell me more about this Marty Sofia, the volleyball game and why you were in the hall when Youth Services was there trying to haul her off. And what do you think happened with this Ricky guy who is now deceased?"

I tell him what happened, going into further detail concerning Marty's relationship with Ricky, the abuse Arnie and I witnessed and the threats we heard him give. I repeat what the cop told me and my response.

"So, this hearing on the fifteenth is just the judge or a district justice. Right? But it could lead to a trial on those charges?"

I nod.

"But the other officer, this Ruth person, she stated that no charges should be filed?"

"Yes."

"Okay." Mr. Hess continues writing. "You have to get back to school. Let me do some more research and Donna Stine—she's our secretary whom you met— will call you and arrange our next meeting. Do you think your parents would be willing to come in and talk with me?"

"I do not want either of my parents involved with this. Dad has stated that I am on my own concerning this trial. As for the business with Aunt Millie, the less they know about what we are looking for, the better."

"They're the problem?"

"Let me put it this way. Dad has never earned more than sixty thou a year, tops. So how did he suddenly afford a new Audi three years ago right after Millie ended up in the nursing home and Uncle Stand died?"

"Oh …" Tom thinks on that one for a moment. "I see. Well, get on back to school. I see we have work to do."

Donna catches me as I am about to head out the door. "Mr. Bain? Do you want us to bill you at your home address? How do you wish to arrange payment?"

Hadn't thought that out yet. No letters I get at home were safe from prying eyes. "Let me give you my e-mail address. When the bill is ready, let me know, and I will stop by and pay. Okay?"

"That will work. You wrote your e-mail address on the paperwork you filled out?"

"I did. And thank you. All this helps." I give her a salute, and I'm out the door.

Thursday both our teams beat the crap out of Kennedy High and we know that we are in for districts. As our teams gather in the post-game circle to cheer our opponents, Mr. Allison gives me such a look that I know that he might be close to crying. His voice, for once, is thick. "I … I will be honest with all of you. I didn't think this was possible. Oh. I knew we had some good players; I knew all of you would give it your best. I figured we might win a few, maybe even most of our games. But to beat Jefferson, then Freeland. You guys did great!"

"Yeah," Bernie butts in. "But it was Bain here: Pete and his brother. They're the ones that made it happen. You guys are the real heroes here."

"Stand together," I hear someone call out. It's Eddy

and the sports reporter from the city paper. They push us together and get the shot of the team and coach, all smiles. Then they want a shoot of both the girls' and the guys' teams together, then finally a shot of just Arnie and myself. I shake my head. *I don't want this, or do I?*

Friday I get a message from the office of Hess, *et. al.* to stop by Saturday morning at nine. That's good, but I guess they have to move with my hearing coming up next week.

Dad asks me to help him with raking and bagging leaves. I decline. "Can't, Dad. Got an appointment."

"Appointment? You just saw the dentist in September. There isn't anything wrong, is there?"

"No Dad. It has to do with the court hearing next week."

"Who are you meeting with?"

"Tom Hess."

"Hess! That son-of-bitch! We told you to go to Jacobs. You do not want the Hess firm involved with this."

I take a deep breath. "I'm leaving, Dad. You told me this was *my* problem. I'm dealing with it *my* way. I may be home before heading to the market. Maybe I can help you then." I walk out.

Dad follows me to the door. I wonder if he intends to grab my arm, but he stops in the doorway and watches me get in my car. I hear a "Damn!" and the door slam as I pull out onto the street.

Tom Hess is waiting by the front door, dressed in

khakis and a sports shirt. He unlocks when I walk up and once I'm inside, relocks the door. "Come on back. We'll meet in the same room we were in before. Coffee?"

"No, thank you." I'm trying to sound cool, but Dad's rage is still bouncing around inside me.

Tom draws a cup and we sit while he adds a dribble of cream, stirs and drinks. "Okay. First thing: I spoke with the prosecutor's office and the Sheriff's department. I think we're going to be okay. I spoke with Officer Marino. She told me that you never touched Officer Monihan, and she's willing to testify in your defense. Anyway, she'll be there. Monihan, the cop who has accused you, apparently has a temper history. You will have to be there and dressed up clean and neat, but I think this may not take long. Can you be cool?"

I nod, then allow a sigh. *Good.*

"Now, the second issue of Millie's will, her great-granddaughter and what happened to her money. I found a copy of Millie's will that she signed four years ago—before her accident and before Stan died." He chuckles. "It was in the folder I had in front of me on Wednesday. It is way different than what you describe coming from Jacobs. If she did write and sign a new will last spring, then her old will means nothing. The problem is, no one seems to have a copy of the latest will. I checked with Jacobs' office. They claim to have seen the will, but do not have a copy. The nursing home claims it no longer has a copy. So, wherever it is, it's not available right now.

"In the will from four years ago … Here, you can read it." He hands me this long document covered in "therefores" and "whereas's." I labor through it anyway.

I look up. "So most of her estate was to go to Stan. Right? But if he pre-deceased her, it was to go to Mary Beng Soo, her great-granddaughter, except for these specified amounts that were to come to Arnie and me which she outlines here. That's a lot of moola. Even Dad and Mom were to get $20,000 each."

"That's right. But there is one wrinkle, and it may be what someone used to gain control of the estate while she was still alive. She granted your father power-of-attorney in the event she became incapacitated. Her fall and hospitalization and Stan's death would have been enough for a power-of-attorney to kick in."

"So dear Dad helped himself?"

"A person acting in his capacity of power-of-attorney can draw on the funds he is managing to cover his expenses, including time spent." Tom shakes his head, obviously angry.

I'm angry too. "Tom, what do I have to do to become an emancipated minor? I want out! I've had enough."

"Whoa! You sure? That's a big step …" He studies my face and I stare back. "You're seventeen now? If you can show the orphan's court that you have a place to live, sufficient financial resources to continue your education and can demonstrate maturity, I think a judge might accept such a petition. It would happen in less than a year anyway. If you want me to, I can draw up the papers and have them ready. But you have to have a place to live and money. Any money in Millie's estate still isn't yours yet."

"I think it is." I take out the letter that Millie left for

me in the security box and hand it to Tom. "There's over three thousand shares in Apple stock in there, as well as over a hundred thousand dollars worth of gold coins. I figure all this belongs to Arnie and myself—unless I find Mary Soo, then most of it will be hers. And in the meantime, I think we have a basis to bring suit against The Woodbridge Nursing Home, Jacobs and my parents."

"You're really willing to burn bridges?"

"Ah-huh." I think what Dad has done is criminal. I do not want to be involved with him when this comes out. "Can you suggest where I can find an apartment—small, clean, furnished, and for not much money—and in the Truman school district? Once I have that, I'll be out of my home the next day. Believe you me."

Tom sighs. "Okay. I'll start on that paperwork. You can get started on finding an apartment. Actually ..." He pauses. "I know a couple of people who might have just such as you have in mind. In the meantime, play cool. Let's get this hearing business over first. Then we'll tackle the Mary Soo business. One step at a time."

"I actually have an idea where to look for Mary. And I intend to check it out next week—after the hearing."

Chapter XV   First Hearing

Districts playoffs start that Saturday. A tough game—girls lose, so they are done—but the guys win, so the season will go on. I care, but not like I did two months ago. The crowd is rowdy, but no one targets me and the refs seem honest.

Again, I have to get out of classes to go to the hearing. I have only one suit—bought two years ago. It no longer fits me in the shoulders. The legs are too short as well. Still, I squeeze myself into it. As long as I don't try to button the jacket, it doesn't look too bad. I drive down to the courthouse, thinking, Mom, Dad, your son could be going on trial, and you're off at work as if nothing matters at all. The hearing is in the smallest of three courtrooms. I check in with a clerk waiting by the door. Tom arrives five minutes later, gives me a smile, checks in as well then joins me. "How's it going?" he whispers.

"Fine." I wish that was really true.

"Look, See that group there, and that party there. They will go first. So this might be a wait."

"Okay. Whatever." I find myself trying to rub my hands dry.

"All hear yea. Hear yea." Tom motions me to stand as the black-cloaked judge enters and mounts to her seat. As we sit down I look around. I note Deputy Marino taking a seat, but not Monihan. Huh? Where is he?

The first case precedes. Something about destruction of a neighbor's fence. The judge orders the accused to be turned over for trial. Second case has the plaintive requesting that the charges be withdrawn. A consultation follows down in front of the judge's rostrum, before the judge allows the charges to be dropped. Then it is my turn. Tom guides me down to a seat at a table on the left. "We are now ready to hear charges of resisting arrest and assaulting a police officer. Is Deputy Monihan present?"

A long silence follows. Finally Deputy Marino stands. "Your Honor, I am given to understand that Deputy Monihan will not be appearing here today." The judge looks around. Finally she turns to my lawyer. "Tom, looks like it's your lucky day. No plaintiff. You didn't want to reschedule, did you? I didn't think so. Well, can't proceed without a plaintiff. The charges are dismissed. Bain, the clerk here will give you a paper which you will take down to the purser's office. They will issue you your bail refund. That is all. Next!"

"Wow." As simple as that. The guy doesn't show up and it's all over. "How'd all this happen?" I stammer.

"Peter, I had a long conversation with Judge Martin several days ago. She agreed that this might be the best outcome. Come on, let's get you your money and get you back to school.

Wait! Who was that who just slipped out the entrance to the courtroom? Marty? I jump up and dash to the door. The hall outside the courtroom is empty. *Marty, was that you? Did you come here, even though there's a warrant out for your arrest?* I hold onto the heavy door and wait for Tom to join me.

One thing down. How many to go? I pick up a check for a hundred dollars, then return to school after thanking Tom as bests I can. End of classes, I head over to the gym.

The moment I see Mr. Allison, I pull the check out of my pocket and offer it to him.

"Home free," I tell him, as he studies the check. "Charges dismissed. Let me endorse that, and we're good."

"That's wonderful. Pete, you've confirmed that decision I made back in September so many times now. I'm so glad I took a chance with you. I understand you're talking in classes now and participating." I nod. "Ready for our next game?"

"You bet."

"Any word on Marty?"

"No. Not yet," I answer before heading to the locker room to change.

Mom and Dad don't say much of anything when I tell them that the charges were dismissed. "That's good," and "I hope you learned something from all this."

Yeah, that some cops are assholes; that others are okay; that having a lawyer does help.

We win the next match, but lose the final districts the following Tuesday. Not the best, but still good. The next night the coaching staff hosts a pizza party in the gym for all of us, along with friends, families, faculty and staff. I think half the school, even the ones who would never dream of going to a volleyball game, show up. Mom and Dad are there, smiling and taking compliments about their sons. No one mentions liars or dead coaches from five years ago.

All of us get some kind of 'Inter-District-semi-finalist' medals, and there's a nice trophy as well. To my surprise, the coaches have our varsity jackets already. The even bigger surprise is when I get one too. "I don't deserve this," I protest when Mr. Allison calls me up.

"It's for being 'most valuable player.'"

I put it on. It's only a little big in the sleeves, dark blue with white cuff stripes and a blue-and-white mariner on the back. 'Pete' is embroidered on the right side above a Varsity 'V' complete with a tiny brass volleyball pin. "Thanks, Coach. Thank you." I turn and bow to the crowd, scrambling down from the stage so no one can see the tears pooling in my eyes.

I'm sitting in the bleachers, waiting for the pizza to be served when Mr. Allison and Ms. Hertz, the women's coach come over. "Pete? Can you get this to Marty?" Hertz hands me another varsity jacket. "We felt she earned it, and she'd put in the money to pay for it. Roger seems to think that if anyone can find her, you can. Would you take it and see that she gets it?"

"Wow! Okay. I have no idea where she might be right now, but when I see her, I'll make sure she gets it."

"Thank you, Peter. She put so much into every game, all the way up to the end."

I'm working my way through my second slice of pepperoni pizza when Arnie and Vicky join me. He grabs my crust from my first slice and it disappears in two bites. Then he picks up the jacket and opens it up to inspect the letter and pin. "Feeling good?" he asks.

"Yeah. It feels good, but I have to find Marty," I

answer.

"A lot of people want to find her. I read that the district attorney is talking of pressing criminal charges. Not good. She's a juvenile, so who knows what jail time would mean."

"Yeah. What a bummer." *You know the game now, don't you, Brother? Don't panic. Think. If you were Marty, where would you go? Where would no one ever think to look? And how can I get anyone to believe she's innocent, if she is?* I take another bite of pizza, but now all I can taste is dull crust and greasy cheese.

Tonight I have two e-mails from Hess and company. One is an invoice for $1159. The original bill was twice that much, but at the bottom is a note saying that Mr. Hess ordered the billed hours to be cut to the rate charged when work was first done for the McClure family. So there goes most of the money from those two coins—but not all of it. The second e-mail contains the name and address for a man who has an apartment over his garage for rent. *Okay. Thanks, Tom— maybe.* No e-mails from Marty, although I have been sending her messages almost every day.

Thursday I phone the number from the second Hess e-mail. A man of 'advanced years,' judging by his voice, answers. I identify myself and ask if the apartment is still available, and would I be able to take a look at it?

"Sure. Come on over. We just got the repainting done last week. Tom said he had a young man looking for a place. If that's you, you're free to take a look." I get the directions and make an appointment for right after school tomorrow.

Friday I drop Arnie and Vicky at Vicky's house where they say they are planning to work on some project for biology. I don't ask any questions, and I don't tell Arnie my plans either. The less he knows, the less trouble he'll be in later.

The house is an ancient "four square" that looks like it dates back to the turn of the last century—centered front door with equal rooms upstairs and down on either side. Neighborhood is older with big trees. The lawns are being kept up, and I note flower beds in many of the front yards. I park in front and knock. It takes a minute, but the owner gets to the door eventually. "You Peter Bain?"

"Yes, sir."

"That's good. I'm Harry White. Lived here for seventy years and mean to stay here another twenty. Just drive your car around back. I'll meet you there. Apartment is upstairs over the carriage house."

Carriage house? I thank him and do as he says. The building looks like a two-car garage with a full second story above that includes a window-filled overhang that shelters the garage doors. Side is asphalt shingles, but they appear to be in good condition. I wait by my car until Mr. White joins me, limping slightly, glasses taped together in the middle, heavy wool jacket buttoned up. "Here. You use the side door. Used to be the stableman's lodgings, then a chauffeur lived here next, then the cook. Had lots of professions go through this door." He gets out a key and fumbles it into the lock. The door is solid but opens easily. Inside, my host clicks on an overhead light and leads the way up a narrow set of stairs to a landing and another door with its own lock. "Same key," Mr. White tells me with a wink.

The inside is cold. No heat. Together we tour the place. The walls are plain but clean with white wainscoting covering the lower halves. The bay window that is part of the overhang fills the combination living room and kitchen with light. A bedroom with a single bed, dresser and stand overlooks the back alley. Beige curtains decorated with shepherdesses and rustic boys playing pipes look like they might grant some privacy. A shallow closet fills part of the wall opposite the bed. Next door is a bathroom that includes a new three-sided, plastic shower stall. Everything smells faintly of fresh paint. The kitchen appliances are recent, the refrigerator is large. There is a microwave and lots of cabinets. A sofa, dining table and two straight-backed chairs complete the furnishings. When I ask, he points to cast iron radiators in the living room and the bedroom. "Heat pipes over from the house. No thermostat. Whatever I set it at, you get. I keep it pretty low, usually around sixty-five in winter. Hope that's not a problem. I cover the other utilities as well, but if my electric goes up by more than twenty a month, I'll be coming to you for the overage." He gives me another wink. "You going to need a telephone, or do you have your own cell phone?

I shake then nod my head. *No. Not a problem*.

"Rent is five hundred a month, due on the first. One month's security. I have a contract that you would need to sign. No repainting without permission. No pets, no loud music, stuff like that. Since Tom referred you, I will take that as your reference. You can park in the garage. I don't drive much any more myself. Sold the old Buick last year. My daughter picks me up for shopping twice a week. There is a key for the garage. Or you can park outside, just stay off of the grass. You don't smoke, drink or use drugs, do you? No. Didn't think so. You don't look like the type. Any questions?"

"No … Can't think of any. Wait. Any internet?"

"Nope. Sorry. But you can use my neighbor's wireless. He's never encrypted his setup. He lets the neighbors use it when he's at work. Trusting fellow." He gives me a third wink. I like this guy.

"Okay. If you have the contract, I'll read it." What am I getting myself into?

Mr. White leads me into his own house via the back door. A contract already lies on the kitchen table. "There you be. I know you'll want to read the whole nine yards."

"Thank you." I take a seat and start reading—four pages, single-spaced. Let's see … Garbage pickup on Mondays. No broken-down cars on premises. Guests allowed overnight, but have to inform landlord if staying more than a week. Available for inspection by landlord at any time. Security deposit may not be used for last month's rent. One year lease, after that: month-to-month. *No bull shit. Pretty much all common-sense stuff.* I take out a pen and sign and date on the lines of both copies.

"You satisfied?"

"Yes, sir."

"Okay." Mr. White takes my pen and signs each copy, then hands me back the pen and one of the copies. I get out my checkbook and write out a check for 1000 dollars and hand it to him.

"When are you planning to move in?"

"I don't know," I answer. "It depends on the home situation."

"Well. Seeing as its already over halfway through November, I will figure on December first as the start date. So the next rent will be due the first of the new year."

"That would be great. Thank you, sir. I may move over a few things starting next week, but I'm pretty sure nothing is going to happen until after Thanksgiving."

He hands me two keys: one for the apartment, one for the garage, we shake and I'm committed. *Phew!*

With no more volleyball practice, my after-school time has opened up. Dad and Mom are never home before 5:30-quarter-to-six, so I use those two hours between getting out of school and their homecoming to organize my stuff and start to move things over. I must take my desk, but that will be a major project and can wait. I start by inventorying the apartment's contents. No food, no dishes and no knives, forks or spoons. No towels or sheets or blankets. Well, here's one place to start. Next day I'm in Walmart buying soups, crackers, cereal (hot and cold), canned fruits and veggies and a bunch of frozen single dinners. Then I go to Target where I buy a set of sheets, two bath towels and two hand towels. I almost buy some dishes and utensils as well but decide to

check out the local thrift store first. There I get lucky. A
collection of heavy, silver-plated knives, forks and spoons—
four place settings—goes for five bucks. It's still in its keeper
chest and includes serving spoons and a big fork. Two knives
are missing. Well, won't need more than one. I also pick up
five plates in the same blue floral pattern on white. All but
one have at least one small chip. I add a mug, a kitchen knife
and two small juice glasses and decide I had better stop for
now. I haul everything over to the apartment, put the food
away and dash home, pulling into my parking place less than
a minute before Mom gets home. *That was close!*

In the evenings after supper I study, working to make
up for all the time lost due to practices and the court case. I
revisit the gold merchant and cash in two more coins. That
gives me enough rent money through the end of March. The
market is paying enough to cover food, I will have no utility
bills. I still have the Aunt Millie 1000, plus all the money I
have been socking away for the last year. I'm good, I hope.
The next trip, I stop at the law offices to pay the bill, then
sneak over a blanket and one of the down comforters that I
used to love to sleep under when I was a kid. I add a few of
my clothes, and my favorite framed poster of the Grand
Canyon after a lightning storm. Place is beginning to feel like
a home.

A week-and-a-half until Thanksgiving and I get a
long e-mail from Hess and company. Drawn from court
records, it provides me with part of the saga of Mary Beng
Soo. As the birth certificate indicated, she was born in San
Francisco on December second, a year later than I was. Her

mother died four years later. After her mother died, Mary was living with Uncle Stan most of the time and Aunt Millie the rest of the time for eight years. Dad had initiated a request to remove her from their care four years ago, maintaining that Uncle Stan was too ill to care for her, that her relationship was unproven and that she was too young to be left alone for long periods of time—as Uncle Stan was doing. Millie and Stan contested the charges. A DNA test concluded that Mary was Uncle Stan's granddaughter and Dad dropped the request. But when Millie broke her hip, Dad stepped in and invoked the power-of-attorney that Millie had granted him earlier. Uncle Stan filed a counter charge but died three weeks later. At Dad's insistence, Mary was assigned to Foster services. *Dad, I hate you.* Mary lived with her first family for three months before requesting a reassignment. This was granted. She lasted two months with the next family before again requesting a new assignment. The Children and Youth Services investigation concluded that Mary was not trying to adjust and refused her request. At that point she ran away. Authorities discovered her in a homeless shelter, took her back in and returned her to the second family she had been reassigned to. She disappeared again. Two months later, she was caught dumpster-diving over by the West Shore strip mall. This time she was sent to the juvenile retention home. She escaped two weeks later and has not been seen since— until this latest event. *What a crummy life!*

West Shore strip mall? That's next to that storage locker place. In fact, I have to go through it to get to the lockers. Hmm. "Okay." *I think it's time I go back there and*

*look through those boxes again, and maybe the suitcases. I've
put off going back there too long.*

Chapter XVI   Reunion

I make careful preparations. I pack a prybar and
screwdriver for forcing suitcase locks in the trunk. I tell Mom
I will not be home for dinner tomorrow, but intend to spend
some time doing some research. She fails the question test, so
I'm free to go. Tuesday after school I stop to cash a check
then I head over to the storage locker place. Third trip and I
know the routine: getting through the gate, turning down the
alley and driving to a space next to the locker—out of sight
from the road and the mall. It's raining, a solid November rain
and miserable out. I step out of the car, suddenly aware of a
change in the silence. What am I now not hearing? I stare at
Millie's locker door. Why was I sure I heard singing? I stand
there in the rain feeling stupid, aware of so much new. I nod,
close the car door as quietly as possible, lock and walk back
to the strip mall where I know there's a Pappa John's. 20
Minutes later I'm on my way back.

Standing outside the locker, I stare at its off-white
steel door. *Well, if she's here, she'll be hungry. If she's not
here, I'll have more pizza to myself. Think positive.* I rap on
the door. "Pizza delivery!"

Silence.

Okay. I put the key in the opener and turn it. As it

starts up, someone inside gasps.

I duck under the still rising door. The futon is open and made up for sleeping. Marty (or is it Mary? Why am I not surprised) is sitting on its edge dressed in pajamas: bottom on, the top half-on, one button secured. Left-hand is on that button; right hand holds what looks like a mace canister. A LED lantern sits on the little table lighting up Marty's pinched and frightened face and the pajamas: once-white with little dancing ponies.

"Oh, my god! Peter! You almost made me die. I damn-near peed in my pants." She takes several deep breaths, then jumps to her feet and wraps her arms around me. I set the pizza box and a bottle of water on the bed and hug her back.

I feel her chest start to shake, aware of how close she is and how naked. *And how much she stinks too.* I lift her dull and obviously dirty hair away from her back and rub her there, then lift her wet face to mine and, without thinking, kiss her on her lips. To my surprise, she kisses me back, her soft, warm mouth filling my head and bod with sudden heat. "Would you close the door?" she sobs while I take deep breaths. *Wow-wow-wow!*

"Yeah. Sure." I let go and lower the door. It gets a little warmer inside, but not much. Mary sits back down on the bed, pulling a blanket around herself, then finishes buttoning the jammy top. I sit down beside her, glancing around the locker with its tiny circle of light and deep shadows. An open suitcase (not one of the two on the dresser) holds clothes. Against the other wall is what looks like a toilet

lid on a stand with a plastic bag underneath. At least six
Pappa John pizza boxes are stacked by the door. Otherwise,
everything is much the same as I remember.

Mary's still crying and sniffling, but regaining
control. "Oh, Peter. I'm so glad it was you."

"Pizza?"

"Pizza! Gad! Sure." Her voice is losing its tremor.
"What kind?"

"Half Hawaiian, half sausage and mushrooms."

"You remembered! How did you know I was here?"

"Marty, or is it really Mary Beng Soo?" She nods,
then opens the pizza box and takes out a Hawaiian slice.
"Yeah, Mary Soo, that's me. How'd you know?"

"The newspaper let the cat out of the bag, but I
figured it out the night you told Ricky that Arnie and I were
cousins. I know you lied a lot, but that didn't sound like a lie.
I knew that someone had to be living in this locker, at least
occasionally. Bunch of other clues: The slip in the book you
gave me, some things you said. I remembered visiting with
you. Met you several times at Aunt Millie's. What I couldn't
remember was your voice, plus, you've grown a bit, you
know. I guess that's why I didn't know you at first." I hand
her a napkin when she starts to wipe her mouth with the back
of her hand and note dirt in the wrinkles of her palms and
under her nails.

"This isn't my voice. Ricky broke my voice last
April. He ... he choked me so badly that I think something in
my larynx broke. I couldn't talk at all for two weeks
afterward."

"Why'd you put up with crap like that? You know he's dead."

"I know." Her voice is a whisper now.

"What happened?"

"When he fell?" She sighs and looks away before answering. "He was standing right outside. I think he was lighting a cigarette. When I broke out, the door must of hit him in the back and thrown him off balance. At least, I think that's what happened. He spun around and grabbed at me. I shoved him away, I mean really hard. I was so pissed! And he went flying down the steps head first. I mean, that's what happened. I guess that did it: killed him. I didn't stick around to check it out." She looks at me. "I heard a cop arrested you for trying to help me."

"I'm okay. The charges got dismissed."

"I know. I was there, hiding in the back."

"So Ricky's death was an accident?"

"I hated his guts, but I never wanted to kill him. I was just trying to keep him off me."

"So if he choked and hurt you that badly, why'd you stick around with him?"

"Long story. I got in deep with him and couldn't see a way out until I got my library job. Even that didn't give me a place to stay some of the time."

"You were sleeping in the library?"

"Ah huh. Cool, huh?"

"What was the story on Ricky? May I ask?"

She nods. "Sure. You can now. I started hiding out in the 'Y' almost a year ago. I would use their gym, shower, then lock myself in one of their back rooms until after the place closed at nine. It worked for a while—until Richard caught me. He was the assistant director. He was real nice—at first—so nice that I confessed as to who I was and why I was hiding there. He let me continue to hide there until one day he suggested that if I wanted to continue being a guest, I had to make 'arrangements' with him. I refused. He promised to report me. I didn't know what to do. I had no way to get around, no other place to stay, really, and I knew foster services was watching for me. I so wanted to stay in school and be normal … So I said okay, as long as he didn't try to touch me below the waist."

"Oh, Marty-Mary."

"Hey, now he was in trouble too. If he reported me, I would have had him on sexual abuse of a minor, or whatever it's called. I think he realized it too after the fact, which is why he didn't push—at first. For three months I put him off. I used every excuse I could think of: claimed I had a headache, told him my period had just started, stuff like that. Then, one night the end of April, he pushed me down on the cot I was using and tried to force himself on me." Her face is so full of sadness now I want her to stop, to shut up, but when I raise a hand, she shakes her head and continues.

"I shoved him away; he grabbed me by the throat and choked me until I blacked out. When I woke up, he was gone and my throat was so sore, I couldn't speak. I wrapped a scarf around my neck to hide the bruising and went to school. I didn't know what else to do at the time." She turns her face away, her voice now so quiet I can barely follow her words.

"Richard found me two days later. He almost cried he was *so* sorry, swore it would never happen again. I told him (actually had to write it down on paper) if he ever touched my throat again, I would report him. It was a weak threat. If I did, they would nail me for running away from the juvenile home. So things continued, but I knew I had to find somewhere else. Richard pretty much stuck to his word until June. That's when I got the job as a page at the library. First time I had my own money, even if only a little bit. Until then, Richard had been buying my meals, even bringing me clothing. I would eat dinners at the Y and he always made sure they were covered. But with the library, I didn't need to stay at the Y every night. Plus I found a weekend job. I got to be good friends with Wanda, the circulation clerk, and she made sure I could sleep in the library any night it was open. I still had to use the Y on Sundays and Saturdays, but weekdays I was free of Richard. Once that happened he started acting really possessive, even nasty. I knew I had to get out. He'd come looking for me at the library. Sometimes I hid here. (Oh, and I found your note. Thank you.) He started picking me up at school. You saw that. I didn't know what to do. If I reported him, or ended the relationship, I knew he's call C&Y Services. But by going out for volleyball, I eliminated the need to take showers at the Y, and I figured I might be able to end the relationship. Then you showed up." She nods and the trace of a smile flickers across her lips, a tiny ripple on a flat lake of sadness. "I knew who you were, and I knew you were one person who would never rat on me. You were the out I was looking for. So I told Richard I was done with him and the Y. That's after he tried to choke me again and I damn near broke his foot. I guess he reported me after the Jefferson game."

"No good deed goes unpunished."

"You're full of sayings, aren't you?"

"I guess." I wish I could really comfort her, take all the pain I'm hearing away and lock it in a Pandora box. "What are you going to do now? How can you stay here?"

"I can't. Not much longer, anyway. It's getting too cold."

"Yeah, I noticed. You been here all these last two weeks? Where's the bug?"

"You mean Miz Tulip? She's parked in the lot in back, hidden under a canvas cover."

"How'd you get to drive her?"

"I just do. Age has nothing to do with being *able* to drive. I've been careful and so far, no one's stopped me."

"You own her?"

"Yup. Bought her from a salvage yard and got her running myself. Took me a year. Guy thought I was planning to take it out when I turned sixteen. I took it out when I turned fifteen-and-a-half. Had to. Needed wheels to get a job."

"What have you been doing for food and water and bathing?"

"Scrounge. Dumpster-diving. Ah ... bathing ...? Hey, are you going to eat that last piece?"

"You can have it."

"Thanks. So not used to warm pizza. Pappa John's has to dump their unsold stuff every night. I think someone knows I'm around 'cause the good leftovers are always in a pizza box set near the top of their dumpster so I don't have to climb in to get it. Ah, pizza, one of the primary food groups. Listen, can you keep this place a secret? I'm not sure where I'm going, or what I'm doing, but I know I've got to move real soon. First snow will give away my coming-and-going in a flash. Seen cops in the strip mall twice in last two days. They were walking around back here yesterday."

"Back here?"

"Yeah, but no way to tell anyone's in these places if the doors are closed."

Why am I finding it so easy to talk to you? Why did I always believe that girls all hated me? "What if I take you over to my apartment? It's got heat, power, a shower and food."

"You have your own apartment? No way! How'd you score that? Dear Dad and Mom know?"

"No they don't—and they won't until they have to know. I'm working on becoming an 'emancipated minor.'"

"What's an 'emancipated minor?'" Mary is cleaning off her fingers with a baby wipe, followed by drying with a rather dirty-looking hand towel.

"It's where someone who's still underage is allowed to act as an adult, free of an adult telling him or her what to do. You see in the news where child actors do it."

"Why would you do that?"

"It's the only way I can think of to get free of my parents and their emotional baggage."

"Hmm. What about this apartment?"

"It's over in the Hartford neighborhood. It's a two-room setup over an old garage. The owner lives in the house in front. Nice guy."

"Would he approve of a girl living with a guy?"

"Ah … Hadn't thought of that. Contract says I can have guests. I guess I'll have to ask."

Mary stares at her hands, her fingers picking at the dirt under her nails. "Could I move over there tonight you think?"

"Yeah … Sure. Can't think of a reason why not. This might be the best night we have. *Think, brain, think.* It might be the only night we have. Can't pull the late night from home every night and there's a chance of snow tomorrow. Won't be many cops out in weather like this. Hey, you should even be able to hide that Volkswagen of yours in the garage."

"Even a garage! Cool. Okay. Let me get dressed and packed. It won't take long." Mary unbuttons her jammy top and takes it off.

"Whoa," I cry in surprise.

"Don't panic. A girl's boobs aren't nearly as interesting as a lot of guys imagine." She picks up a bra and fastens it in front, rotates it around, puts herself in and pulls the straps over her shoulders. "There, you feel better?"

No.

"You can turn your back, you know. It's not like I have another room to change in."

"Hey, we're cousins."

"And your point?" She's got on a tee-shirt now and adds a long-sleeved tee over that.

"Okay. Second cousins, once removed, is hardly

close," I admit.

"I *did* feel a response to your bod when I hugged you. What? Are you blushing now?"

I sigh. "Just finish getting dressed."

"Okay." She smirks and steps out of the blanket, takes off the jammy bottoms, picks up panties and puts them on. Jeans follow and she's decent. She sits down and works on socks and the cheap, pink running shoes I remember from school. "See. I feel safe with you. You're my good-buddy. You've always cared for me."

"What was on that chain you're wearing around your neck?"

"One of Pop-Pop's dogtags. It helps me to remember."

"Oh?"

"When Pop-Pop went back to Thailand to find my grandmother and mother, he found my mother wearing this tag around her neck. She had gotten it from her mother. That's how Pop-Pop knew she was his daughter."

"Oh. Can I help pack?"

"This will only take a minute." Mary grabs a backpack from the floor and shoves it full of the rest of the loose clothes, puts on her coat and a wool cap. "This, that bag and that suitcase go." She pulls the sheets off the bed, folds them and puts them in the suitcase. "Blankets can stay. Just fold them and leave them on the bed once I get the futon set back up as a couch."

I help her set up the futon, then lay the blankets back where I remember them from before. Mary adds textbooks to the suitcase, a spoon and a cup, then closes it up. "That should be it. What's the address?"

"277 East Maple? You know how to get there?"

"No, but I can follow you?"

"You're taking the Volkswagen?" A thought enters my head. "Why don't I drive the Volkswagen and you the Volvo. That way, if a cop sees the VW, he'll see me behind the wheel instead of a missing girl. Make sense?"

"You drive stick?"

"I drive an old Volvo, remember?"

"Yeah. The ugly brown job. You're making more sense than anyone I've talked to for years."

Mary turns off the lantern and I raise the door, checking outside when I have it part way up before letting it run to the top. The overhead light does not go on. We shove the suitcase, her bag and a plastic bag of 'stuff' in my trunk. "Where's the bug?" I ask as I close the locker door and check to make sure it locks.

"Back here." We're both whispering and I can feel my heart beating against my chest. I follow Mary around the end of the lockers to a parking lot. The bug is there, almost unrecognizable under a grey canvas cover. Off it comes and we jam it in the back. I note that the flowers no longer sprout from the antenna. Mary hands me a key and key chain consisting of a link with a LEGO Wonder Woman at the other end. I give her the keys to the Volvo. I get in, belt up and start the engine. It complains briefly before turning over. I cringe as it lets out a familiar roar. "I'll come around and you can follow me out the gate. I'll be turning right on Garland. Keep close enough not to lose me," I tell her.

"Got it." With an okay sign and a wave, Mary splashes back to the Volvo as I ease around the end of the lockers and head for the gate. Ten feet from the gate and I can see the Volvo pulling in behind me. We're set to go. Never did see any of the records I came for. Well, next time.

Gad, this car is cold! I look for a heater knob but find none. The defrost is pathetic and I find myself cocking my head to peer out of the lower left corner of the windshield. Looks like half-a-tank anyway. Don't have to worry about needing gas yet. I feel more nervous this trip than I was the day I went for my driving test. A police car pulls across in front of me at the first light but never looks my way. I sigh and check the rearview. I can see Mary behind me, both hands tight on the wheel. Two blocks later, another police car passes us going the other way. I can see its brake lights go bright half-a-block behind. Is he turning around? *Shit, yes*. I catch a glimpse of the Volvo making a right turn onto a side street and the cop is behind me. *Double shit*. Now what? I continue on, waiting for the top lights to flash. Where did you go, Mary? What am I supposed to do?

As I approach the next red light, the police car pulls into the left hand turn lane and comes up beside me. He looks over. I turn toward him and give him a nod. The left-turn lane light goes green and he pulls out and disappears. I let out a deep breath. *Where's Mary*? Do I circle back, or pull over and wait. I have to move, the light is green for me now. I drive on, looking for a place to turn around but before I find one, the Volvo is once more behind me. *Thank you, God of refugees.*

I take a slightly longer route to get to the apartment, just in case that cop has circled around to follow, but I see no sign of him.

It's close to eight-thirty when we pull into Mr. White's driveway. I take the bug all the way in and turn it around, open the garage doors and back the car in.

"Home, sweet home," I announce to Marty, who is already out of the Volvo and standing under the stile, holding the backpack. I open the door for her, hand her the key for the upstairs door and return to the Volvo for the suitcase and plastic bag. "This is beautiful," Marty cries to me when I join her. "Like a palace for some long-lost princess."

"It's not that special, is it?" I set the suitcase down and offer her a hand in taking off her coat.

"It's the first place I will call 'home' in almost three years. Yes, and it is beautiful. Thank you, Peter." For a second, I'm sure she is going to start crying again. "Grandma wanted me so much. She was always telling me how proud she was of me. And I never got to see her again. Three years she was alone in that stupid home, and I couldn't even visit." Two tears are shining on her cheeks now. "And I thought I'd never see you again either."

"What?"

"You were always the nice older cousin. Even when you stopped talking to your mom and dad, you'd say 'hi' and talk to me when you knew your parents weren't listening. That evening you and Arnie came in Northside, I knew it was you. I was so excited, except you acted like you didn't know me. And I couldn't just say 'Hey, I'm Mary, not Marty." But then when you came to volleyball practice, I decided that even if you didn't remember me, you were still the same nice guy *I* remembered. I needed you, and you came through—just like I dreamed." She looks down at her hands, her lips turning upward. "My knight in shining armor." She takes a deep breath. "I'm okay. This is great." She smiles and pats my arm.

"You sure? Listen, I've got to get home before the wicked witch and the wicked warlock start to wonder where I went. Can you manage? I'll let Mr. White know tomorrow that you are here. There's some food in the cupboards and there's towels and sheets."

"Where's the shower? Any shampoo? Do you have a razor here?"

"In there. Yes, there's shampoo and soap. There's an ejectable razor in the cabinet. Keep my key, just don't lose it. Oh, one more thing." I reach in my pocket and take out my wallet, count off ten twenties and give them to her.

"What's this? I can't take your money."

"It's not *my* money. It's your money, part of your inheritance." I explain about the bank security box and its contents and the key from Aunt Millie. "There's more, but I suspect that it is just the crust of what that nursing home and Dad tried to dig out and make off with."

"Yeah." Mary folds the bills over and puts them in her pocket. "Most of it's still in those suitcases back in the locker. All he would have gotten were her social security and retirement fund checks."

"What's in there?"

"I don't know. Tons of papers. Nothing I could cash."

I have to think on that. I turn to go. "I'll be back tomorrow right after school.

"Peter." She takes my arm and pulls me into an embrace. "Thank you." Deep breath. "Thank you."

"Thank you," I answer. This time we kiss together.

"What have I just done?" Remorse sets in before I'm half-way home. If trying to help Mary escape got me into deep trouble, aiding and abetting a criminal on the lam has to be even higher on the list of jail-time offenses. What if someone asks me "Do you know where Marty Sofia/Mary Soo is?" What do I say? I will not lie. But I sure had better get hold of Tom Hess and get some advice.

Chapter XVII   Mary's Story

Arnie grabs me the moment I am heading upstairs. "Hey, Bro, what gives? Where'd you go tonight? Sure could have used the ride home."

"Sorry. Important business that couldn't wait."

"And I'm out of the loop right now?"

I unlock my door. "Right now, yes. I want you safe and ignorant in case there's trouble."

Arnie follows me inside my room. "This have to do with the inheritance and Mary Soo?"

"Yes."

"And that locker next to West Side?"

"Yes."

"You find anything?"

"Yes."

"Can you fill me in. Please, pretty please?"

"If I fill you in, you could be guilty of the same thing I am now."

"Oh. Later?"

"Yes. I'll fill you in later."

"Do I get a ride home tomorrow?"

"Be ready to leave immediately. I do have things to do."

I enter my room, close the door and stare at my desk. "I did a good deed. I hope I don't get punished for it. But, God, I'm sure glad I found you, Mary."

Eleven o'clock, in bed and still awake. I keep remembering the feel of her lips, the brief view of her pale breasts. So good, yet how does she see me? Why wasn't she concerned about my seeing her naked? Does she want me to … My forehead twists as I squeeze my eyes knowing that sleep is no nearer than England or France. Or … did Ricky do this to her? Does submitting to rape—even half-rape—strip away one's soul so nothing matters? Does she really care or want me? Tiltman and his lies sure did a number on me. *God, what a world of shits we live in.*

In the morning I make another appointment to meet with Tom Hess. It's set for nine on Saturday. The guy must be doing me great favors to come in on a Saturday, but he knows I'm in school. Why are some adults so understanding? I focus on classwork and get a bunch done during study hall. Lunch, and who should join me but eager-beaver Eddy Clancy.

"Season's over. Do I get my story now?"

"What story?" I make room for Eddy and his lunch tray.

"You promised you would give me the story of your volleyball playing after the end of the season."

Yeah, I did say that, didn't I? "So what do you want to know?"

"How did you get so good, when Coach Tiltman wrote that you were the worst would-be player he had ever attempted to help?"

I hoped that all that would finally be over. *Why is the ghost of Tiltman never going to let me alone?* "I never was a poor player, just young. What Tiltman wrote was a lie to divert attention away from what I had accused him of. Do you get that? Can you understand what I'm telling you? I never was a poor player—never! If you don't believe me, if you insist on publishing the same crap that I've had to put up with for over five years, forget it! This world is full of sick adults. Kids shut up, because if they say something, no one believes them." *Like Mary.*

"But Coach Tiltman was so good with teams. And he was an outstanding teacher. Everyone says that."

"Ed, you're Catholic, right?"

"Ah … yes. Why?"

"You go to mass and watch everyone parading up front to get their wafer. Right?"

"Ah-huh?"

"How many are truly repentant sinners? How many are deep, committed Christians who love their neighbors? Yet there they are, confessing their sins and going forth to 'sin no more?'"

"You have a point. Can we get back to volleyball?"

So I tell him about practicing, about the line in the garage and Arnie and I serving and volleying a ball back-and-forth for hours. I tell him about finally getting enough courage to risk a denial, and how Marty helped convince the coach to let me try out. "Coach Allison took a chance. He's the real hero here. I know he got a lot of grief until I helped win that first game I played in. We had a really good team this year. All good guys willing to play their hearts out. It's been great to get to know them. It was great that they got to know me."

"So, you're on the team for next year?"

"I think so."

"So what do your mother and father think of all this after all these years?"

"I … I wish I knew."

The snow starts at noon, but it's so warm that no more than an inch is on the ground when I pull into Mr. White's back lot after dropping Arnie off at the domicile. Getting out I catch a glimpse of a face peeking out of the curtains of the bay window. I go knock on the main house's back door.

"Come-in, come-in," Mr. White invites. "Looks like we might get winter before Thanksgiving this year."

"Yes. It does look that way. Sir, a slight change has occurred, which I wanted to tell you about as soon as I could."

"Oh? What is it? You're not leaving before you arrive, are you?"

"No. My cousin is staying in the apartment. She'll be staying there along with me. I hope that's okay."

"Your cousin? Ah, where will she sleep? Awfully small space for two, specially a boy and a girl."

"I know. She'll have the bedroom. I'll bring in a sleeping pad before the first and make a bed in the front room. We'll work it out. I hope it is only for a short while."

Mr. White studies my face, hands folded together, index fingers tapping each other. "All right. But keep me posted if she leaves. That her car in the garage?"

"Yes."

"Let me get you a second set of keys, and tell her to stop down some time so I can meet her and add her name to the lease. I do need to know who's in the place."

"Thank you."

I take the second set of keys and head over to the apartment. Mary is waiting at the upstairs door, dressed in clean jeans and a purple hoodie. Her hair looks so clean it shines, and the unwashed body smell from last night is gone. Her smile is both shy and confident. "I've been waiting for you." She takes off her glasses and turns her cheek toward me. When I kiss, she turns to bring her lips to mine. "Hmm. Best yet, 'Kissing cousin.'"

"What does that mean?"

"I don't know. Just a saying I've heard over the years." She walks over to the little kitchen table and sets her glasses down next to an open notebook and a stack of texts. No wonder that suitcase had felt so heavy last night.

I take a seat in one of the two chairs. "How'd your day go?"

"Quiet, but busy. I been doing a lot of studying, trying to make up for missing two weeks of classes. I ate some of your food. I hope you don't mind."

"I have an appointment with Tom Hess, the lawyer that helped me get off, tomorrow morning at nine. I think it might be smart for you to go with me and meet with him."

"Won't he just call the police?"

"I don't know, but you're gonna' have to do something. This can't be a safe place forever."

"I know."

"I think he can help you, negotiate, maybe get the charges dismissed or reduced. Then you could go back to school. He might even be able to help you get back your inheritance, and get you free of Children and Youth Services."

"Let me think about it."

"If you do not want to go, may I ask Tom some questions that might help you?"

"Okay." We sit a while. Silence had seemed so right,

but not any more. What did Mary's voice once sound like?
Would I recognize it if I heard it? "Make you some tea before
you go?"

I look outside, aware of the growing darkness. "Sure.
Thank you, then I have to go."

Mary gets up, grabs the only pot, fills it with water
and puts it on the stove. "Earl Grey okay?"

"Fine. Thank you." *Remember to bring over another
mug.*

"What went wrong with your foster homes?"

Mary sighs. "Long story. In an egg shell, first parents
were a couple of Bible-beaters. Would not allow me to use a
phone or a computer. Insisted I pray with them every night.
Seemed to think I was some kind of piece of sin that they had
to convert and save.

"Second family was even worse. First thing they did
after the worker left was check my arms for needle marks!
Went though my suitcase, lookin' for drugs. Curfew was at
seven; bedtime at nine. It was like some kinda' prison." She
pours the water into the mug and over a teabag, stirs, takes
out the bag and hands it to me.

"Thank you. What about you? Aren't you having
any?"

She tosses her head. "Save me half." As I hold the
mug, breathing in the bitter-sweet scent, I remember. Earl
Grey was the tea that Aunt Millie always served me. Never
with cream or sugar. Sometimes with a bit of honey.
*Remember to bring over one of the honey bottles from the
cupboard.* Mom never uses any. I doubt she'll notice one of

the bottles is gone. I continue to add to the mental list. Get some bacon and scrapple at the market tomorrow. Eggs too, for a proper breakfast. Milk, OJ, lemonade: stuff for the refrigerator.

"Penny for your thoughts?" I am aware at how tentative and concerned Mary sounds now.

"Just making a mental grocery list."

She laughs. "You're cute."

"How'd you come up with the name Martina Sofia? How'd you get it to work with school?"

"She was a real person, a little girl in San Diego who died falling out of a moving car when she was eight." Mary nods, her eyes briefly full of sadness. "Had the same birthday as mine. I read about her at the time she died. When I needed a new name, I thought, why not? Besides, Sofia means 'truth.' Richard constructed a phony shot record for me. I tested into ninth grade since I couldn't get the schools in San Diego to send a copy of 'my' records. Somehow it all worked out. Slicky-dicky-doo."

"So. Which name do you want me to use?" I get up and place the mug in the sink.

"You *could* call me Mary McClure. Pop-Pop and Grandma Millie were trying to adopt me. That would be what I am, if it went through."

"Did it?"

"I'm not sure."

"No Beng; no Soo?"

"No, but I may have to *sue* your parents to get what Grandma Millie wanted me to have." She laughs again. I don't ever remember seeing her so happy.

"I have got to go. Got to be home before the parents."

She nods, a cloud crossing her face.

"So you're set here for now? I'll pick up more groceries tomorrow after work, and let you know what progress Tom has made concerning Millie's estate. I'll still stop by tomorrow morning at eight, and you can let me know then if I you want to go with me. Okay?"

"Okay."

I get on my coat. She grabs my lapel and gives me a kiss. "Thank you for listening to my stupid story. I'll be here."

She had seemed so happy until I said I had to leave— happiness that turned to a yearning, almost pleading tone. How must it feel to live alone and have no family when you're only fifteen, while knowing that there are dozens of men and women out to get you? Was that why she let Ricky take advantage of her? I have lived alone in silence for so long that maybe I feel what she is feeling, but I never have had to hide in a storage locker or scrounge in restaurant dumpsters.

This time I'm later than Dad and Mom. "Where have you been?" Dad demands as soon as I walk in the door.

"Visiting a friend. Lost track of time. I'm sorry."

"We're having pizza tonight," Mom calls from the dining room. "We already ate our shares. I doubt your slices are still hot. Put them in the microwave if you want them heated up."

Nothing worse than zapped pizza. Crust always gets hard or rubbery. "I'll take it warm." I get it cold, but don't complain. This must be the way Mary's been eating it for the last two weeks.

I'm working on homework, even though it's a Friday night, when Arnie knocks. "Where you been?"

"Visiting a friend." I close the book I'm reading. *Here goes nothing.*

"A friend named Marty Sofia? Come-on, Brother. I'm not stupid. She's got to be somewhere, and you tracked her down, didn't you?"

I point to the door to my room. Arnie closes it and secures the bolt. "Okay. Truth: I did find Marty—or Mary McClure as she prefers—and yes, I have been seeing her for the last two days. This is not something you will tell anyone, especially not our mother and father. Understand?"

"I understand. Where does the 'Mary McClure' come from?"

"That's the name she prefers. She *is* Mary Beng Soo, yours and my cousin, the cousin that lawyer and the nursing home appear to have screwed out of an inheritance."

"But still the Marty Sofia you have the hots for?"

I chuckle then nod. "Yeah, the same."

"So what's going to happen?"

"I wish I knew."

Chapter XVIII   The Best of Times, The Worst of Times

It's snowing! And still just the weekend before Thanksgiving. Mary is warm and dry and fed, or should be. I think about the many others in this town and elsewhere who are homeless and for whom a turkey dinner must be but a dream as I head for Tom's office. I told Dad I had to be to the market by 10:30 and want to get an errand run first. This is one of the busiest weekends of the year and I will head to work as soon as I'm done at Tom's.

Climbing up the stairs of the apartment I hear voices coming from inside. Who? But it turns out to be just Mary and Mr. White. I sigh. "Good morning, you two. I see you've met." I'm trying to sound unconcerned.

"Yes," Mr. White answers with a smile. "A delightful lady, but younger than I thought she was going to be." He gives me one of his winks. Mary is dressed in a cream-colored blouse, a short green jacket and black jeans. She has her hair tied back with a red scrunchie. She looks quite dressed up and quite young. "I met her this morning when she came down to use the washer and dryer in the basement. She said she had an interview today and needed nice clean clothes."

"I'm ready," she tells me. "Oh. And, thank you, Mr. White. I'll be over to sign that lease when I get back." She pats his hand and we head out the door. "Can you make it by yourself?" I ask our landlord as he starts down the steps.

"No problem. Been doing it for seventy years. I'll lock up. You two go ahead and go. Take your time on those streets."

"So, you decided to come along?" I pull out in traffic,

aware that Mary is once more out in the open.

"I got thinking last night. This has to end sometime."

"Got something in the Kohl's bag for you.'

"What is it? A varsity jacket! For me? This was only my second year on team."

"Allison and Hertz said you earned it."

"Looks nice and warm. Oh, thank you for bringing it over. Maybe I can wear it …" She fingers the name 'Marty.' "… Maybe not. We'll see."

"Who's the friend?" Tom asks when he unlocks the door to let us in.

"Tom, this is Mary McClure, or, as she is also, Mary Soo, or Martina Sofia."

"Oh. Your cousin, right?"

"Yes sir, and we, she, needs your help."

"Well, come on in. Let me see what we can do."

We sit in the conference room and Mary talks. Tom takes notes, occasionally referring to his files. When Mary and I finally run out of story, Tom sits there silent, tapping his pen.

"Okay. I believe your story. I believe what you did was not intentional. But it's not my judgement call. It's going to have to be a judge's call, or a grand jury's or a trial jury. But you can't just hide out. The problem will not go away. Sounds like Ogden was a schmuck, but the public and the district attorney don't know that. So, first-things first: you, Mary, need to turn yourself in at the DA's office. I can contact the office and arrange such a turn-in. I can go with you as your lawyer. If you do turn yourself in, I think we can get a low bail, and start to negotiate a reduction or dismissal of the charges. But nothing will happen until you cease to be a fugitive. Do you understand."

"I do," Mary whispers.

"*I* will not turn you in. There is such a thing as lawyer-client privilege, which certainly ordains here, so what we discuss today remains confidential." He looks at his notes. "Now, you have another problem. That is that you are already a fugitive from the juvenile home, and Children and Youth Services is not happy about that. You show up, and they're going to be after your blood. And if they find out that you are living alone in an apartment supported by Peter here, they will be even more unhappy." I raise my hand. "Peter, I know you have been doing the best you can. You're trying to do the right thing. Coming here, Mary, was the right thing.

"I will not go back to that juvenile home. I am not a criminal, Mr. Hess. Why can't I just stay where I am and go back to school?"

"As Martina Sofia? As Mary Soo? Or as Mary McClure? Mary, this is a mess. And you're using someone else's name in order to avoid C and YS only makes it worse."

"If I had Grandma Millie's money, I could pay some sort of fine, but I don't have that." Mary is looking like she is ready to cry. "Why do the abusers get away with everything, and the abused get nothing but trouble?"

"Amen," I breathe.

Tom and I exchange looks, then he studies his notes for almost a minute. "All right, tell you what I'll do. You've met Harry White, correct? Nice guy. Actually an old friend and colleague of mine. Can you meet me here on Monday at 8AM? I will call the DA's office first thing and ask one of their people to come over and we can negotiate terms before you turn yourself in. If they agree to meet you here, it will be on our turf. A lot easier on you and easier on their office too, I think. Prosecutors who come down hard on children do not look good to the public. Would you be willing to do that?"

"I could go back to the storage locker."

"No," I cry out. "That's no different than my silence. I lot of good that did."

"Okay. I'll be here at eight. You'll get me there?"

"I'll get you there," I promise.

I drop Mary back at the apartment and head for work. She is obviously depressed now. What can we do otherwise? Move out of state? I suggested that at one point, but Tom pointed out that with a possible murder charge, Mary isn't safe in any state. I park behind the market, grab my apron and head in to start work.

"Where've you been, Pete? We're practically screaming it's so busy."

"Sorry, Bill. Had a nine o'clock appointment that I didn't think would take that long."

"Well, get busy. Lady there needs brussels sprouts."

I get one ten-minute break all day, barely time to grab and eat a pretzel sandwich. By 5:30, I am beat, but there is no way I'm going to the domicile without stopping back at the apartment. I get there close to six. The lights are on and when

I reach the upper door carrying two bags of groceries and a third bag with a new can opener in it. Mary runs over to let me in. "How's it going?" I ask as soon as I get inside.

She shrugs. "I hung your poster. Is that all right? And I unpacked most of my things. And look, Mr. White brought over a geranium. He said we needed some color in the place. He's a real sweetie. You know he's ninety-two? I hope I'm still mentally and physically together and in my own home at ninety-two."

She sounds so cheerful, but when I open my arms, she folds into them and starts to cry. "I don't want'a go to jail; I can't go back to that stupid juvee home. That's a prison too. I want to be free! Why can't I be like any other fifteen-year-old girl?"

I let her cry, rubbing her back and shoulders, feeling useless as a goldfish for comforting. Then Mary straightens up and lets go of me. "Stay for supper. Please."

"I'd love to. Let me call the home police and get clearance." I take out my phone and hit the instant dial. Mom answers.

"Mom, I'm eating at a friend's tonight. I'll be home later, okay?"

"Peter, you've been gone all day. I think you've been out enough."

"Mom, this is really important." I've had no problem for weeks. Why now?

"Just a moment." Now Dad's on the phone, and he sounds pissed. "Peter, you need to come home, and come home now. I don't know what's going on, but we were at the market this morning at 9:30. You weren't there. Where were you?"

"I told you I had an appointment. I went to work at 10:30."

"An appointment? With whom?"

"I can't tell you."

"What the hell is that? You will tell me whom you saw, and now."

"An attorney. Thomas Hess, junior, to be specific. I believe you may have known him at one time."

"Shit. You're *still* seeing him? I thought your court business was done. Well this is a fine how-dee-do. Where are you now?"

"With a friend."

"I want the address, damn it."

"Dad, I will be happy to discuss this with you when I do get home, but not when you're screaming profanities at me over the phone. I will be home this evening—late." I hang up.

Mary and my eyes meet. "That went well," is her only dry comment. She starts unpacking the veggies and dairy stuff I got.

"So what's for supper?"

"I thought we might be able to celebrate our new home, a little bit anyway. I found some frozen tortellini, and canned mushrooms and a jar of white sauce. So I thought we could boil the tortellini, cook up the mushrooms, add sauce and that might be nice. It's not from scratch, but it's something. Oh, I see you brought some broccoli. I'll steam that for a veggie."

"Okay, but only under one condition."

"What's that?"

"I get to help."

It takes almost an hour, but in the end we sit down to what's got to be the most special meal in the world, complete with dimmed lights and a red candle in the center of the table. We hold hands across the table and silently say a grace. As we eat, I find myself playing footie. Mary keeps giggling whenever my toes start to climb her shins. She curls her toes around my ankles. We say hardly a word the whole meal. "Next time, Farmer-John cheese."

"'Farmer-John?' Oh, Parmesan. Peter, you're funny sometimes. Yes, it would have helped."

"I think this is the best home-cooked meal I have ever had."

"Better than any your mother *ever* cooked? That's a stretch, but, yes, it was good. Wish I had thought of a dessert."

I get up and walk over to pull two fortune cookies from my jacket pocket. "Not appropriate to the meal, but will these do?"

Mary giggles, takes one and unwraps it. "But is it a fortune, or just the usual Chinese saying?"

"I don't know." I unwrap mine and crack it open. "Long journeys begin with a single step," I read. "Where have I read that one before? But maybe appropriate." I lay the slip of paper on the table and eat the cookie.

Mary breaks hers and takes out the paper. "The stars are many. Good friends few, but they outshine even the sun."

We clear the table and I start right into washing the dishes, glad that I thought to buy a scrubby, dish soap and a dish drainer. So many things to think of when you don't have a dish washer. Afterward, we curl up together on the couch. I think about love-making, wondering what it will be like, but not sure this is yet the time, or whether Mary will let me. Would my hands and mouth feel different than Ricky's? Based on that night in the locker, Mary is pretty easy-going about her body. I can see what might happen, but … wait. Wait until I'm free, and Mary's free? When will that be? Maybe never. Still, my hands can't keep from touching and holding her tighter. "Is this … is this better than before?"

Mary slowly nods. "Better." She takes my hand and sets it against her waist then sighs.

"What was it like … I mean with Ricky? I'm sorry. I shouldn't ask?"

Mary closes her eyes, her words soft breaths and distant as echoes. "Like … a dog was pawing at my chest: poking and grabbing at me, or worse. I never looked at him, never kissed him back, never touched him. I would close my eyes and do homework in my head."

"What!"

"Yeah." Mary nods. "I would write English essays, repeat German vocabulary, solve math problems—all in my head. It did help. If I wasn't there—in my mind—then none of it could be real, could it?" she lets a sob escape, then gives me a weak smile. "But your fingers feel fine. I'm not thinking about math problems now."

I pull her closer and we kiss, lips parted, tongues

briefly touching. *Oh, my God*. Then I have to pull away to
breathe.

"You might want to uncross your legs, lover-boy. I
don't think you want to go home with your balls in agony."

"Mary, you are so sweet and lovable. Crude, but
caring."

She laughs. "Just the voice of a little experience. You
walk in that door with your Dad waiting with his whip: one
look at you bent over in pain, he's gonna' know exactly what
you've been doing and be even angrier than he is already."

I ease away and uncross my legs and spread them
wide. "Why do these things happen?"

"Hormones. I don't know." She kisses me on the
neck.

"No hickies, please?"

"None at all," her voice, so close to my ear, is like
some ancient harpist's dream chants to the gods.

I sigh, sit up, get up and walk around. The longer I
stay here, the worse it will be. "Maybe I had better head
home. Depending on the riot act reading tonight, I may or
may not make it back tomorrow. If I do, I'll bring more stuff.
Otherwise, I'll be here Monday when Hess makes the call.
Sound good?"

"Sounds like a plan. Thanks, Peter. And, Peter …"
She takes my hands in hers and turns them over to stare at the
palms. "You are a sun in a sky of stars. I love you."

"As a cousin?"

"We aren't related close enough for that to matter."

I hug her and lean down to kiss her forehead. "You're

right, and I love you too."

Anyone who claim's that the greatest fury is a
spurned lover never saw my parents in full rage. I'm home by
8:30, but I might as well have slept the whole night away
from the domicile. Dad and Mom are both waiting in the
living room. Arnie's nowhere in sight. The second I'm in the
door and announcing that I'm home, the television is shut off.
"In here, Peter," Dad orders.

I take off my jacket and hang it up in the closet. I'm
not sure if this will allow a cooling of the air or add to the
heat. I walk to the doorway into the living room. "Sorry I
missed supper."

"Peter, come in and sit down," Dad points to the
empty wingback.

Okay, this is going to be fun. I take a seat.

"We ordered you to come home. Instead, you openly
defied us and stayed out anyway. We will *not* allow you to do
this. We have to have trust in order for there to be love. *Oh,
Dad, you're in the preaching mode tonight.* Trust comes from
doing what we tell you to do when we tell you to do it. It does
not come from sneaking around and visiting shylock lawyers
and shacking up with girlfriends whom we know nothing
about. Wait! Your mother and I have already made some
phone calls. We know you have been seeing this Mary Soo, or
Marty whatever she calls herself now. She is not your cousin.
She is not any kind of a relative. Even if she was, she would
not be someone we would allow you to date or see or
whatever. She's a juvenile delinquent, a con artist, and, if the

latest news is any indication, a murderer as well. As of now, you are grounded. We will drive you to work tomorrow morning, and pick you up after work. You will take the bus with your brother to school on Monday, and you will come straight home afterward. If we find out that you are not coming home on the bus, one of us will pick you up after school and take you home. This will not end until you apologize for your actions, and promise never to do anything like this again. And if you do go off on your own, we will contact Children and Youth Services ourselves and turn you in. Maybe you'll end up in the juvenile home with that criminal girlfriend of yours. Do you understand?"

"Dad?"

"Do you have anything to say? Say it now."

"You have already convicted me without a trial or a judge, so I don't know if either of you will listen to anything I say. I've lived around the lies of others so long, that when I find truth, I want to embrace and hang onto it forever. You've just made a bunch of statements about Mary Soo, none of them really true, and some totally false. I believe though that you have a personal, vested interest in maintaining *your* story. No, wait. I am not through talking! I think I know a lot more about Aunt Millie, Uncle Stan and Mary Soo than even you, with your twist on history, do. Go ahead, ground me, Try to keep me away from Mary, but remember that, when this thing is over, truth will still be there, and that is what I will stand for."

"Truth? You, the liar, say you stand for truth. What do you know about truth? That's enough. Get up to your room. And, remember: no driving. You're not going anywhere."

I get up and head for the stairs but can't resist a parting shot. "And what is the truth of where the money came from that got you your precious Audi?"

"Peter!" But I don't wait for the next waves of fury to reach me. Instead, when I reach my room, I unlock and open and close the door without going in my room, then tip-toe back to where the ventilation grate comes up from the living room. Dad had it put in when we got the wood stove to carry some of the heat upstairs. I take out my cell phone and set it to record.

I can clearly hear Mom ask. "What did Peter mean by that remark about the Audi?"

"I told you about that long ago. I bought it with that promotion bonus I got from the company two-and-a-half years ago."

"And that paid for my Mini too?"

"Ah … yes."

"Funny that Peter never brought that up or questioned it before. What are you going to do about Mary Soo?"

"I'm going to call the DA's office first thing on Monday and tell them that I want them to throw the book at her. I'll tell them that she's corrupted my son, and that unless they lock her up, she's likely to encourage him to run away like she has. Helen, this has got to end. I will not have my own son destroy everything I have worked so hard to set up for these last three years. With Millicent dead, I thought we were finally clear of all this. Now, not even Woodbridge knows where her records went to. Jesus, just when I have the lock on that property over on Hanscomb Heights." I hear them get up and the click of one of the living room lights being turned off. "For three years, I've been trying to get that Mary Soo out of our way and buried. Now she's sucked in our *own* son!"

I grab my phone, retreat to my room and quietly open the door. As I'm about to close it, I catch sight of Arnie standing by his own bedroom door. I nod. He points to his ear and nods back, then both of us retreat to our own inner sanctums.

"Well, now what, Peter?" I take a deep breath and drop onto my bed. I stare at my ceiling. No one I can phone; no way to get anywhere. It's like Dad's screwing me to the wall, tighter and tighter. Why can't he give? Why does he hate Mary so much? I nod. Because she's standing in the way of his dream: a mansion on the heights with everything that symbolizes. Well, dear Dad, I don't want that. I just want a mom and dad who trust and believe in me. I guess that's too much to hope for.

Emancipation can't happen too soon. But how can I get the rest of my stuff out of here? How can I even sign papers, or meet with a judge? *Tomorrow. Deal with this tomorrow, Bain.* I get up and head for the bathroom to shower and brush my teeth.

Chapter XIX Trial by Lawyer

Crap night. Not much sleep, but I'm up by six and down for breakfast by seven. Market opens at eight on Sundays, and I intend to be there on time. Of course, with current restrictions, that means Mom or Dad has to get up early too. They hate to get up early on Sundays. Too bad. At 7:30, I'm knocking on their bedroom door. "Mom, Dad, I have to get to work."

I can clearly hear the moans through the bedroom door as they struggle to wake and get going. Five minutes later, Dad emerges, unshaven and his few remaining top hairs hanging off his pate in all directions. "You ready? Let's go." His voice is still rich with sleep.

"I'm ready. Do you want the keys to the Volvo?"

"Oh, yes." I hand him one set, then follow him out to the garage and get in the Audi. I don't bother to tell him that I have another set in the desk. Nor do I remind him that I still have my cell phone.

The drive to the market proceeds in dead silence. Only when I'm getting out at Bill's do I tell him that I will be done at four, and whoever picks me up should drive around in back, and I would meet them there. With that I head inside without a wave or good-bye. I hear the Audi spin gravel as Dad, now thoroughly pissed, heads back to the domicile.

The first hour I spend most of my time helping unload and lay out the veggies, freshest to the back, yesterdays unsold to the front. About half our stuff is indeed locally-grown—that's what Bill advertises. The rest comes off the truck in big cardboard boxes: don't ask, don't tell. The oranges and lemons sure aren't local. All set, I start helping customers. It is busy, busier than most Sundays, which usually don't get going until close to noon when the after-church crowd stops in on their way home. It's close to ten o'clock before I get a short break. I already have Mr. White's number in my phone directory. I phone him, praying that he is not a late Sunday morning riser. He answers on the third ring.

"Hello, Mr. White? It's Peter Bain. I need to get in touch with Mary right away. She doesn't have a phone in the apartment. Would you be willing to go up to the apartment and get her and have her call me back at this number, I would be eternally grateful."

"Where are you, Peter?"

"I'm at the farmer's market where I work on Sundays. This is my cell phone number. Here, let me give it to you. It's really important I talk with her. Tell her I'm grounded and can't get her tomorrow. She needs to get a hold of Tom Hess and make new arrangements."

I hang up and wait. Will Mary get the message? Will she call back? I'm back on duty. Brussels sprouts and pumpkins are the big things. Yams are going like there never was a Thanksgiving before, and the South is rising again. By one, I am bushed, and no one has called back. Then there she is, dressed in her windbreaker and purple hoodie. "What happened?" she asks.

"Hey, Marty" the boss calls out, "You here to help, or keep Pete from working?"

"I'm here to help," she answers.

"Here's a change apron. Go for it."

Mary takes the apron and gives me a smile. "I'll talk

to you later. I didn't see the Volvo in the back, so you really are grounded?"

"How'd you get here?" I stammer.

"Mr. White called his daughter, and she drove me over. He talked to your Tom too. I'd have been here earlier, except that Tom told Mattie (that's Mr. White's daughter) to take me shopping. He insisted I had to have certain clothes for tomorrow. Mattie's picking me up around three, I think. Hey, I get to earn my own money again today. Not bad with the library job on hold." She sounds in high spirits today. Not sure why with tomorrow coming all too soon. "Your Mr. White is a real nice guy. You know that, don't you? His daughter's nice too." She blesses me with a grin that shoots through my chest and dances up-and-down my spine, then heads for the carrots section to help a customer.

We finally get a slight break around two as the after-church crowd fades. "So what happened?" she asks

I tell everything including the recording.

"This is deep shit. What about tomorrow?"

"I don't know. I have to go to school."

"Well, here's what happened to me. Mr. White came up to the apartment. I was already up and dressed—good thing. He told me to come over to the house, that he had talked to you, talked to Tom, and talked to his daughter and that she was on her way over to take me shopping at Tom's orders. So, Mattie arrives. She's a sweetie, just like her father, but only in her sixties. Her married name is Black, can you believe that?"

"If she has a son, did they name him Gray?"

"YES! I couldn't believe it when she told me. 'David Gray Black.' He lives in upstate New York. But he goes by just David."

"What a hoot! Weren't you worried going out shopping with the cops still on the lookout for you?"

"I haven't had my picture taken in over three years. I doubt anyone in the general public knows what I look like. Harry and Mattie figured I would safe if I was with Mattie." Mary shakes her head. "Yeah. She sure was a talker too. I think she told me half her life history. Her father: Harry, Tom's father and Grandma Millie go way back together. Mattie knew Pop-Pop too. God, I wish I had known all these people three years ago. Anyway, she took me to Kohl's where we picked out a dress for tomorrow, then I stopped at one of those phone kiosks and bought one of those real cheap phones with a hundred hours of pre-paid minutes. Here it is, since I suspect you want to have the number."

"You bet." I take out my own phone and thumb in her number. "How's Bill know you? I never saw you working here before."

Mary laughs, a happy sound. "Saturday mornings until eleven. I doubt you ever saw me—except as a customer."

"Oh, my god. That is *so* weird. We'd better get back on the job."

An older woman with wavy white hair and a pleasant smile arrives just before three. "I've got to go," Mary tells Bill. He writes some figures on a pad, then takes three tens out of the till and hands them to Mary. "See you later," he tells her.

Mattie Black waves to me. "Nice to meet you personally, Peter. Mary was telling me so much about you."

"Nice to meet you, also, Mrs. Black—in a role other than a customer."

She laughs. "Yeah, I know. You've waited on me here many a Sunday and never knew who I was."

The place feels silent and empty with Mary gone. It's dead too, most of the shoppers gone. I start cleaning up: stacking empty boxes, consolidating batches of fruits and vegetables. Most won't be sellable by next Saturday and will go into dumpsters. That's the way the system works.

Mom rolls in just after four. I get in and we head home without a single word between us. I sense the ping on my phone warning me that a text message is coming through, but have to ignore it. I guess Mom misses it.

Dad is watching the tail end of a pro football game. I walk right past him. He ignores me. As I walk down the hall to my room, I notice dust and pieces of wood splinters on the floor. "Oh, shit!" Where the hasp of my lock had been secured to the door jam is a fractured mess. Where the deadbolt closed is now a hole. My room is no longer secure. I take a deep breath, push the broken door open and look around, careful not to touch anything. Things inside actually don't look *too* bad. I guess the fury and energy went into breaking in. My bed covers have been torn apart, and all my books pulled off their shelves but then put back—in a haphazard fashion. My dresser drawers are half-open and my clothes have obviously been gone through. Closet is standing open. I wonder what Dad thought when he found the dresser and closet almost empty.

The big concern is the slant-top desk. I approach it and run my fingers across the surface. It does not appear that the secret door has been disturbed. I dare not check it now, not with Mom hovering around just down the hall. It is not an easy cache to locate. The first release is not too hard to find, but pulling it doesn't appear to do anything, and the second lever won't do anything either unless the first lever is held down. Even then the door won't open unless you lift its corner just so. I got a lot of things in there now: rental contract, bankbook, checks, bank statements, receipts for the gold coins I've sold, cash from the market job. Dad and Mom will have a shit-fit if they find it. Mom's probably wondering what I did with the thousand I got from the nursing home's will since it didn't go in the account we share. I've got to get out of here, and get this desk out of here too.

I open the slant top and lightly touch my laptop that takes up a third the desk's work surface. It doesn't look like it has been moved. Dad must know the whole thing is encrypted to the eyeballs. It'd take the NSA to crack it—I hope.

I turn around and Mom is standing by the door, watching me. "I'm sorry, Peter. You can't lock yourself away anymore."

"I can see that. Now will you please leave me alone."

She nods and walks away.

The text, to my surprise, is from Tom Hess. "BRNG DRS-UP CLOS 2 SCH I WLL PK U UP." What does that mean?

Dinner is a study in non-communication. Except for "Pass the biscuits" or "May I please have more potatoes" type stuff, we eat in silence. Afterward, Dad settles down in the recliner for another sports event, Mom starts on the dishes, Arnie and I retire to our rooms. Studying is difficult—too much tomorrow to worry about, but I do get all my math problems done and some reading for social studies. *What a day ...*

Next morning, I carefully pack my sports coat and a tie in my gym bag before joining Arnie and Mom for breakfast. Dad has already gone to work, and Mom fails the personal dress inspection test. She never asks why I'm wearing a dress-up shirt, or my good slacks and black shoes. Arnie and I ride the bus, ignoring the stares of classmates who have never seen us ride before.

"Dad must have had a hell of a good time breaking down my door."

"He was swearing so much even Mom told him to hush up and remember that the neighbors have ears. Once he was inside, I was sure they were going to ransack the whole place, but they left after half-an-hour. What have you done with all your stuff? Mom noticed that even your Grand Canyon poster is gone."

"It's all with Mary. It's safe. The moment I get my wheels back, the rest of it is going too."

"You're really serious about this moving-out business?"

"Well, wouldn't you be, if you were I?"

Arnie nods. "So what's going to happen with Mary?"

"I don't know. I may find out this morning."

"Huh?"

"Be cool, and I'll tell you later, maybe at lunch. Okay?"

"Be careful. I think Mom was planning to follow the bus to school to make sure you got there."

My phone beeps. C U SOON. MM.

I smile.

End of first period bell and I see Mrs. Garcia, the school's receptionist, standing outside my classroom. She waves to me when I exit. "Come down to the office. Someone here to meet you." I stop and grab my gym bag out of my locker and hoof it over to the front office.

Tom is waiting. "Good. I see you got my message. Let's go. You can put the tie on while I'm driving."

I sign out and follow Tom out the door. "How'd you get me out?"

"I know Mr. Smelz. Mary's at the office already. A Mr. Abbott from the DA's office is to meet us at 9:45. He does not know Mary is there, but he does know that it concerns her."

"How's she doing?" I think I have the tie's knob straight. I get out my jacket and brush it off and try to rub out the creases.

"Better than I thought she would be. She's a strong girl." He nods. "… been forced to grow-up a lot. I think we'll be all right."

The law office is bustling, with two secretaries typing and a lawyer-type in a silk blouse, fitted black skirt and pumps directing paperwork. "Hi, Tom. Working on your golf day?" she asks.

"Work needs to get done," he answers and leads the way to the conference room.

Mary is waiting there. She gives me a big grin when I walk in, then stands up and slowly turns around for my approval. She's wearing a new shirtwaist dress in a dark green cotton covered with tiny printed pink roses. Over that she has on her varsity jacket. Her hair is done down in a single, long dark braid and she is wearing what look like new glasses— new frames anyway. No lipstick or makeup. She looks like she could be thirteen, fourteen max, certainly not a threat to anyone. *Maybe that's the intention.* "New clothes. First dress I've owned in nearly three years, and look: stockings. What do you think?"

"Nice. Beautiful."

She comes around the table and we give each other a peck on the lips while holding hands.

I note Tom shaking his head. "Okay, you two, sit down at the far end so that Mr. Abbott does not see you right away. Let's go over what may happen and discuss how you want me to deal with each possibility." It is then that I notice the video-recording camera on a tripod facing into the room.

Mr. Leon Abbott, dark suit, bright silk tie, smooth, young face, arrives fifteen minutes later. When Donna brings him in, he takes in all of us but zeros in on Mary. The surprise on his face is worth a painting. He turns to Tom. "Tom, I didn't know Mary Soo was going to be here. What are you trying to do?"

"Have a seat, Leon. I think we can have an open discussion here and reach some conclusions that will benefit justice and my young client." He introduces Mary and myself, referring to me as an interested family member and next of kin. *That's a little bit of a stretch, but mostly true.*

Abbott shakes our hands, firmly with me, gently with Mary. "Bain. Bain? Don't I recall your name in connection with Mary Soo before?" Leon takes a seat, opens his brief case and sets out a audio recorder. He adds a notepad and is ready. Donna rejoins us with some kind of recording machine which she types notes on.

"Leon, I met Mary Soo last week after Peter here brought her in from the cold—literally. I have spoken with her, interviewed her and convinced her that meeting with someone from the DA's office was in her best interests, as well as in meeting the demands of justice. Mary?"

"Mr. Abbott, I would like to enter a plead of not guilty to any charges that you might bring against me concerning the fall and death of Richard Ogden. I would state that his fall was accidental and not intentional on my part. I did not push him."

"Now hold on a minute." Abbott looks up from his note taking. "Can you prove that?"

"Leon. You have heard what she just said," Tom butts in. "Now stop and think before you follow through with the charges you would like to make. I am certain that you have no physical evidence that would show an intentional crime. Mary is the only witness, and she is denying that she pushed Ogden. If you accuse her of deliberately causing Ogden's death, consider whether you would ever be able to prove that to a jury."

Leon does a slow burn. "Then why did you run off? If you are innocent, why did you drive away?"

Mary looks at Tom. He nods. "Go ahead. This is not a courtroom, nor are you under oath, but Leon here needs to hear you."

"Mr. Abbott, I left because Children and Youth Services with two police officers were trying to grab me for running away from juvenile detention. I had been placed in the juvenile home because I refused to accept the foster parents that Children and Youth Services continued to insist that I live with—not because of any crime I ever committed." She takes a deep breath. "It is very hard when you're only thirteen to appeal a decision when you have no money, no friends, no relatives who will acknowledge you, and no one like Mr. Hess here to stand up for you. I have friends now and I have a lawyer who believes in me. If we are negotiating anything here, I would be willing to plea guilty to running away from the home, but I will not admit to any charges relative to the death of Mr. Ogden. I did not cause his death."

Abbott sits back and stares at Mary. Then he rubs his chin. "Let me make a phone call to the boss."

"Go ahead," Tom prompts him. "We're all here."

Abbott punches a number. "Yes. Leon here. I need Charlie on the phone now. Yes. It's in regard to the Mary Soo girl." Pause. "Charlie? I'm going to need to put you on speaker phone. Yes. It's about Mary Soo. She's here, with Tom Hess. Yeah. Surprise."

"Are you serving the warrant, or negotiating a plea bargain?" I hear the voice on the other end ask.

"We're negotiating. And what Tom and Mary are saying is that a charge of murder, or even involuntary manslaughter ain't gonna' fly. It was an accident."

"That's crazy."

"Charlie, I may agree with you, but I doubt that you will get a conviction with Tom at her side. Charlie, she's a young girl. It'll be hard to charge her as an adult in any case. I've met her. I shouldn't say this, but she's attractive, clean-cut, poised and looks very young. She'll have a jury crying for her."

"So what is Tom pushing for?"

"He wants any charges relating to Ogden's death dropped. Mary and he are willing to fight the charges that led to her being sent to the Juvenile Center."

"I can't do that," Charlie's voice says.

"What are we going to do? She's the only witness and she denies pushing him. All his injuries were from hitting his head on those bottom steps."

"So how *did* he fall?"

"He was standing on the top step when I ran out of the school," Mary puts in. "I almost ran into him. When he

turned around, he lost his footing and fell off the steps."
Hmm. That's not exactly the story you told me before.

The other end of the line is silent for at least half-a-minute. "Charlie," Abbott speaks. "We're not going to win this one. I think we're better off folding our tents before this turns into a bigger manhunt and media circus than it already has become."

Charlie's voice lets out a sigh. "I would have no problem with that, but I've got pressure from, shall we say, other interested parties that are demanding this to go to trial. —including a phone call this morning."

"Will that serve justice?" Tom puts in. "Or will it save money? How expensive will a trial be if you lose. And believe me, this is one court case you will lose. I will make sure of it." *Wow, Tom can tighten a screw! I am so glad I hooked up with this guy.*

"All right. You win for now. I'll tell the sheriff's office we're dropping the charges against Mary Soo in regard to Ogden's death 'based on new evidence.' Go ahead and work out a deal concerning her other, outstanding charges. I've got to go. Thanks for bringing me in. And, I'm glad to hear Mary's not running around in a dump somewhere. Try to make a happy ending for the press. We could use that right now. Talk to you later." The phone goes dead.

Abbott puts his phone away. "You heard what the man said. You win. Richard Ogden's death will be ruled accidental. So Mary, in regard to that, you're home-free. Tsk. We are not, however, done with the foster care and runaway business. Are you willing to go before a district justice and make a plea? Will you be willing to abide by a justice's decision?"

"I guess." Mary pushes her glasses back up to the top of her nose. "If Tom is willing to be there as well."

"I'll be there, Mary."

"So will I," I add.

Abbott nods. "Okay. Where are you living now, Mary? Do you have a home? Are you going to school? Do you have anyone who can watch out for you?" I almost raise my hand, but Tom wags his finger at me and I keep quiet.

"I'm living with a Mr. Harry White. He's a friend of Mr. Hess here." She smiles. "He's ninety-two, but still spry— I guess you'd say. I have my own place there, make my own meals, have my own bedroom and bathroom. His home is in my school district, so as soon as I leave here, I'll be able to go back to school. I need to catch up on the almost three weeks I missed. I have some money from a job I had at the Northside Library, and I work Bill's fruit stand in the market on Saturday mornings. I am not a burden to anyone."

"You're old enough to work?"

"Library pages can start at age fourteen. Working in a veggie stand is considered farm labor, so I can work there too."

Abbott takes down notes. "Okay. I know who Harry White is. Tom, you can vouch for all of what she's saying, I take it?"

Tom nods. "Yes, I can."

"Okay. What's your address? Do you have a phone number where the DA's office can reach you? You should get a notice within the month, certainly well before Christmas, as to the date and location of the hearing. I will also contact Children and Youth Services as to what is happening so they aren't continuing to look for you. That make you happy?"

Mary nods, grinning. "I can go back to school! Thank you. Thank you, sir." She jumps up and grabs me and gives me a hug, then reaches over to hug Abbott and Tom as well. "Oh, thank you. Can we go now?"

"Go wait out in the vestibule, you two. I need to talk with Leon for a couple of minutes. Then I'll take you both back to school."

Mary and I hi-five, then leave to take seats in the outer room. I give Donna a thumbs-up. She smiles. "Congratulations," she says.

"You'll have to give the school office your new address," I point out.

"Yeah. Not a problem." She laughs. "Oh, God. I never thought it would be this easy. Thanks, Peter. Thanks for everything."

"Yeah, but home is the shits now, and I'm not sure what to do."

"What happened?"

I tell her about the broken door and the ransacking. "Dad knows I have something hidden. He didn't find it, but it's only a matter of time. I've got to get that desk and my bod out of there permanently."

"Yeah, but if he finds out you're moving in with me, what will he do then?"

Chapter XX   Truck Attack

We're both in school before eleven, Tom dropping off Mary first over at 'B' before taking me over to 'A'. I brief him on the weekend's events before getting out of his car—including the recording of Dad and Mom's overheard conversation.

"You have that?"

I pull out my phone, find the conversation and play it for Tom.

"Oh, geez. That sounds awful! These are your parents? May I have a copy? No, I guess not, not unless you can get it to my office."

"I might be able to forward it to you as an attachment to an e-mail."

"Do that. As soon as you can." I get out. Tom promises me he'll stay in touch. Inside, I check back in, ditch the coat and tie and head for my 11 o'clock class.

Arnie joins me at lunch, along with Vicky and a couple of girls from volleyball. "Hey," one of the players named Jodie calls out. "I heard that you went to some kind of hearing in regard to Marty, or is it Mary now?"

"It's 'Mary,' and she's getting that straightened out today. She should be back in class even as we speak."

"Yay! Marty is such a cool player. Hard worker too." The other girls clap and wave their hands.

"You know Dad called the school right before you got back?" Arnie puts in. "Checking to make sure you were here. Ms Myrtle saw me and told me. I don't know what the office told him. I don't think they appreciate calls like that in the middle of a school day."

"Thanks, Arnie."

"So what's the news?" Vicky asks.

"The District Attorney is dropping all possible charges against Mary in regard to the Ogden guy's death. She still has to go to a justice to explain why she ran away from her foster care, and explain what and where she'll be in the future."

"Is that good or bad? I mean, the dropped charges over Ogden are great. I hear he was kind of an asshole, but what about the juvenile detention?" another girl whose name I can't remember puts in. "Will she have to go there?"

I would like to say 'no way, José,' but I really don't know. "I guess we'll have to burn that bridge when we get to it. I hope children's services don't want her back."

All but Arnie and Vicky return to their own tables. "So, what's next at home?" Vicky wants to know between sips of her diet cola.

Arnie and I exchange looks. "We wish we knew."

"Yeah, if we can get my desk out of there, then all my paperwork would safe anyway."

"My dad has a Ford pickup. It's huge in back. I bet he'd be willing to help you move it. Want me to ask him?"

"It was a bear last time when we put it up there."

"Dad so wanted to throw it away. What will you tell him when it's gone?"

"When is he not there except when we're at school?"

"Yes, Vicky. That would be great. Ask him, and if he says okay, I'll let you know a time."

I come home with the bus, study and text Mary. She has no computer of her own, which explains why she never answered my e-mails. She always used the library computers. Dad and Mom do not bring up my absence from school, so maybe he didn't find out. I do not attempt to repair the door. I figure that's their problem. Dad broke it; he can fix it. I do add a hook-and-eye on the inside so no one can come barging in when I want some privacy.

Mary answers my texts via her new phone with happy little notes. She's making up her school work and believes she can still pass all her courses this marking period. She washed and waxed Miz Tulip, but hasn't attempted to drive anywhere. Then Black Friday evening when I get a phone chime, there she is in living color. "Hi, Peter. What do you think?"

""Ah … Great. But I didn't think your phone would let you do this."

"It's Black Friday, remember? I called Harry, and his daughter took me to the mall and I traded up for one of the cheaper iPhones. You prop it on a stand, dial and skype. Cool?"

"Yeah, cool. And I love you. But I don't know when I'll see you again. The lock-down here continues."

She makes a sad face. "I wanted to tell you. I baked a tiny Turkey yesterday with chestnut stuffing. I took it over to Mr. White. He was so surprised and thrilled. I guess he'd gone to his daughter's for dinner, but she forgot the turkey in the oven and overcooked it, and no one was happy with the results. I gather she isn't much of a cook."

How does one forget a turkey? "Oh, Mary. I wish I could have shared a turkey with you."

"How was your Thanksgiving dinner?"

"Ah … Strained? Quiet. Bird was good, but the dinner kinda' sucked. You know, I never used to say anything to Dad. Drove him nuts. Now he's the one not talking to me."

"Hang in there."

"I'm sure trying." *Like the kitten on the poster hanging by one paw.*

I get an e-mail from Tom. He wants to meet with me about further investigations into the missing Woodbridge Nursing Home will. I want to, but how can I even go anywhere? It's not just the lack of wheels, but I can't walk out the door without Mom or Dad demanding to know exactly where I'm going. I finally suggest the market. That might work. Mom says she will continue to take me to work on Saturdays and Sundays.

So Saturday I'm on my way to work again. It feels strange to think that ever since June, Mary was working there Saturday mornings, and I was there Saturday afternoons, and we never met or knew it. I have Mom get me there at noon. No problem. She does a little grocery shopping while I get started. After she leaves, I send a quick text to Tom, letting him know I'm here. He rings me back almost immediately. "No can do, Peter. Sorry, but family and a bunch of stuff just came up. I might be able to make it tomorrow. By the way,

Mary has her hearing date: December Tenth at 10:45AM. I can't believe how fast that worked. Usually takes almost a month. Something is not right. And I still have not gotten an answer from Woodbridge on that will. I'm sure they're stalling. I'm going into the courthouse on Monday. They should have a record of when it was probated."

Bummer. "Thanks. Keep me posted." Something's definitely strange about this whole business. But as the afternoon business picks up, I have to push this problem to the back of my brain.

"Hi, Peter. Hi, Bill. Can you use me for a couple of hours?"

"Sure, Marty. Grab your apron."

Man. I can whistle or dance now. "Hi, yourself. How'd you get here?"

"Harry drove me over in my car. He still has his license, believe it or not. It was quite a ride. He's careful, but kinda' slow. I thought we were gonna' get rear-ended twice. And there was this guy in a big Ford following us almost the whole time."

Big Ford? "It wasn't a Crown Victoria, was it?"

"How would I know?" Mary is weighing mushrooms for a customer, but I know she's still listening to me.

" 'Cause that's what cops drive."

"Oh. Why would a cop be following me or Harry now?"

"I don't know, but watch your back."

"I was. That's how I knew he was back there."

Mary works for three hours, then leaves at three. We

kiss—lips open, tongues touching—but I've got a lot of
packing to do before I leave, so I force myself to keep it short.
In the brief moment of body contact I can feel a tension and
stiffness I hadn't felt when she arrived. "What's wrong?"

"I don't know. I thought that when the DA dropped
the Ricky charges that everything would be finally okay. But
there's something still going on. Why would a cop be
following me now? And I thought I saw someone walking
around the carriage house last night around ten. Neighbor's
dog started barking, and it woke me up. This morning, I found
footprints in the flower beds next to the apartment door." She
snaps her jacket closed. "Look, you need to get back to work.
If I think I can't handle this, I'll get a hold of Tom right away.
Okay?"

"Okay." *Not okay.* My own stomach is starting to
twist like it's at the end of a bungie rope.

I hear the growl of Miz Tulip pulling into a space
behind Bill's stand. I snicker, trying to imagine Old Harry
driving that car with Mary sitting next to him. She's probably
a better driver than he is now. I bet she worries the whole trip.
I pick up a stack of emptied orange boxes to go in the
dumpster and wave to Mary as they leave.

A minute later comes the sound of plastic hitting
heavy metal at high speed: Bam! Rip! Tinkle, tinkle.

"Oh, my god! Bill, I'll be right back." I ditch my
apron under the cash box and run through the center aisle and
out the front of the building toward where the parking lot
exits onto the highway. Right there is Miz Tulip, her right
side a mangled mess of depainted and crumpled steel. This

huge grey pickup is backing away. What happens now is beyond belief. The driver of the pickup continues to back up until he's well clear of the Volkswagen, then he suddenly accelerates around Mary's car and takes off, shedding pieces of bumper and bits of metal as he disappears. "Holy shit!"

I'm running for the bug now, and reach it along with several other bystanders just as the passenger door snaps off its hinges and slides to the ground. "Mary? Mary, are you all right?"

"Call 911," I hear someone shout. "Don't try to move," orders another. "Kid, stand back." That's aimed at me. I ignore the order and get close enough to look inside. "Mary, Mr. White? Are you all right?"

Mary slowly raises her left hand. "I think I'm okay. What happened?" She lifts her right hand next. It's covered with blood.

Chapter XXI   The Stakes Higher than Freedom

An ambulance arrives in less then five minutes. By then Mary has managed to undo her seatbelt and climb out of where the door used to be, despite the advice against moving coming from half-a-dozen would-be Samaritans. Someone guides a stool under her and she sits, slowly going over her body. I help her get her right arm out of her jacket, then pull out a handkerchief and wrap in around the biggest, deepest cut on her forearm, then raise her arm high. As she peals off her jacket and raises her shirt, I can see bruises all down her right side as well as on the right side of her face. "God, I hurt all over," she admits. "How's Harry?"

"Sitting there cursing a blue streak, and mumbling about something X," I answer.

"Let us take over now," a medic tells me, and I nod and step back. I watch as he slowly works his way over her body, legs and arms. He takes off my handkerchief, which I quickly retrieve, and slaps a pad of gauze on the wound. "That's going to need stitches," he tells her. "Let's look at your face. Any bruises on your scalp. Did you hit your head?" Harry's out of the car now, walking slowly, still mumbling and looking like he's in shock. Another medic guides him over to the ambulance and helps him to lie down.

Time passes. I reach past the medic and take Mary's left hand. She gives me a weak smile and squeezes. The medic takes it all in, but says nothing, so I hold on. I know I should go back inside and pick up my pay. Mom's probably already there wondering where I am. What if she sees me out here with Mary? I dismiss that thought. I doubt Mom knows what Mary looks like.

Presently a flatbed wrecker rolls up. "Where are the police?"

"I don't know," I hear someone answer. "Usually they're the first ones to arrive."

Others chime in with a range of speculations, but I know why. This was not an accident, although they'll claim it was Harry's fault: ninety-two, driving a strange car. This was an attempt at vehicular homicide. "They just tried to kill you."

My voice sounds funny, like a snake has crawled in my throat.

"I know," she answers and gives me a faint smile. "You'd better go. Don't give your folks reason to make things worse. I'll see you in school."

"You sure?"

"I'm sure. Thanks, and I love you."

"I love you too." I let go of her hand and walk away, looking back again and again, still wondering if the police will ever show up.

The market is almost empty, ready to shut down when I get back to the stand. Bill and Mom are waiting. "Bad accident?"

I nod. "Very bad. A huge pickup creamed an old Volkswagen. Just drove into it at high speed, pushed it twenty feet down the road, then backed up and drove off."

"Not the first time. That's a dangerous intersection. Anyone hurt?"

I'm studying Mom's face, but see nothing but fear and concern. "The people in the Volkswagen are both hurt. Truck who hit them drove off."

"Hit-'n-run?"

"Yup.

"VW …? That wasn't Marty's car, was it?"

I turn my back to my mother and wave a hand for Bill to cool it. He stares at me, then nods. "Badly?"

"I don't know. There was blood everywhere." My hand gives him an okay sign.

"Excuse us, Mrs. Bain. I know you want to get home,

but I have something I must show Peter before he leaves. He'll need to get on it first thing when he arrives tomorrow." Bill points and I follow him outside to the back of the box truck that he uses to bring in the veggies.

"How is she?" he asks the moment he knows we're out of earshot.

"She's got a bad cut on her lower right arm, lots of bruises and scratches. She looked awful, but I think she'll be okay. Mr. White looked badly shaken, but I saw no injuries."

Bill sighs. "Well, the old VWs were small, but they had good steel in them. No plastic. Sounds like she could have been killed."

"I think that was the plan."

"You've got to be kidding me. Who would want to kill Marty?"

"Maybe someone determined to keep her from inheriting a small fortune."

"Money? Marty's never had even two dimes to rub together."

"I know, but it's a crazy world."

"Okay. Take your pay out of the register. Get on home. Let me know what you find out about Marty. I'll see you tomorrow."

"That's what I plan on."

Riding home, Mom breaks the silence. "That's such a dangerous intersection. It's too close to the traffic light. People on the highway see a green light and just whip around that corner and bang, hit someone trying to pull out. Sad, so sad. When you drive again, be careful."

"I always am," I reply. *No, Mom, that was no accident.* Harry may be old, but Mary said he was careful. She would have been watching too. And if it was an accident, why did the trucker drive off? Why didn't the police ever show up? They'll never catch the guy who did it, because they have no description of the vehicle. If Mary had been killed, it would have been a perfect crime.

Home and in my room: I wait until I hear the TV going full blast before calling the local hospitals. Playing the 'closest relative' game, I find out she's gone to Jefferson Memorial. Makes sense. It's the closest hospital. Mary has been 'treated and released'—which has to be a good sign. Mr. White was admitted "for overnight observation." Yeah, not much a doctor can do for bruises. I bet she'll be a colorful sight in school Monday. So no internal injuries or broken bones. Mary, you are so lucky. Oh, Mary, someone has you in their sights. What am I to do? Who wants to kill you? Answer: whoever benefits from you being dead. Woodbridge? Mom and Dad? I call Bill at home to let him know. He thanks me for letting him know several times before saying "See you tomorrow."

Sunday is quiet. Work goes same-same. Bill asks again about Mary, but I can tell him nothing new. I try to phone Mary twice before she answers. She admits to having been asleep. She sounds awful, but promises to see me 'soon'—whatever that means.

I'm eating my Monday lunch when I feel a nudge against my elbow and when I look up, Mary's there to join me. "Holy cow. I never thought I'd see you here."

"Move over and don't touch. I'll scream like a rock star groupie if you do. How do I look?"

"Honest answer? You could try out for the role of the living mummy and get the part on the first audition. Do you feel as bad as you look."

"Thanks. Yeah, I feel like crap."

Arnie sets down his tray on the opposite side of the table. "Man, that truck really did a number on you, didn't it?"

Mary nods and starts in on her sub sandwich. She doesn't look too bad on her left side, but her right cheek is swollen and her forehead and right ear sport bandages. Her whole lower right arm is wrapped in gauze. Every time she lifts the sandwich to her mouth, I can follow the ripples of pain crossing her face.

"Why'd you even come to school."

"Because I feel safer here than anywhere else. This place has armed guards that aren't on the take, unlike our local police."

"I wish I couldn't believe you."

"Cops ever show up?"

"Not while I was still at the market."

"Ruth Marino—you remember the Sheriff's deputy you told me tried to get your buddy Monihan to back off?"

"I remember."

"She showed up at the hospital right when I was ready to leave. Royally pissed at having to do what she thought was a routine followup—until she found out that no one had spoken to me or Harry before, and no one had interviewed any witnesses. Then she got even more angry. She left looking like she was packing for bear."

"How'd you get over here now?"

"Walked. It's not that far. Couple of friends in 'B' are covering for me in the cafeteria."

"That truck hit you deliberately."

"I know that. When he backed off, he looked like he was ready to hit me again. I rolled against Harry as tight as I could. Next thing I knew, he was gone. Big cloud of dust."

"He was dropping pieces of his bumper and part of Miz Tulip all down the road."

"Poor Tulip. She was a collectable antique. I once had someone offer me three thousand for her. Now I don't even know what junkyard they took her to."

"I saw the wrecker come. It had the name Baker on its door. I can probably find out. Anything in her I need to get out?"

"No. Not much. I left my mace in the glove compartment. I think I left my gloves on the floor. If you get there, look around. I can't think of anything else. I won't go there myself. I know if I do, I'll end up bawling."

"You get a hold of your insurance company?"

Mary snorts. "What insurance? I've never had insurance since the day after I got the plates and registration."

"What!?"

"How was I to get and keep insurance when I don't even have a driver's license?"

I guess that makes sense. "I'll find out what I can." My meal is done. I get up.

Mary eats the last bite of her sub and stands up as well. "Thanks. See you tomorrow, if I can."

"Please, take care. I love you."

"Hey, I love you too. You know, you were the first guy I ever slept with."

"What! I haven't ever slept with you."

She shakes a finger at me, a smirk on her face. "Grandma Millie told me a long time ago. I was four and staying with her. It was right after my Mom died. You came over for some reason. We played together, then both fell asleep. Grandma put us both in her bed. When she checked on us later, we were both still asleep, but you'd wrapped your arm around me, like you were trying to protect me." She turns and heads for the tray dropoff. Somehow I get my jaw back in place and follow her. Then I'm laughing, so hard that half the cafeteria must be staring at me.

The accident doesn't even make the paper, but I do notice that Dad is even more irritable than ever—if that would be possible. Right after supper he retires to the front parlor without even excusing himself. He closes the door, but I can hear him yelling at someone or other on his cell phone while I'm loading dishes in the washer. Then Mom rejoins me in the kitchen. "Why don't you get on upstairs and start on your homework. I'll finish these."

I set in the last plate and leave. Wish I was a fly-on-the-wall in the parlor right now.

Next morning I'm up before Mom. As I head for the kitchen, I realize that I haven't been in the parlor for weeks, maybe even months. Dad and Mom never used to keep the door closed so it was more like part of the house entry way. It sure has been closed for a long time now. I ease over, listen for Arnie or Mom, then try the door. Locked. Hmm. I check the lock. It is one of those in-the-door types that uses a skeleton key. Shouldn't be too hard to break into. Easier than my room was. I decide to wait until after school during the post-school, pre-parent time break time—which is not as long as it used to be since I have to ride the bus.

Mary joins me for lunch again. She looks better today. The bandages are gone from her head, and some of the bruises are turning yellow. She still doesn't try to use her right arm much. She confides that her right thigh has more colors than an Andy Warhol painting—whoever he was. I fill her in on the strange doings around our home. She, in turn, reports that she knows that the house and her apartment were under watch again last night. Mr. White is home again and seems to be recovered, but he's sure he'll never want to drive again. We both express a certain sadness over that. "You give up driving and a chapter of your life ends," is the way I put it. Today we part with just a cautious hug, but the smile Mary gives me, and I return, feel the same as the words we exchanged yesterday.

I brief Arnie. We get home just before five, which means we have maybe a half hour to do the deed. I pull out the old key box from a back kitchen drawer and start sorting, picking out any keys that look like they might work. Arnie takes the first three that look likely to fit while I continue to sort. "This one works," he calls from the hallway. I quit sorting, dump all the keys back in the box and join him. Together we enter the parlor. It looks the same: a couple easy chairs that came from Mom's side of the family, still with antimacassars on their backs. A stereo set with a four-foot high speaker cabinet fills half the north wall. It must date back to before I was born. So far, so same. "What are all these rolled up maps?" Arnie picks up one of the white sheets lying on the library table. He opens it up. "What is this?"

I look over his shoulder. "It's a blueprint for some house. Looks huge." '445 Hanscomb Heights' reads the label. Dad was talking about Hanscomb Heights in that conversation I recorded. It's the hoity-toity part of town, where the one percent live. *Where would we ever have the money to build a place ...?* "Close it up and put it back, right where you found it. Let's get out of here." I wait to make sure Arnie has followed instructions, then retreat back to the hallway. I relock the door, but pocket the key, put the other two keys back where they belong. We head upstairs as I hear the sound of a car coming up the driveway.

"Why would Dad have blueprints for a place in Hanscomb Heights?" Arnie whispers as we take seats on his bed.

"I don't know. Do we look rich enough to even buy a lot up there, let alone build a house? Not only that, the floor plan looked like it was part of a big house." *That's where we stopped on our way back from the will reading. It has to be.*

Chapter XXII   Thrust and Counter-thrust

Back in my room I suddenly realize that I haven't heard from Tom Hess. I didn't hear from him Sunday or Monday. He said he was going to go down to the courthouse to check will probates. Sounded like that was going to be a Monday priority.

And what about the hearing before the District Justice? That's the tenth—next week, Thursday. Mary and I need to be ready for that as well. I don't usually pay much attention to the newspaper, but … I head downstairs, ignoring Mom's questioning look and rummage through the recycle bin until I find today's paper. There, above the fold, first page of local news: "Pedestrian struck in hit-and-run incident by courthouse." I rip out the page and the third page after where the article continues. "What are you doing, Peter?" Mom starts to get up.

"Getting an article for some research I need to do," I answer. I fold the pages over so the article doesn't show and head back to my room. Please. please let it not be Tom. But I know it is.

"Pedestrian Struck by Hit-and-run Next to Court-house Monday Morning.

"Thomas J. Hess, local retired lawyer, was struck down as he was crossing Jefferson Street, one block from the courthouse. Witnesses described a large grey pickup truck seeming to 'come out of no where,' hitting Hess, then driving off without stopping. Hess was thrown clear and landed 20 feet away. He was life-flighted to Valley Regional where he remains in critical condition.

"No identification was recorded for the truck, although witnesses agreed that it was a light grey and probably a Ford in the 150 series.

"It was like he was going airborne," witness Sharon Fry described seeing the truck hit Hess.

"Papers were flying everywhere. Afterward someone was going around picking them up, but that person did not say where he was taking them."

I scan the rest of the story which is mostly bio: "Hess —long respected member of the Valley bar association, active with youth groups and the Rotary. Son of the late Thomas Hess, Sr, who established the firm of Hess, Hess and Hidderschmidt in 1960. Active in the firm until two years ago." But what happened to the papers he was carrying? Had he found something out about the will? *Mary, we are all in the deepest shit imaginable.*

Mary phones me as I'm getting off the bus the next morning. Had I heard? What are we going to do? She can't get over for lunch today. I can almost hear the tears over the phone. Who can I trust or talk to now?

At lunch, Vicky lets me know that her dad and the truck are available this Friday, if we want to move the desk. "Yes. Oh, great. Yes!" Way I figure it, if we all jump in the truck the minute school let's out and rush home, we should be able to get the desk out of the house and over to the apartment, and get back home before Mom or Dad show. I hope so. If we don't make it, I'm going to be in even deeper trouble than I already am.

Who can I trust? I stop by Mr. Allison's regular office before the end of lunch period. He's not there, but I wait. A minute before the one o'clock bell he shows up coming from the faculty lunch room. *Why didn't I think to look there*? "Mr. Allison, could I have a minute of your time?"

"Hi, Peter? How's it going? Minute's all I've got. What's up?"

"Sir, I need some help. More like advice."

"You free after school?"

"I doubt it. I have to take the bus. Parents won't let me drive."

"What happened?"

"Mary's in deep trouble. Someone tried to run her down and kill her on Saturday. On Monday, someone hit and almost killed our attorney. We don't know what to do."

"Have you gone to the police?"

"They know about it; don't seem to be doing anything."

"Okay. Stop by this office after your last class. We can talk, then I'll get you home. Probably make it before the bus does."

"That should work. Thank you, sir." I give him a tiny salute and head for class as the first bell sounds its warning.

I text Arnie to not look for me on the bus. I text Mary to give her a heads-up on the desk and tell her I'm seeing Mr.

Allison after school.

"WHR?, she texts back.

IN HS OFF, I answer.

"So, what's happened since the end of season?" Coach asks when I enter his office at 2:30.

I take a seat. "I helped Mary move into an apartment, I went to a meeting with the Assistant DA, I got my car taken away, Mary's car got smashed by a hit-'n-run with her in it. She's okay, but Tom Hess, our lawyer isn't. He got hit on Monday and almost killed. Mary has a hearing with the District Justice next Thursday and without Tom, we don't know how to handle it. And I'm grounded. Other than that, it's been pretty normal."

"Wow," Coach whispers. "Start at the beginning."

So I do. I'm up to Mary's moving day when she shows up, backpack in her left hand, a worried look on her face.

"Hi, Marty. Or is it Mary? Come on in." Coach offers her his chair and takes a seat on the edge of his desk.

"It's Mary. Thank you. Pete, I am so beat. I can't take this any longer. You want to know what's just happened? I just got a note from Children and Youth Services demanding that I return to the juvenile home—"Pending a decision at the hearing next week." I'm just getting my courses back on track and have almost all my work made up. I can't do it."

"Okay. Sit down, Mary. Let me hear the rest of Peter's story. Then we'll see what we can or cannot do."

I finish out my narration while Mary sits, alternately

wringing her hands or playing with the paperclips on Mr. Allison's desk.

"Mary, you're a good student. You are sure you can't make up your work in the juvenile home?" Mary shakes her head to Coach's question. "Okay. Let's go see if Mr. Smelz is still here and talk with him."

"But he's not my principal."

"But he knows your principal, right?"

"Dr. Thompson? I guess so." She gets up. I give her left arm a squeeze as we head together out into the hall.

Mr. Smelz is still in his office. When Coach, Mary and I show up, he motions us in and listens while first Coach explains the problem, then listens to Mary tell her story. "It sounds like C and YS could find better use of their time," Mr. Smelz decides. "You've never been convicted of any crime or misdemeanor—other than running away from a foster home and the juvenile home?"

"No, sir."

"Do you know if they intend to try and pick you up tonight?"

"I don't know sir. I'm afraid they plan to."

"Al, why don't you take her home to your house for tonight. I'll talk with Doc Thompson in the morning and we'll see what we can do. What do you think?"

"That would be wonderful," Mary answers, and both Coach and I nod agreement.

Mr. Allison drops me off at the domicile first, then continues on with Mary. 15 minutes later, Mary is on the phone. "Peter, I can't believe it. I wanted to stop by the apartment to pick up some things before going to the Allisons. There were two police cars and C and YS people all over the place. I could see Harry outside talking to them. It was awful. What if they come to school tomorrow?"

"Did they see either you or Coach."

"I don't think so. No one followed us."

I don't know what to do. I don't dare use my phone a lot in the house for fear that my *dear* parents will remember that I still have it. Texting leaves electronic memories. I visit Arnie in his room and fill him in. He doesn't know what to do either. I end up doing nothing—not that this makes it possible to sleep.

Next morning I call Tom's office on our way to school—partly to beg for help, partly to find out how Tom is doing. Donna returns my message at lunch time. Tom is not much better. He has a broken thigh, ribs, shoulder and some internal injuries. Police have talked to him, but he can remember nothing about what happened. As for help for Mary's problems, Donna offers no ideas, other than to talk to Harry. What help can Harry offer? Still, I pass that suggestion on to Mary.

She answers that she understands that C and YS has been told not to come into the school looking for her, but she knows a vehicle is waiting outside. What a nervous day! I want to run out there and yell at who ever is in that car to go away; I want to break their windows and hit them so hard they never want to come back; I want to can my temper and get back to that soft, quiet state I was in back in August before this whole business got started.

Moving the desk is a welcome distraction. Vicky and Mr. Sutherland, her dad, pick me up as soon as the last class ends. He drives over to the domicile at speeds that average five-miles over the limit. I run in, drop my bookbag in my room, take out my computer and set it on the floor, and start handing empty drawers to Vicky. With the desk as light as it's going to be, Mr. Olsen and I maneuver the desk out into the hall, down the stairs and out the door. In less than fifteen minutes we have it tied down and we're on our way.

I spot the sheriff's department car parked on the curb as we approach Harry's place. I get out and help direct the truck to a spot just short of the side door. Drawers go inside and up the steps. Then Mr. Sutherland and I off-load the desk and angle it back-and-forth until we have it inside and aimed up the steps. The cop gets out and, hand on his phone, walks over to watch. "You guys need a hand?"

"No, thanks. I think we have it," Mr. Sutherland answers.

"This for the girl living here?"

"We're just storing it here for now," I answer as we lift the desk up the next step.

"Sure you don't need an extra hand?"

"Nope," I say.

"And you are?" he asks.

"I'm John Sutherland, and this is my daughter, Vicky. We're just friends from Truman's varsity volleyball." I keep my mouth shut.

"Hey. I heard you guys done real good this year.

Almost took the inter-district playoffs."

We're almost to the top. I'm on the top end, so the cop can only see Mr. Sutherland and talk to him.

"Thanks. We'll be going for the state championships next year. Wait and see." Two more steps to go.

"That'd be cool. My son loves volleyball in gym class."

"How old is he?" One more step. I have the top end on the landing.

"Twelve. He's in seventh grade, but big for his age."

"Tell him to keep at it, and try out when he hits ninth."

"I will." We're inside and I cannot hear the cop any more. "Over against this wall. Yeah, that way." Vicky and I fit in the four lower drawers. "Let's head home. I still have to be in the house before mom gets there."

"Will Arnie be home already?" Vicky asks.

"He should be." I relock the apartment and we all head down. Harry is standing outside waiting by the truck, the cop beside him.

"Hi, Mr. White. How's it going?" I greet after locking the bottom door.

"Fine, Peter. You seen that girl of mine?"

"She's fine. She has her hearing next Thursday."

"She told me. Will you be there?"

"If they let me. Will you?"

"I might be." And he gives me one of his winks.

What does that mean? We get in the truck, Vicky in the middle and head for my home.

Arnie is waiting by the front door when we arrive. I immediately dash inside while he, Vicky and Mr. Sutherland talk. I grab the card table out of the downstairs closet and carry it up to my room where I set it where my desk used to be. I put my computer on top and plug it back in. My desk's safe from Dad's searching, but how am I to get to it? And what if someone breaks in the apartment while Mary is gone?

As I anticipate, the evening does not go well. Arnie and Vicky are still making doe-eyes at each other when Mom gets home. She doesn't like it, but maintains a civil tongue for the Sutherlands. The near-train wreck occurs when Dad gets home and happens to past my room coming back from the upstairs bathroom and looks in while I'm not there to close the door.

"Where the hell is your stupid desk?" he screams in a voice so loud that two neighborhood dogs start howling. "Peter, get up here and explain this to me."

"What do you need, Dad?"

"You heard me. Where's the desk?"

"In storage at a friend's house."

"What friend? How'd it get moved? Why is it not here? Peter, answer me."

"My friends moved it in their truck. I don't need it right now. It's an antique and I don't want you trying to tear it apart looking for things like you did my room."

Dad does a slow burn.

"Honey, do you want Chinese tonight?" Mom calls up. "I'm beat and don't feel like cooking. I'll order and pick it up." Dad hesitates." Do you know what you want?"

"General Tso, chicken and dumplings, The usual. Oh, and teriyaki beef, if you're getting it from Mandarin House."

"Their teriyaki beef *is* good. So's their teriyaki chicken. I'll order both. You boys want anything special?"

"No, Mom," I call down. "It sounds like you have it under control." *What a perfect diversion. Dad loves Chinese.*

Dad stares at me, then turns away and heads downstairs. Arnie and I exchange thumbs-up.

Well, that went better quickly. Why is Dad in a better mood? It can't just be getting Chinese. It seems now like every time something goes wrong for Mary, Dad gets cheerier and more relaxed. *You're directing this whole war against Mary, aren't you, Dad? I sure hope you aren't the guy paying the thug who almost killed Mary and Tom.*

Chapter XXIII   The Hearing, Part One

I work the weekend, but don't see Mary. She's still staying with the Allisons, in a room with their senior daughter. She doesn't make it over from B for lunch either on Monday, Tuesday or Wednesday. She's afraid of C and YS grabbing her whenever she leaves the building. I learn where my part comes in on Wednesday afternoon. Coach grabs me as I'm heading for the buses. "Dress up as best you can tomorrow."

"I'm going to get to go to the hearing?"

"Yup. You may be a witness and have to testify.

Principal told me: make sure he's there. Be ready at nine. I'll stop by your classroom and will drive you over to the mall where the district justice court office is."

"Yes!!" I shake my clasped hands at him.

Of course, going to school all dressed up will not be easy. "How will you get your clothes?" I ask Mary when we skype on the bus.

"It's planned out. Harry and Mattie will have my clothes to me tonight," she answers.

"What plan?"

I see her look away. "Harry and I discussed everything. He promised that everything is going to work itself out. I don't know how or why, but he seems to know something he's not telling me. He winks all the time. You've noticed that, haven't you?"

I nod.

"It's like he's sharing a secret, only I'm still not sure what the secret is yet. Oh, and he asked if you have any paperwork with Grandma Millie's handwriting on it?"

I think a moment. "Yeah. There were a bunch of letters from her in the security box. I brought most of them home and put them in my desk."

"The desk that's in the apartment now?"

I suddenly realize that she was never in my domicile room, so she wouldn't have seen it before. "Yes."

"That's Grandma Millie's old desk, the one with the secret compartment, isn't it?"

"Ah, yes. You know about it?"

"Both the desk and the compartment. She used to do

all her writing on it. I used to make drawings on it whenever I stayed with her."

"Well, the letters are in the compartment. Bring whatever you and Harry feel is best."

"Will do. I'll tell Harry about the desk and what to look for."

That night, I pack my suit in the gym bag along with the dress shoes, shirt and tie I wore for my hearing. Dressed in regular school clothes I head for school the next morning. We get there ten minutes before the first bell. I use that time to run down to the gym and change. The moment first period ends, I'm hoofing it down to Mr. Allison's office. He's waiting by his door, all dressed up as well. "Mary's on her way?"

"I assume so. She's riding with someone else, I think Dr. Thompson."

I nod, impressed.

The district justice's office and courtroom are at one end of a strip mall on the west end of the nearby borough. I don't know why, except that maybe this is where the juvenile home is located. The outer room is a pond of bored or nervous waiting people plus three state policemen. Various clerical types stand around behind a cage-fronted counter. Mr. Allison takes me over to that counter where I get in line and register as a witness for the case of Mary Soo vs. the Valley County Office of Children and Youth Services. Lady tells us to take a seat and wait until the case is called. Two minutes later I see

Mary arrive, dressed in her pretty dress, wearing her glasses and varsity jacket. The patched sleeve of the jacket hides her bandaged arm. With her is Harry White, his daughter and Dr. Thompson. Harry is also dressed up in a dark-blue, pin-striped suit complete with a small white rose stuck in his lapel as a boutonniere. Mary gives me a little wave and smile before the four get in line to check-in. What is going on?

The four of them join Coach and myself. "Everyone here?" Harry asks.

"Who else are you expecting?"

"Donna from Tom's office. She has the rest of the paperwork."

"Hmm." I give Mary another wave. She wiggles her fingers at me and adds a shrugging smile as I realize that something's different. Mary is still Mary, but she doesn't look like a kid. I spot earrings and a faint blush of lipstick and know I'm seeing a Mary I've never seen before: Mary *grown-up*—not someone that needs the care or protection of a youth services.

Donna gets there at twenty of, carrying a briefcase which she gives to Harry. "I think I have everything you need here." Harry takes the case and starts going through its contents. He nods and tsks, licking his fingers to separate various pages. Finally he pulls out a three page document set inside a dark blue binder. He hands it to me. "Check the signatures for me, will you? Can you verify that the signature under Millicent McClure's typed name is your great-grandmother's signature?"

I have no idea what I am looking at, but the

handwriting I see has no resemblance to the handwriting I remember in the letter she left for me asking me to find Mary. "I would be willing to state that this signature is not Aunt Millie's." I tell him.

"Good. Then maybe we are ready to go. Look's like the last case is finishing up."

A guy in a fancy suit—maybe a bit too fancy with several gold chains around his open-collared neck—comes out accompanied by a short, dark-haired man in a grey suit carrying a briefcase. "What'll I do now?" Fancy suit demands of his companion.

"Pay me," is the response.

"This is shit! Absolute fuckin' shit!"

One of the state cops moves in. "Please control your language and the volume of your voice," he orders. Fancy shirt deflates. "Where do I go now?" The cop points toward a cage with a sign over it that says Bursar. *I think he lost—even with a lawyer.*

"Mary Soo?" calls a voice. A woman also dressed in a cop-type uniform is standing by the door Fancy Suit just came out of. Mary gets up and slowly lifts her hand. We all get up. "This way," the lady cop directs. We follow her into a room set up as a miniature court room, complete with a dais flanked by the American and state flags. In front are two tables. Mary and Harry take the table on the left. I hesitate, then join Mr. Allison, Dr. Thompson, Mattie and Donna in chairs behind them.

We wait. A strange woman and the man I remember from the night C and YS tried to abduct Mary come in and sit down at the other table. A moment later Mr. Jacobs joins them. *What the hell is Woodbridge's sleazy lawyer doing here?* Another young man in a polo shirt and and leather jacket comes in, nods to Jacobs and takes a seat behind the C and YS people.

More people are coming in, including Mrs. Hertz. Arnie is there as well. He gives me an okay sign. No more persons join the other side. We wait some more.

"All rise," the lady cop calls out. The district justice, wearing a black robe like a judge enters from a side door and takes his seat. He inserts a name tag in a holder that reads 'Beltran.' A wave of his hand and we all sit down. He looks to be around forty, trim with his silvery hair cut short. He puts on half-lens reading glasses and examines some paper.

"Melissa Carver? You have a petition and charge here for this court."

The C and YS woman gets up. "We do."

"You may approach the bench."

She does and holds out a binder. Justice Beltran takes it, opens it and reads through the single page. "You are petitioning that Mary Soo, who was once in your custody, be returned to that custody until such time as she turns eighteen, or until you determine she no longer needs to be under your control?"

"That is correct." I hear soft voices behind me. I look back to see my father and mother, all dressed up, tip-toeing in to take seats in the back. Beltran gives them an irritated look.

"Are you acting as attorney in this matter?"

"No, Attorney Ronald Jacobs here is."

"Okay. You may sit down." Beltran looks back down at the paperwork, then turns to the left table. "And you are Mary Soo?"

Mary whispers a yes and nods her head.

"Do you have representation here?"

"Mr. Harry White here is acting as my attorney," Mary answers.

"And you are a lawyer?

"Yes, your honor. *Juris* from Yale Law, class of '55. I was president of the Valley Bar Association from 70 to 75. Worked with your father back in the early Eighties. It's been a long time, I know, but I feel I can still do the job when I have to."

"Ah. I do remember." Beltran smiles and nods. "Mr. Jacobs, you may call your first witness."

"I call Melissa Carver." She takes a seat up front and the lady cop swears her in.

"Would you describe Mary Soo's experience with Children and Youth Services of this County?" Jacobs instructs.

"Mary has had a long association with our office," Carver answers. "We first became involved in her case shortly after her mother drown herself in Lake Noxhatchy on December tenth, twelve years ago to this day. There was no father, and there appears to have never been one. Nor did she leave a will. Stanley McClure, who claimed to be her grandfather requested guardianship. Our office reviewed the request, but felt that it was not a good fit. Although Mr. McClure obviously cared for Mary, other family members cast

doubt on the relationship, testifying that she was not a blood
relation. There was also a concern about McClure's health.
He was already suffering from cancer. His mother, Millicent
McClure, stepped in to verify the relationship and offered to
help care for Mary, if that need would arise. Although
skeptical, we approved that plan. Three years later, again at
the insistence of other relatives, a DNA testing was
completed. The results were inconclusive. *Huh*?

"Three years ago, Ms. McClure fell, breaking her
hip, forcing her to move into the Woodbridge Nursing home
for recovery. A month later, her son died. This left Mary
with no family willing to take her. At that time Children and
Youth Services determined that the best outcome would be a
foster family until which time a more permanent
arrangement could be made.

"The first placement did not work out. The foster
parents complained that Mary was uncooperative, at times
belligerent and consistently insistent on doing everything *her*
way. While her schoolwork remained up to high standards,
her social skills were poor. After three months, she requested
and the family agreed to a reassignment. This we granted.

"The next assignment lasted two months. It ended
when Mary ran away. She was located in the St. Johns
Homeless Shelter when the workers there, concerned due to
her age, reported her. She escaped again and remained at
large for six months before being located in a dumpster
behind the West End mall. She refused our offers of a
placement back with the second foster family. Feeling that
we had no choice, the County Committee felt it necessary to

place her in the juvenile home until a better situation could be found. She stayed there less than three weeks, climbed a chainlink fence in the middle of the night and disappeared. For those three weeks she was stubbornly quiet and uncooperative concerning even the slightest routines. And if you doubt my word on this, I can bring in several members of staff willing to testify as to her behavior.

"Justice Beltran, we feel very badly for Mary. She is intelligent and could have a bright future, but with no family or financial resources, the County cannot refuse its responsibilities for this child.

"Please. I am not finished. Last month, Richard Ogden, the Assistant Director of the YMCA, reported that he had located Mary. She was living part-time in the YMCA while attending Truman high School, and going by the name Martina Sofia. She was sneaking in, then hiding in the back rooms. She would spend the night there before leaving before opening time to go to school. He confirmed that she was apparently using the YMCA at least two or three nights per week. He could not state where else she was living. With the knowledge that she was a student at Truman and that she was a member of the girls' volleyball team, we attempted to catch her the night of the Truman-Freeland game. I need not go into the details of that fiasco. We caught Mary as she was attempting to leave, but then she got away, injuring one of our team members in the process. Our efforts to re-catch her ended when it was discovered that Mr. Ogden had fallen down the outside steps of the high school and seriously injured himself. A riot was starting up in the gym over the end of the last men's game. One of the sheriff's departmental police had just broken his hand. The other deputy had to place Mary's boyfriend under arrest. In the midst of this, Mary escaped again. That is the history of our most recent attempt to bring in Mary Soo.

Jacobs clears his throat. "Humph. If she has not been living in the YMCA, where has she been living."

"We do not know."

"Is there any chance that she has been using sexual encounters as a means to gain shelter and food?"

Whoa. What kind of question is that?

"We do not know. We do know that this is a common means of survival that many runaway girls her age turn to in order to survive."

"Justice Beltran, we must object to this speculation and innuendo. If Ms. Carver here has no personal knowledge of Mary's actions, she should remain silent."

Wow. Mr. White, where did you come from?

"So noted. Mr. Jacobs, you will withdraw that question. Any other questions for Ms. Carver, Mr. Jacobs?"

"No, your honor."

"Mr. White, do you wish to question the witness?"

This is getting more and more exciting. I find I'm rubbing my hands on my pants again and again. I can't see Mary's face since she is sitting in front of me, but it must be a work of art.

Harry gets up and slowly walks around to the front of his table. "Ms. Carver, did or did not Mary Soo ask for a new foster family prior to her running away?"

Carver takes a long deep breath before answering. "Yes ... she did."

"And why did you, or your office turn her down?"

"I don't remember. It ... a different department was handling such matters at that time."

"Hum." Harry studies Carver for at least 30 seconds. "Now, you admitted that you do not know where Mary Soo was living except those few times when Mr. Ogden knew she was staying at the Y. Did you make an attempt to find out that information once Ogden reported her to you?"

"Ah. No."

"Did you contact the school prior to this attempted seizure? Did you enlist their cooperation? Did you ask them what address Mary was giving them as her home address?"

"Ah. No."

"In other words, you decided to act alone without coordinating with any other agency who would have been required by law to grant you assistance? Is that true?"

"... Yes, but we were given to understand that she would not be easy to catch and fast action would be necessary."

"And who told you this?"

"We ... I received two phone calls. The first was from Mr. Ogden. The second was from a Mr. Daniel Bain. He was most insistent that we had to act quickly."

"I see. And you just took them at their word?"

"Yes."

Harry tut-tuts. "It is a strange business when a government agency makes decisions on the basis of a couple of private tattle-tales. How many foster homes do you work with?"

Carver thinks. "Thirty-six, I think. The number changes almost every quarter."

"And you couldn't find any other home for Mary except the two that were obviously creating problems?"

Carver throws up her hands. "We can't just go moving clients every which way! We'd been told that she had problems and needed a firm, disciplined home environment. The McCormick and Lamar families seemed to be the best fit."

"And this person who told you she needed a 'firm, disciplined home environment' wouldn't have happened to have been this Mr. David Bain, Would it?"

"Ah ... yes."

"No more questions, Ms. Carver."

Beltran sighs. "I can see that this is going to take more than the normal fifteen minutes we set aside for these hearings. Bailiff, would you let the clerk know that this is going to run half-an-hour at least, and ask her to tell the next plaintiffs to make new appointments or be prepare to forgo lunch. Thank you. Jacobs, your next witness?"

The man wearing the leather jacket swears his oath and takes the chair.

"You are?"

"Roger ... a ... Harris."

"And where do you live, Mr. Harris?" *Why is Mr. White taking such an intense interest in this guy?*

"I live on West Seventh Street."

"And your business is?"

"I own and run a used CD, DVD, Blue-ray and video store on the corner of sixth and Jackson."

"And how do you know Mary Soo?"

"Not by that name, but I do know her face."

"And you see her here now?"

"Yes." The guy points at Mary.

"Thank you. Continue."

"I never knew her by that name, but she used to come in my shop at least once or twice a week. At first, I didn't pay much attention to her, but then I noticed that whenever she visited, as soon as she left, I would be missing some of my more popular titles."

"And what did you do about this problem?"

"I set a trap."

"What kind of trap?"

"The type that a lot of stores use now. You try to take something without running it through a decoder and the moment you try to walk out the door, an alarm goes off. Caught her the next time she was in there."

"What did you do, and what did she do?"

"I demanded she return the Blue-ray she was hiding in her bookbag. She started crying, begging me not to turn her in. Then she offered to show me some 'fun' if I forgot all about the stealing and gave her enough money to buy a couple of meals."

"Did you take her up on her offer?"

"No. I declined. Nor, I admit, did I call the police. I just warned her never to come in my store again."

"Has she been in your store since?"

"No. Haven't lost any more movies either."

"And when was this incident?"

"Last summer. First Monday in July. The second, I think."

"Thank you, Mr. Harris."

"Do you have any questions, Mr. White?" Beltran does not sound like he expects any.

"I might have a few. Mr. Harrison, that is your name, correct?"

"Ah … yes?"

"I'm curious. How long have you had your pickup truck?"

I suck in my breath.

"Bought it two years ago, new. Why?"

"And it's the Ford 150 with extended cab that's parked at the other end of the mall, around the corner from the Best Buy, am I correct?"

"What are you talking about?"

"It's a grey truck, with a License plate that starts with XAD 7, am I correct?"

Jacobs is on his feet. "What does this have to do with Mary Soo?"

Mr. White holds up his hand. "Were you out driving the Saturday after Thanksgiving?"

"I don't know; I don't remember." Mr Harris is turning as surly as a dog who's just discovered the cat already got to its supper.

"Well, Mr. Harris, or Harrison, whoever you are, who

was driving that same truck when it slammed into Mary Soo's Volkswagen at high speed when it was about to exit the farmer's market at about 3PM that Saturday? And who was driving that same truck with a patched bumper the next Monday when it hit Tom Hess while he was attempting to cross Jefferson Street minutes after he had been in the courthouse locating a copy of a will that supposedly turned much of Millicent McClure's assets over to the Woodbridge Nursing Home?" Harry turns around, his eyes sweeping the crowd. "I would suggest to this court that a thorough examination of that same truck will show that it has a patched or replacement front bumper not more than a week-and-a-half old. And a forensic examination might also reveal paint marks from Mary's car.

"Who hired you, Mr. Harris, or Harrison, to kill Mary Soo, or Tom Hess? Who hired you to lie about her here in this court?"

Shit! The whole place is in an uproar. Beltran is banging his gravel and two state police are joining the bailiff. "Order. Order now." The room settles down a little.

"All right, quiet," Coach suddenly calls out. The room becomes like a tomb.

"Thank you. Now, if we may continue. Any more questions for Mr. Harris, or is it Harrison?" Beltran can't quite hide a line of sarcasm. I can see a bead of water starting to run down the guy's right temple.

"Just a few more, your honor." Mr. White turns to the witness who is looking like he either wants to run or punch someone. "Tell me, Mr. Harris, or Harrison, who paid you, and how much did they promise you to first eliminate Mary Soo, and when that failed, to eliminate her lawyer, whom your employer knew would cut a long series of holes through Youth Services Stories argument?"

"No body paid me nothing."

"You see, Mr. Harris or Harrison, I was the driver of that Volkswagen you tried so hard to destroy. I saw you at the wheel as you whipped by, and I was able to catch the first letters of your license plate, a plate registered to a Roger Meldoni. That wouldn't be you would it? You did lie about that store robbery attempt just now, didn't you? You never saw Mary before in your life before you attempted to kill her coming out of the market? Correct?" Mr. White is visually shaking now. "Justice Beltran, I think I am through with this witness. No further questions."

Meldoni steps down, but when he attempts to leave, one of the State police stands in his way. Beltran clears his throat. "Mr. Meldoni, you may have stepped down, but this court is not done with you. Please have a seat, and do not attempt to leave. Mr. Jacobs, do you have any more witnesses?"

Mr. Jacobs looks like he has aged 20 years. "I would like to call Mr. Daniel Bain to the stand."

Chapter XXIV   The Hearing, Part Two

Dad comes forward. When he and Mom had arrived

here, he had a smile on his face. Now he looks like he would rather be in the deepest jungles of the Amazon, or on the north slope of Siberia in January rather than be here. Still he takes the oath and sits down. He's sweating more than Meltoni was when Mr. White got done with him.

"Mr. Bain," Jacobs begins. "You are related to this Miss Mary Soo?"

"So my cousin and great aunt claimed."

"But you never believed that claim?"

"No."

"Could you explain why?"

"Let me present some biographical information."

Jacobs nods. "Proceed."

"Stanley McClure, Millicent McClure's son and my first cousin, was a major in the Air Force during the Viet Nam War. He was stationed for over a year at Phanom Air Base in Thailand. He later claimed to have met a Thai girl of Chinese background while there and had a relationship with her. Aside from a few snapshots of Stanley and a girl standing together, I know nothing about this relationship—whether it was real or just casual. Twenty years ago, Stanley claimed to have located her again and flew back to Thailand in an attempt to find her. Instead, he came home with a young woman named Lie Beng Soo whom *he* claimed was his daughter. The woman he introduced to my family spoke no English and had bad teeth. She did appear to be of half European, half far eastern background, but that was all it seemed that Stanley had to go on. But he was convinced. Aunt Millicent was convinced. The two did everything and anything for Lie—got her enrolled in English classes, got her to a dentist, bought her anything she wanted. My wife and I would visit the McClures and Lie would be lying around, eating candy, ignoring us and watching movies. Then in 1998, she flew out to San Francsico to, and I quote Stanley on this, "to visit an aunt she has located." We heard nothing more about Lie for almost a year when Stanley suddenly flew out to San Francisco himself. That Christmas, he and Lie returned with a new baby that was apparently her daughter, conceived as a result of what Lie claimed was a rape by some sailer she met one evening while walking along Fisherman's Wharf. She named that daughter Mary.

"Four years later, on this same date, December tenth, Lie took Mary out of Millicent's apartment and walked north to Lake Noxhatchy, abandoned Mary then walked out onto the ice until it broke under her weight. She fell in and drown.

"I'm telling this story because it does relate to the question of who Mary Soo is and whether she would have any claim to any assets that Millicent McClure might have once had. Having assets can be an important part of any determination you must make concerning Mary's welfare. Correct?

"Helen and I were sure that Mary was not Stanley's granddaughter, because we believed that Lie Soo was not Stanley's daughter, that she had gulled Stanley into believing she was, in hopes that she could get a free ride to the United States. But we could not convince either Stanley or Millicent of that truth."

I so wish I could see Mary's face now. She has her

face in her hands. But then Harry takes her arm and she sits up, brushing hair back away.

"So, you asked that a DNA test be done?" Jacobs prompts.

"Yes. Helen and I insisted on one. Stanley finally agreed, but later told us that the report was promising, but inconclusive. We were never shown a copy of the results. But I guess that didn't matter. He was determined to raise Mary as their child, whether she was a granddaughter or not. Three-and-a-half years ago, in March, 2010, Millicent let us know that she planned to formally adopt Mary and name her as her primary heir. We were appalled, but felt we could do nothing. Then that December, Millicent fell while going downstairs in her apartment. She suffered serious injuries, including a broken hip, broken ribs and other more minor injuries. Stanley was so ill by then himself that he was unable to help. As far as Helen and I could tell, Mary was effectively raising herself, coming and going whenever she pleased. We took it upon ourselves to get Millicent into the hospital, then into a rehabilitation clinic, then into the Woodbridge Nursing Home when it became apparent that she would never be able to live on her own again. By this time, Stanley was dead. Suddenly we were faced with the question of what to do with this supposed great-grandniece who was just thirteen at the time, had no personal resources and no family. We recommended that she be put under the care of Children and Youth Services, and that is what happened."

"Humph. A pretty sad story, Mr. Bain. So you did not feel it appropriate for you or your family to take over care of

Mary?" Jacobs asks.

"No. We did not. We have only a small house, and two sons. Helen and I have decent incomes, but not ones that would make taking on a third child with undoubted special needs an easy burden. We felt she would have a better chance with a new home and cared for by someone who would give her the attention and support she needed." *And maybe affection and love?*

"Thank you." Mr. Jacobs sits down.

Beltran points to the other table. "Mr. White, your witness."

Harry gets up and stretches his back. Limping a little, he approaches Dad. "Millicent McClure? Would that be the widow of Walter McClure?"

"Ye ... es."

"Walter McClure of McClure Limited?"

"Yes."

"Mr. Bain, you imply here in your testimony that Mary Soo had or has no resources other than what the county here could provide, yet she is the great-granddaughter of the McClures, founders of one of the largest companies in the Valley. Do you know what the current value of McClure Limited is?"

"I would have no idea."

"Are you sure? Well, I checked stock numbers this morning at the opening bell. McClure Limited is currently valued at 36 dollars per share. Walter and Millicent, as first owners and major stock holders owned 59000 shares, or a little over one third of the stocks issued. That would come to over forty-five million dollars in assets in their own company alone. That does not include any other assets that Millicent might have owned. If Millicent had adopted Mary, as you have just stated she indicated to you that she intended to do, would there be any question as to whether Mary would have had the resources to place her in any home environment that she chose? Tell us now, what happened to all those assets? And what did Millicent's will say about the disposition of her estate?"

"I … we don't know. We could find almost no records of any of Millicent's holdings. All we had to go on were her social security payments and retirement records. Any other records were gone. And I assure you, we looked. *I bet you did, Dad.*

"Come now, Mr. Bain. You had power-of-attorney for your great aunt, a responsibility you eagerly took on once Stanley died. Do you mean to say that you had no access to her records, did not know who her broker or accountant was? Do you know what her will stated?"

"Ah, excuse me," Jacobs is standing, holding up a triple sheet of paper. "This here is a copy of Millicent McClure's last will and testament, one she signed this last March. This would be the document this court will need."

"I see." Harry looks at Beltran, then at Jacobs. "We will get to that will presently. Now, Mr. Bain, do you know whether you were to benefit from Millicent's former will?"

"I believe Helen and I were to receive gifts of 20,000 dollars each."

"And your sons?"

"I'm not sure. Perhaps similar amounts."

"And Mary Soo?"

"I'm not sure. Except for her gifts to my family, Stanley was to get everything."

"But if and when he died?"

"I'm not sure."

"Do you mean to say that after Millie McClure told you she intended to adopt Mary, that she then made no provision for her in her will?"

"I ... I don't know," Dad answers.

Mr. White appears lost in thought, then he eyes Dad again. "Would you tell this court why you thought it so necessary to call the district attorney's office to demand they follow through with charges in connection with Richard Ogden's death."

"I felt it important as a concerned citizen. That's all."

"It would have nothing to do with the fact that if Mary were to inherit the estate which was her due, you would be denied the riches you were seeking for yourself?"

Dad sputters, but does not answer.

"All right, Mr. Bain. I have here a recording of you speaking with your wife, Helen Bain. I would like the permission of the court to play that recording now."

"When was this recording made?" Beltran asks.

"Last Saturday evening in the Bain house."

"Who made the recording?"

"Peter Bain, their son."

"Go ahead."

Mr. White places a small tape player on the edge of

the dais and pushes play. The voice of Dad and Mom come through clearly. A minute later, the conversation is over. Mr. White shuts the little machine off. He turns to Dad. "Mr. Bain, that is your voice, is it not?"

"Ye ... es." He sounds like he's drowning.

"No further questions."

"Mr. Jacobs, do you have any further witnesses to bring forward?"

"No, sir."

"All right. This has already gone on far longer than any simple hearing. We are moving into areas that might be outside the focus of whether Mary Soo should be or not be returned to the care of Children and Youth Services, but I believe that what I am hearing to be important. I declare a ten minute recess." He glances at his watch then takes off his glasses. "We will reconvene here at twelve fifteen. And Mr. Meldoni, or whatever your name is, you are not to leave this room." Justice Beltran stands, we all stand, and he walks out.

The room half-clears out. I stretch and join Mary and Harry at the front table. Mary gives me a tired smile. We hug.

Harry sighs. "I've got to get to the head, same as Justice Beltran there. When I get back, we need to talk about the next step." He waves and leaves.

"Did Harry find the letter in the desk I described to you?" Mary nods. "And you have it here."

"Yes."

"I'm not sure why Harry wanted something in Aunt Millie's writing."

"He told me. He thinks the Woodbridge will is a

fake."

"Oh. But how will a letter from Aunt Millie to me prove that? I've read that letter a bunch of times. It doesn't say anything about wills or her money."

Mary shrugs. We both sit and stare at the dais, hands held under the table.

Harry rejoins us. "Long line in the johns. Okay, Peter. You're gonna' be my first witness. I'm going to ask you about this letter. You will need to authenticate it. Can you do that? Just say that you recognize the handwriting and describe how you came to possess it. Then I'm going to ask you to look at the signatures on the Woodbridge will and compare them to Millicent's handwriting. Got it?"

"Yes, sir."

People are piling back in, Dr. Thompson and Coach Allison among them.

"Let's get started," Beltran strikes the gravel once. "Mr. White, call your first witness.

"I call Peter Bain."

I stand, come forward, recite the oath and sit down in the back-facing chair.

"Peter Bain?"

"Yes?"

"Are you familiar with your great aunt's handwriting?"

"Only a little."

"But you do have a letter that she sent you that is in her own writing. Is that true?"

"Yes."

"Is this that letter?" I take the letter which Harry hands me. "Would you describe its contents and explain how it came into your possession."

"It is a letter from Aunt Millie addressed to me personally. She asks my help in locating Mary and confirms the relationship. She then tells me about a storage locker located behind the West Shore mall where Uncle Stanley was supposed to have placed some of her goods that month before he died."

"And how did you come into the possession of this letter?"

I take a deep breath. Even though nothing Harry is asking is hard, I can feel twenty or more eyes staring at my face, twenty ears listening and considering every word I'm now saying.

"It was in a safe deposit box in the north side branch of the Merchants National Bank. Aunt Millie gave me the key two years ago."

"And your name is on that security box?"

"Yes. Mine and my brother Arnold's."

"Okay. I have here a copy of what is being referred to as the 'Woodbridge will.' Without going into its contents, would you look at the signatures at the end of the will, and compare them with the signature of the letter that Millicent set aside for you."

"Objection." Jacobs is standing. He is not a happy guy. "What does this have to do with Mary Soo?"

"Jacobs, sit down. Let Mr. White finish this out," Beltran orders. Jacobs throws his pen at the table, but he does resume his seat.

I look at Harry for guidance. "Go on," he says.

I compare the two signatures. "There is no way that the same person could have signed both these documents. This is Aunt Millie's handwriting." I hold up the will. "Who knows who wrote this."

"Thank you." Harry takes the two papers from me and carries them over to the dais where he hands them to Beltran.

The justice puts on his glasses and studies the letter and the will. "They certainly do not look anything at all alike to me. Are you saying that Millicent McClure never signed this will; are you implying, or stating that this will is forged?"

"I am," Harry answers.

"So, where does that leave Mary Soo?"

"That is what I am getting to, your honor." Harry pulls another document from his briefcase. "Barring the Woodbridge will, this is a copy of Millicent McClure's most recent will. We located it in the McClure file at the office of Hess, Hess and Hidderschmidt. Tom Hess was Millicent's attorney for many years until her death. It is dated October 21st, 20—, witnessed by Tom Hess and Donna Stine, Tom's legal secretary and notary. You will note that the signature at the end matches the signature on the letter to Peter Bain. It states that her son, Stanley, is her first heir, but that, except for certain payments outlined thereafter, Mary Soo, her adopted, or about to be adopted, great granddaughter is to be her next heir in line if Stanley does not survive her more than thirty days. Obviously, she outlived her son by several years.

Mary Beng Soo is heir to the McClure estate. We see no reason that Children and Youth Services would have any claim to control Mary when she has the resources to make whatever arrangements for her care that she will approve of."

Dad is waving his arms around. Jacobs is staring down at his notes. Carver and her buddy look like they've just walked into a wall.

Beltran waits for the room to settle down. "Any more questions?"

"No, sir," Harry answers.

Beltran turns to the other table. "Attorney Jacobs, Do you have any questions for the witness?"

Jacobs shakes his head without looking up.

"Attorney White, do you have any other witnesses to bring forward?"

"Donna Stine, Dr. Mel Thompson, Mary's high school principal."

"Okay. Let me tell you what I am going to do at this point. There are obviously several matters here that are of criminal intent, and outside the purview of this court. That does not mean that they will not be considered by a judge or in a trial, but that is for the prosecutor's office or a grand jury to decide. However, I may and will make a decision concerning the welfare of Mary Soo. To do that, I would ask that you, Mary Soo, please stand. Bain, you may step down."

I can't keep from sighing. I rise and walk back to my seat.

Mary stands. "Mary, did you know about this money?"

She shakes her head. "I have had access to documents on Grandma Millie's estate since she died, but I did not know what to do with them. I was afraid to tell Mr. Bain about them. Whenever I spoke with him, he kept asking about them. He kept demanding that I tell him where any records were. 'Did I know? Did I know?' He made me so afraid, I couldn't say anything. You know, I thought that something would be there for me. I mean, Grandma Millie kept telling me that she had provided for me."

"How old are you?"

"I turned sixteen last week."

"If we were to allow you to leave the custody of Children and Youth Services, where would you live? How would you get around? Do you think you are capable of living on your own?" Beltran suddenly smiles. "I guess that's a silly question, isn't it. You've been living on your own for two years. Let's put it this way: is there someone, an adult, willing to take responsibility for you until you reach age eighteen?"

"Sir, yes, I have been living on my own for almost two years." Mary lifts her head to look the justice in the eye. "I'm in tenth grade at Truman High and getting As or Bs in all my subjects. I work at the Northside Public Library where I am a page. I work at Bill's in the Farmer's Market on Saturdays. I have an apartment owned by Mr. White here. I will have transportation as soon as I get my license and a new car."

"Your honor," Harry puts in. "I would be more than willing to take responsibility for Mary."

"So you have your own income, a place to live, and,

with Attorney White here, an adult to watch out for you?"

"Yes, your honor."

"Okay. Mr. White, you may act as her temporary guardian. Mary, you are free of the custody of Children and Youth Service as of today. Ms. Carver, see that this gets taken care of." Beltran gets up. "This session is over. Jacobs, Meldoni. Do not leave. The rest of you will leave now."

We rise and file out. Mary is jumping around, all smiles. She grabs my arm and we hug. "We did it; we did it! Oh, my God! Thank you, Harry. You were so great! And, Pete, you were so cool. I can't believe that that truck driver showed up. We nailed him. Can we get him to replace Tulip?" She sighs, sad-faced once more. "I'm going to miss her, even if she was noisy and hard to start half the time."

"What now, Mr. White?"

"You two need to get back to your classes. Children and Youth Services can appeal this to up to a regular judge and the county court. But I doubt they will. They look pretty bad already. Mary, when you get back to the apartment after school, come over to the house, and I'll go over what you will need to do next."

Coach and Dr. Thompson join us.

"Al, I'll get these two back to school. you go ahead and get to your next class," Dr. Thompson tells Coach. "Bain, you're gonna' have a hard time tonight with your parents. How do you think it will go?"

"I don't know, sir." Something I haven't really thought about."

"What about lunch?" Mary puts in.

"I think we can work something out. Cafeteria in B school is open until 1:30."

"Okay. Let's go." I lead the way out of the building, then follow Dr. Thompson to his car. Mary and I smuggle in back. We wave good-bye to Harry, waiting for Mattie by her car. I look around but do not see either my parents or Arnie. I guess they left.

Chapter XXV   Threads Woven Together Complete a Circle

"Mary, you need to complete paperwork to insure that all your grades and classes are in your name, instead of this Martina Sofia," Dr.Thompson tells her.

"I think I got that all taken care of last week, but I'll stop by the office," she promises. "I think the rest of this day might be a loss—class-wise—anyway."

"Mary, any idea why your mom killed herself?" I ask.

"Because of your dad."

"What do you mean?"

Mary straightens up but continues to squeeze my hand. "Grandma Millie told me. All her life, Mommy'd been abused in Thailand for not looking pure Thai. So when she came here, she hoped that people would be kinder to her. She spoke no English. All she knew was that the dog tag necklace she had was Pop-Pop's and her mother's. But she never fit in here. And your dad, apparently, treated her something awful.

Never in front of Grandma or Pop-Pop, but he never let a chance go by when they weren't nearby. That's why she went to San Francisco—to get away from your dad. But when I came along, she felt she had no choice but to come back here. She tried to love me, but your dad never let her forget how I was conceived."

She shivers. "Cold weather and snow depressed her even more. That December, your dad told her right out that she didn't belong here and should never have been born! I think she intended to kill herself and me as well. Pop-Pop told me that when Mommy and I got to the lake, I refused to follow her out on the ice. I was too heavy for Mommy to carry. I remember her crying and shaking, then she set me in a swing, started it rocking, and walked away. Pop-Pop told me that I was probably crying for hours before someone heard me and found me." Mary sniffs, then buries her head against my shoulder.

"What a hole my Dad has managed to make of your life."

"Yes, but not any more, Peter. Not any more," she whispers.

"Peter, I'm surprised that no one questioned your integrity, considering your supposed past." Dr. Thompson puts in.

Changing the subject? "I was surprised a little too. I seem to have a lot of support now." *And it feels good to have friends.*

"Strange business. Did your father get anything from the estate?"

"I think he must have had access to some of Aunt Millie's accounts. He's spent a lot more money on stuff over the last few years than he did while Aunt Millie was still on her own."

"You saw the old will in Tom's office. Did it mention Arnie or yourself?" Mary asks next.

I stare at the ceiling, trying to recall what I had read. "It does. Both of us were to get lump sums of 150 thousand dollars when we turn eighteen. In addition, there was something about some stocks and bonds in our names. It was hard to follow all the legalese."

Is that what the Apple stock is about? I'm a rich young man, or so it will be. Not much, but maybe enough to get me through an undergraduate degree without taking out loans. I start chuckling.

"What are you laughing at," Mary whispers. She's still leaning against me, left hand on my thigh.

"Nothing. Here I never expected anything, yet Arnie and I get something. I think Dad was hoping, or trying to get a fortune, and he got almost nothing."

"What will happen when you get home?"

"I don't know." *If he gives me too hard a time, I grab the Volvo and just leave.*

"Can't you just leave?"

"I may have to."

After a quick lunch in the B school cafeteria and a kiss good-bye from Mary, Dr. Thompson drops me off at the A school door and heads back to his own office. I go in, sign back in, go to my locker and pick up books for my next class

—the last one of the day. No one in the office asks for an excuse; they all know where I've been.

"So, Liar, you finally got your day in court." It's Jason Small, as usual. I ignore him and head to class.

I take the bus home. Arnie isn't on it, which I find strange. Riding the bus feels almost normal now. I sure miss the Volvo—even if it is an old-fogy kind of car. Soon, soon this part of my life will be over—I hope.

As I get off at the bus stop, I see Jack, wearing cold weather clothes, but otherwise the same, striding down the sidewalk with his lumpy-lumpy gait, arms swinging, face red. "Hi, Peter," he calls out when he sees me."

"Hi, Jack," I reply and give him a smile and a wave. Sometimes it would be nice to live in a world with no enemies and a smile for everything the world sends your way.

As I enter the domicile by the back door, I note the silence, the wag-a-tail clock's ticking seeming as loud as our wood shop's grinder. Where's Arnie? Did Mom and Dad actually go to work after the hearing? I spot the Volvo keys on the kitchen counter. I snag them, then grab a ginger snap cookie from the jar before heading upstairs. My room is empty except for a single pile of my stuff sitting in two big cardboard boxes in the middle of the floor. Dresser, bed and the card table are gone. *Well, looks like good, old Dad has made the decision for me. I guess I move out today.* I wonder where the dresser and bed went. Maybe in the garage? I pick up one of the boxes, surprised at how heavy it is considering it's mostly my clothes. I carry it downstairs. That's when I hear a snore from the parlor.

The door is locked, but I have the key. I shove my copy in the hole and hear something metal fall on the floor on the other side—probably another key left in the lock. "Dad?" I open and look inside. Dad is there, in one of the easy chairs, the floor covered with drawings: floorplans, profiles, elevations, all of what I assume are for the mansion up on the heights. Dad is asleep, his face slack, a spot of moisture hanging like an icicle bud from the lowest point of his mouth. An almost empty bottle of Dewars Scotch sits on the side table, an empty tumbler beside it. How could anyone drink even a glass of that stuff? "Ugh."

Dad blinks then opens his eyes. "Who the hell said you could come in here?" He struggles to sit upright and wipes his mouth. "Well, I see you're here anyway—the great hero come home. Hi, Liar." He lifts one hand, then lets it drop. "They believed you this time, didn't they? Moving out and in with your Chinese, Thai— whatever she is ?" He feels around, as if unsure whether he's on dry land, or swimming. "Good work. You made me look like the liar, a criminal and a generally heartless bastard." He licks his lips, grimaces and squeezes his eyes before focusing on me again. "You leaving?"

"Dad, you stink. Where's Arnie?"

"Arnie? I don't know. Same place as your mother— wherever she is? You leaving?"

"Yes, I guess I am."

"Good luck. I'm sure Bill pays enough for you to support her and yourself. Don't come back. Ever. You are a bastard and ungrateful son." He nods and pain crosses his face. "Ha! Can't be both at the same time, can you? Hadn't thought of that angle." He squeezes his eyes shut and shakes his head. "I should *never* have allowed you to play volleyball. I was better off when you weren't talking, wasn't I? Good-bye. Close the door when you leave."

"Dad, go to bed."

He gives me a silent wave then reaches for the bottle as I close the door.

I load my crap in the back of the Volvo, then make a once-around tour of the house. It feels even more empty and silent than when I got here. The walls hold the cold like they're trying to suck up any spot of warmth that might bubble from even a cup of hot chocolate. I sense and see the greyness as the rooms fade to mouse fur dusk. When was there warmth and light in this place? I try but can't remember. The pain I feel in my chest makes it hard for me to breathe as I block a sob, close and lock the back door, get in the Volvo and drive away.

I call Mary on my way over. She's already home, and has the outside light on when I pull into Harry's driveway. The minute I put my key in the door, she's opening it and taking the box I'm carrying from me. "Any more?"

"One more, computer and printer. I'll bring it up." When I do, she's waiting at the top of the steps, ready to help me maneuver the second, larger box through the door.

Inside, the living area smells of lavender salts and turkey soup. A vase filled with red and white flowers graces the open desk's surface. A rolled-out mattress with pillow, sheets and a blanket lies on the floor between the desk and the dining table. "Where'd that come from?"

Mary laughs. "Harry brought it over. He *is* a little old-fashioned and concerned. It is wider than the bed in the bedroom, don't you think?"

"Ah … yeah." Then the second I set the box down, she's folding herself into my arms. "Mmm." We kiss. "Aunt Millie always smelled of lavender."

"I know. She taught me to use it."

"This is home now."

"I know. Mine too." And we kiss again and the pain fades.

The two suitcases in the storage locker turn out to hold ten years of records covering the long fight between Aunt Millie, Uncle Stan and my parents—attempts by Dad again and again to deny Mary her potential inheritance. They also contain records of investments, stock certificates, CDs, municipal bonds, etc. Aunt Millie had money planted all over the place. No wonder she had been afraid of Dad getting a hold of that stuff. If he could have controlled all this, we'd have been on the heights in that mansion for sure. Why hadn't she revoked the power-of-attorney? Who knows? I guess it was too late after she fell. Tom's office has a lot of work cut out for them to make sense of everything, and set up trust funds for Mary to draw on.

Harry White is to be Mary's guardian for the next two years and she is no longer considered a ward of the state.

Harry insists that to make this legal, she needs to have a bedroom in his house. He never goes upstairs anymore, so Mary has the whole second floor to herself. She does sleep there some nights, but the apartment is *our* real home. There we eat together, study together and spend the evenings together—whenever she is not at the Northside Library— rebuilding our shared pasts and planning a shared future.

As for the Woodbridge will? County Orphans Court has ruled that invalid. Apparently, Dad and Jacobs cooked that up together and got Woodbridge to go along in order to hide the search for the real goodies. Woodbridge's director and assistant director are under investigation and may be looking for new jobs by the new year. The leftover money Woodbridge had claimed has already come back to Mary.

Tom is recovering, although he will never be as healthy as he was. The Ford truck driver, Meldoni, is in jail, set to go on trial for attempted vehicular homicide. Turns out he has a rap sheet that must go back fifteen years. We're sure that Jacobs or Dad hired him, but everything was arranged through anonymous phone calls and cash payments, so we may never know. I think that I never want to see Dad again.

When the call comes four days before Christmas, it's Arnie on the phone.

We've been seeing each other at lunch time. We talk, but never about Dad or Mom. We never talk about the might-have-beens.

"Bro, you'd better come over."

"To the domicile?"

"Yeah. Please. Dad's gone missing. Mom's hysterical. She says she needs you now."

At first I don't know what to say. I think about my own dreams, broken by Dad's lack of trust and greed. I think about his hatred of Mary and her mother, and all his plotting to deny her inheritance. Why should I come now? He threw me out. But ... "What's Mom saying?"

"She says he's gone up to the lake."

"Lake Noxhatchy?"

"Yes."

"I'll be right over."

"What's happening?" Mary is decorating our little fir tree with paper cutouts and strings of cranberries she threaded together herself.

"Dad's gone suicidal. Arnie thinks he's gone up to Lake Noxhatchy."

"Oh my god, no!" Mary's mouth stays open and her eyes get this thousand-yard stare before she turns to look at me. "I'll go with you." She sits down in the chair by the door, pulls on her winter boots and grabs her knit cap, coat and gloves.

"What do you mean? You don't have to."

She nods, lips set in a firm, thin line. "Your father destroyed—ruined—the first sixteen years of my life. He ruined your life. But if I don't go now, if I let him die without my being there, it's ... it's gonna' destroy the *rest* of my life. I don't want that to happen; I don't want regrets anymore."

"Okay. Are you sure?"

Mary nods and stands by the door waiting, while I put

on my own coat. Together we head down to the Volvo.

A city police car is parked in front when we get there. I park across the street. "You want'a stay here?"

"I'm going in with you."

"You still want to?"

"I have to." We both get out, cross the street holding hands while watching for traffic. A small crowd is gathered outside, including Denver Jack.

"Hi, Jack," I call to him as I head up the steps.

"Hi, Peter," he responds in the same high voice he's always had.

"Who's that?" Mary asks once we're inside.

"That's Denver Jack. Down Syndrome. Nice guy, sweet. Always the friendliest person you are ever likely to meet."

"Denver Jack? That's a weird name. How'd he get that?"

"I'll tell you later. Hi, Arnie. Hello, Mom. What's the word?" The vestibule is a confusion of bodies: neighbors, family friends and two police officers, including Monihan from the sheriff's department. I spot him right away; he sees me, goes red, then we both look away.

Mom hears me and comes over. She has been crying, her cheeks strawberry-raw and wet. "Oh, Peter, what's happening? Dan's has been so different and unhappy ever since you left. Oh … Hello, Mary."

"Hello, Helen." Mary takes Mom's hands and holds them tight. "I'm praying for him. Is that all right?"

"Thank you," Mom answers and the tears start all

over again. I let her hug me. I hold her close, feeling her chest shaking, her mouth making sad whimperings.

"Call coming in," The other cop announces. "What do you have, Mike?" Pause. "They found the car. The Audi? Yes, the Audi. Unlocked. No one in it. Where? West shore, near the swing sets in the playground. No sign of Bain anywhere."

"The playground? Look on the ice," Mary suddenly cries out. "Look out *on* the ice!"

"What? Where? You hear that. Girl says look out on the ice." Cop turns toward us. "They're looking." He concentrates on the other end. "You think you see something? They think they see something that looks like a body, way, way out. They're checking it out."

We all stand, silent, breaths held. Mom lets go of me, but continues to hold a hand. Mary wraps her left hand around my arm, her head close to mine. She's still careful with her right arm; there'll always be a scar.

I can hear distant voices coming over the Cop's phone. "They say they can see a person lying on the ice. It's him. It's Bain!" A wave of warmth sweeps across us. Mary grips my arm tighter. "He's alive. He's alive! Ambulance just rolled in. They're sending out a stretcher." A long silence, then: "They're bringing him in. Will be heading to the hospital momentarily. Okay, folks, show over. Is Mrs. Bain there?"

"Yes," Mom whispers.

"They're taking him to Jefferson Memorial. You might want to head there, but take your time. The roads are slippery."

I drive with Mom in front, Arnie and Mary in the back seat. We park as close to the emergency entrance as a vacant space will allow and trot in. Three layers of paperwork and personnel later and we step into a curtained off room presided over by a state cop, a rack of machines and one technician. Dad looks like he got rolled down a dirt road head-first. His forehead and stubble-covered checks are grey and purple, His arms are swollen, a plastic wrap-around filled with tubes covers his chest. I guess to try to get his body back up to temperature. But he is conscious. When he sees us comes in, a faint smile twitches across his lips and eyes. Then he looks away. "I'm so sorry," he whimpers."

I lean forward. "Dad, be home for Christmas. You do, and we'll all be there."

"Mary? Mary, you'd be there?"

"Yes, Mr. Bain. I'll be there."

"Was that? Was that where your mother died?"

"Yes, Mr. Bain."

"The ice refused to break. I'm so sorry."

"I forgive you, Mr. Bain. Get well and come home."

Then he smiles again, feels the pain and relaxes. "Thank you."

Mary and I are on our way home. "You were going to tell me why that Down Syndrome boy is called 'Denver Jack.'"

"Oh. Yes, I was. He hates the word Denver. The local bullies know that and some of them, any time they see him, tease him. It always makes him cry or scream. I asked him one day, nice-like, why he hated Denver. You know, Down Syndrome people almost never hate anything. He told me that Denver hurt him, made him hurt Denver. So, that's all I know.

Mary is silent a long time. "What was Coach Tiltman's first name?"

"It was Dennis … You don't think, do you?"

"Get someone Jack trusts to ask him. If what happened to you, happened to Jack, he might remember it as pain. Jack might have seemed an easy victim."

"Oh, my god. And he's lived almost next door for as long as I can think."

When I come in the high school door the Monday after the Christmas-New Years holiday, I look for and spot the change. The rectangle of lighter shade buff paint on the wall betrays where the wreathed and framed portrait of Dennis Tiltman, 'beloved coach and teacher,' used to hang. I shake my head, marveling how one is a liar, but two makes truth. And how quickly truth can change everything. I head for my locker. Jason Small is coming the other way. "How's it going, dude," he waves as he passes me.

"It's going great," I answer, "And you?"

"It couldn't be better."

"You're right. It couldn't be better."

– The End –

M.W. Loder

Forbidden Games